MW00781251

The Mermaid Broker

A Vega and Middleton Mystery

Sue Hinkin

Sue Hinkin

Literary Wanderlust | Denver, Colorado

Other books by Sue Hinkin

Deadly Focus
Low Country Blood
The Burn Patient

PRAISE FOR DEADLY FOCUS

4 out of 4 stars! "Deadly Focus: A Vega and Middleton Mystery by Sue Hinkin is a compelling, fast-paced thriller that takes readers on a treacherous journey in search of truth and justice."

—ONLINEBOOKCLUB.ORG

"An exciting series opener that delivers murder, drugs, and romance."

—Kirkus Review

"I was bowled over! It's fantastic!!! Gripping. Gritty. Instant and vivid characterizations. Suspenseful. Surprising twists! Holy cow!"

—Sonja Massie is the author of more than 60 published works including the highly acclaimed Savannah Reid Mysteries under the pseudonym G.A. McKevett and the bestselling novel *Far and Away* adapted from the movie by Ron Howard starring Tom Cruise and Nicole Kidman

"The pacing is breathless, but don't turn the pages too fast, so you can enjoy all aspects of this well-built mystery."

—Susan Myhre Hayes is the author of Peace in the Puzzle: *Becoming Your Intended Self* and uses her book to support groups and individuals as they search for their unique purpose.www.peaceinthepuzzle.com

"All in all, a satisfying, well-crafted, fast-moving read, with characters that stay in your mind and leave you wanting more. Sequel, please.

—Carolyn Olson Adams, Amazon Reviewer

PRAISE FOR LOW COUNTRY BLOOD

Silver Falchion Award finalist in the Thriller Category
Killer Nashville 2020

"Hinkin's second Vega and Middleton Mystery...reads like a thriller, successfully blends multiple ingredients: fast pacing, romance, danger, humor, and a crazy wild ending. A spirited reporter dealing with her past and helping police solve a murder in the family makes this novel hard to put down."

—Kirkus Reviews

"*Low Country Blood* has energy to burn. Published by small but mighty Literary Wanderlust in Colorado, *Low Country Blood* measures up with mainstream mysteries from major publishing houses. The story immerses in a taut yarn and takes us to a land that is malleable and shifty as quicksand."

—Mark Stevens writes the Allison Coil Mystery Series-
Antler Dust, *Buried by the Roan*, *Trapline*, *Lake of Fire* and
The Melancholy Howl.

"Author Sue Hinkin hits the ground running in her second novel, *Low Country Blood*. From the initial murder, to an Afghani heroin cartel, to a kidnapping by one of the cartel henchmen who turns out to be a sadistic killer with history in Savannah, Hinkin keeps the story moving with intense action and gripping plot twists. Her affinity for the people and understanding of Savannah's deep, tangled cultural roots give the book its unmistakable heart."

—Colorado Book Review

5/5-Stars! "Author Sue Hinkin's compelling work, *Low Country Blood*: A Vega & Middleton Novel, embodies an exciting story with memorable characters – not to be missed!"

—Readersfavorite.com

PRAISE FOR THE BURN PATIENT

5/5-Stars! "This is a fast-paced, intelligently plotted, and deftly written story that will have readers on the edge of their seats."

—readersfavorite.com

4.5/5 Stars! "With likable heroines, depraved villains, and a cast of interesting supporting characters, Hinkin proves she is more than just a writer of thrillers, her writing is a thrill to read as well."

—Colorado Book Review

4/4-Stars! "This is an action-packed tale that will keep readers on the edges of their seats. It was gripping from the first page, and the breathless suspense was maintained throughout the story."

—OnlineBookClub.org

"No spoilers here. Take it from me, this is a crackerjack high voltage mystery from beginning to end. Once you read this, you'll want to read the rest of Sue Hinkin's novels. Great!!!"

—Ted Elrick is the co-screenwriter of the feature motion picture, "Home Sweet Hell," he has been the longtime editor of the Directors Guild of America Magazine and his mystery and science fiction short stories have appeared in numerous publications.

Published in the United States by Literary Wanderlust LLC, Denver, Colorado.

www.LiteraryWanderlust.com

ISBN Print: 978-1-942856-75-7
ISBN Digital: 978-1-942856-79-5

Cover design: Pozu Mitsuma

Printed in the United States of America

The Mermaid Broker

Chapter 1

She'd spent much of her life underwater. Friends had even teased her about being half fish. For Isabelle "Izzy" Abbott, studying oceans and its inhabitants was her profession—but this time was different. Something was off. The taste on her lips was not the saltiness of her beloved Pacific, but the coppery tang of blood.

Isabelle's pulse rate accelerated. Pale light flickered from the darkness above. The moon? Her feet kicked hard; fingers stretched desperately toward the illumination. She followed the rise of silvery bubbles. Not too fast. The nitrogen build-up could be lethal. Where was her emergency tank?

Lungs near exploding, she broke the liquid surface, gasping for breath. Then, her hand felt something solid. Isabelle was not underwater but lying on a rubbery mat, soaked in her own sweat. When she tried to move her body, restraints bit into her skin. Zip ties? Handcuffs? Her heart hammered like a trapped animal trying to escape its cage.

Where was she? What had happened? A car accident? Was

she in a hospital? A jail? So many questions. Isabelle forced her eyes open. Her lids were made of concrete—heavy and gritty. The room spun.

Faint, distant strains of music tinkled—discordant wind chimes accompanied by the moaning, agitated sounds of whales. What the hell? As a marine biologist, she recognized the vocalizations immediately as those of animals under grave stress. What sicko would want to weave animal misery into a song? She gulped hard.

Cool, damp air moved across Izzy's skin and smelled of salt. Goosebumps rose. She widened her eyes, blinking, trying to acclimate. The small, square space around her appeared to have tiled walls like an operating room or a lab. It was illuminated only by a large window into a deep blue aquarium similar to those at the Aquarium of the Pacific in Long Beach.

A school of dark greyish fish, hundreds of them the size of dinner plates, glided by and disappeared. Black piranhas, a South American species she wasn't terribly familiar with. Izzy shuddered. A thin, black lateral line stretched along each body from tail to pectoral fin. It was a sensor that indicated distress in the water and a call to attack wounded prey. She held down a pang of nausea. Unable to completely focus, her head ached as if she'd been clubbed by a two-by-four. Maybe she had been. *What was going on?*

A body lay on a cot across from her. A girl about the same age as her biology students at Santa Monica High School. Pale skin, lank hair, face smeared with gold paint or makeup. Sleeping? Dead? Was she wrapped in a straight-jacket? Yes.

Izzy tried not to panic. Was she in a mental institution? This couldn't be a dream, it seemed vividly real. She tried to call out to her roommate, but Izzy's throat was so dry, all that came out was a whisper. She licked her parched lips and tried again.

"Hey! Hey, over there! You awake?"

The girl's eyes, pallid and sunken, fluttered open. Izzy gasped, stunned by the dim pools of utter despair staring up at her. Anxiety exploded in her chest like fireworks. This was not a hospital, this was something else, something not in the realm of Isabelle Abbott's experience.

Struggling against her bindings, the girl banged her head against the bedframe. "Help me, please help me. I can't breathe," she pleaded. "I'm claustrophobic, can't handle tight spaces—this thing is destroying me."

Isabelle winced at the aching sound of desperation in her voice. "I can't reach you. I'm cuffed to the bed." Again, she pulled hard against her restraints, but there was no give. "Where the are we?"

The girl started to cry with big, deep sobs, then she stopped herself, slowed herself down, struggling for control. "We're in hell," she gasped.

Isabelle sensed the girl was right. "How did you get here?"

"A dive trip off Catalina. They drugged me." She paused and shut her eyes. Bruises shadowed her cheekbones. "I remember the stink of something weird over my face, in my mask."

The memory of something foul began to crawl into Izzy's consciousness too. The koi, the empty pet store. "We're moving to a larger space," the kindly man who'd met her at the door explained. He invited her in to see the rare specimen she was seeking.

He poured lemonade. *A bit more, sweetheart?*

Had she been roofied? It was all a jumble.

The girl began to sob again then struggled once more to settle herself. "Breathe in, breathe out, slower, slower," she murmured to herself.

Isabelle knew if she herself was wrapped in one of those contraptions she'd go off the rails, too. Her head began to pound. "Why did they take us? What do they want from us?" She tried to position her body more comfortably on the rubber mattress, but it was impossible.

"Rape. Female bodies to mutilate. Murder." The girl began to shake uncontrollably. "I never believed this could happen.

Only on TV, not to real people."

Stomach tightening, Isabelle felt another wave of nausea. *Chill, girl.* They both had to calm down and think clearly if they wanted to survive. "What's your name?" she asked gently.

There was a sustained, almost fearful hesitation, but finally an answer. "I'm Celeste."

"I'm Isabelle. People call me Izzy most of the time. How long have you been here?"

Another pause. "Maybe a week or ten days, near as I can tell." Slow tears tracked her cheeks.

"So, how does this all go down?"

Celeste now lay still as vulnerable prey hoping to avoid notice, breath shallow. Only her mouth moved. "The clients, they're on a world sex adventure tour. Ventura is the "Mermaid Fantasy" experience. They make us wear exotic mermaid costumes like players from *Cirque de Soleil* then they put us in a huge tank, big as a gym, bigger." Her eyes flitted to the aquarium window, then closed tight. "We swim around, and they turn off our air if we don't perform." Her voice dropped an octave. "Assholes pick mermaids to fuck. Afterwards, they can choose to let us live, or watch us die."

"Die?" A hot gush of adrenaline coursed through Izzy's veins. She gagged.

"Yeah, beyond sick. Then, they're off to Japan and Thailand."

"How do you know this?"

"One of the customers filled me in. A Saudi guy." She attempted to turn toward Izzy. "I think he might have been gay but had to play the macho role for his friends. He was kind of sweet, didn't do anything to me, just wanted to talk. I was lucky, this time."

"They actually *kill* people? Like a snuff thing?" Her brain wanted to reject the information, but here she was, handcuffed in the darkness in a room that smelled of dead fish.

Celeste gulped and swallowed a cry. "One woman was murdered yesterday. They threw her into the aquarium filled with piranhas, the kind that can clean a cow down to the bones in minutes."

Isabelle shook her head. "That's an urban legend." But maybe the huge black piranhas she had just seen would prove the legend to be real.

"It's not! They went crazy and took huge chunks out of her. Maybe they starve the fish to make them hungry. Maybe they're a weird breed. There are sharks, too. Big ones." Celeste trembled. "I freaked out. That's why I'm in here. They tased the hell out of me. The next tour group comes in five days. I'll be eaten alive." She began to hyperventilate.

"No, no, we'll get out of here." Isabelle's eyes wildly scanned the room for an opportunity to escape. Nothing. "We're not going out this way, Celeste."

The young woman laughed, then screamed in fury.

A fast tap-tap-tap of footsteps came toward their room.

"Oh, shit," she said. "I'm so sorry."

There was a dinging sound before the door flew open. Blue light filled the room. An orderly, a thick-set man with a bulbous nose and low-hanging ape-like arms, whipped a taser from a tool belt around his waist and hit the lithe blonde in the neck. Her body convulsed, and she passed out. *Small mercies.*

He turned to Isabelle. "You wan' summa dis?" His voice was deep with an Eastern European, Arnold Schwarzenegger-type accent. The taser whined as it powered back up. "Or you be good girl?" He stroked Izzy's damp hair then ripped at it, brutally, with his rubber-gloved hand.

Izzy choked, quaking. "I'll be good." *Until I can get that taser and make you pay, you sadistic prick.*

He licked his wormy lips and turned toward his victim. Checking Celeste's jugular with his fingers, he nodded his head. Foamy saliva leaked from the corners of her mouth. With a last dim smirk at Izzy, ape-man shuffled from the room.

The lock clicked hard, like an empty chamber in a game of Russian roulette. She shuddered—if they didn't find a way out fast, and if Celeste was right about what the kidnappers were up to, they could be dead with the next spin of the revolver.

Chapter 2

Beatrice Middleton, an attractive, African American woman in her early forties, sat in her corner office at the West Coast branch of CNN-STAT gazing at the distant Hollywood Sign. In the late afternoon smog, it was the brownish color of the weak tea sitting cold on her desk. The bustle outside her door was young, intense, and energetic. Laughter, loud opinions, excitement—too bad she was feeling none of the above.

I want you to come up with a new take on the human-trafficking narrative, her boss, Winfrey Chambers, had announced earlier in the week. Perhaps he had more confidence in her than she deserved. Over her career, Bea thought she'd covered this subject from every depressing, awful angle, and if there actually was something new, she didn't want to know about it. Perpetrators had once crept too horrifyingly close to her own thirteen-year old daughter for her to maintain any detached journalistic objectivity. She still had nightmares about what could have been. Maybe that rawness was why Chambers wanted her to step up on this one. *Damn it all.*

Nothing was happening in her brain but avoidance. She picked at the pale green nail polish her manicurist had talked her into. *Be bold, try something different.* Bold, shit—it looked like anemic pond sludge against her dark skin.

Bea's cellphone buzzed. Lucy Vega, her closest friend and her news photographer of choice, was on the line. Whenever she got a chance to hire a stringer, Lucy was *numero uno.*

"Hey, Luce. What's up, girl?"

"You still stressing over that trafficking assignment?"

"Was just about to go to Chambers and beg for an alternative topic. Got a serious block on this puppy. I'm ready to break out a gossip mag and file my nails, that's how inspired I am."

Lucy chuckled. "Well, maybe I have a lead. I ran into Bijan at the taco truck on 10th and Ocean Park at lunchtime."

"I thought you were supposed to be on complete bed rest with this pregnancy."

"Don't nag. I'm losing my mind, Bea. I need an occasional Tito's Taco fix or the baby's gonna be looking at a psychotic mama."

"Too late on that one, girlfriend. Poor tyke. So, how's our bad boy, Bijan?" Bea and Lucy loved him. A bushy-bearded game developer and forensic accounting consultant with expertise in trolling the dark web, they occasionally enlisted his help, especially in following the money. He could sniff out wandering *dinero* like a hound on a blood trail.

"He's fine, just fine, says to tell you, *hey*. But I called to let you know he stumbled across something weird on one of his deep net dives. Could be that new edge you're looking for."

The dark web. Bea felt her neck muscles tighten. "Oh, no. I don't really want to hear it."

"No, you probably don't. Say the word and I'll let it go."

Bea paused. She couldn't allow personal issues to get in the way of doing her job. With a hard-won position at the top of her field, she wanted to stay there. She took a deep breath. "Okay, lay the ugly on me."

"International sex tourism—pricey, elite, extreme."

Bea was relieved it was something she'd already covered. "Old story."

But Lucy wasn't finished. "Ending in a spectacular murder of the trafficked victims who are dressed up like fish."

"Like fish? So freaky. A snuff ring of some kind?" The image of dead fish washed up on the sand lit up her mind for a fleeting moment. "Fake?"

"Maybe. Bijan thought it looked real."

A thin, rainbowy film had formed on the surface of Bea's tea like oil in a puddle. She drained it anyway. "Well, thanks for the idea but we don't have the resources to track down international stories. Plus, snuff stories aren't new either. Chambers can pass it up the food chain to the brass in New York."

Lucy continued. "Except there's a site somewhere in Southern California perpetrating this shit. Bijan really went after it hard online, but details are as tight as my Spanx after the Golden Corral buffet."

Bea laughed out loud. "Liar. You've never even been near the GC—been trying to drag you over there for years."

"Yeah, true. But anyhow, reach out to Bijan if you decide to pursue."

"Of course." Bea pressed on the bridge of her nose with her fingertips and closed her eyes.

"He's waiting to hear from you. See ya later, Beebs. I'm heading back to the ranch. They started framing the new barn this morning. Love you."

"Okay, Lucy, love you, too. Happy barn-raising. And girl, for heaven's sake, stay out of the construction zone and observe from a hammock."

"Yes ma'am."

Just as Bea clicked off, Chambers, a tall, professorish, light-skinned African American man with a slim build that made her wish for a piece of his metabolism, poked his head into her office. "Ideas yet?" He fingered his gray goatee.

Bea slumped in her chair and pushed back from her desk. "Yeah, maybe. Have a seat."

Chapter 3

A woman in her early thirties, Casey Abbott had just moved into a modest duplex in a neighborhood near the San Buenaventura Mission in Ventura. Through scrimping and saving, plus a small inheritance from her mother, she'd managed to break into the SoCal real estate market. To her, this little *casita* was nine hundred square feet of heaven with a distant view of the Pacific to match. Sheer curtains swelled in the breeze from the ocean. Her yellow-eyed black cat, Sebastian, sat on the window sill and watched a swarm of hummingbirds at a feeder hanging from an avocado tree just beyond his reach.

Casey glanced at her watch. She scrubbed her fingers through her spiky brown hair then retied her well-worn running shoes. Her sister Isabelle was almost two hours late for their bike ride to the Saturday morning craft fair and farmer's market. Izzy was never late for anything and since their parents had passed on, taking this time together from their busy schedules held increasing importance to both of them.

She punched the speed dial for Izzy. The call went to

voicemail. Again.

"Iz, where the heck *are* you? The seafood guy is gonna be sold out of crab legs by the time we get there."

Agitated, Casey sat at her desk and proofread an article she'd written for the following day's posting. She made a spare but livable wage as a freelance website designer and blogger. Her phone buzzed. She pulled it from the pocket of her denim shirt and checked caller ID.

Her heart sank, it wasn't her sister.

The caller was Izzy's neighbor, Titus, a retiree who worked part-time as a dog walker.

"Hey, Titus, what's up?" Casey asked, not waiting for him to answer. "I've been trying to get my sister and I can't reach her. You seen her?"

"That's why I'm calling," he said. "Her car's been gone since yesterday, and Booker's been barking for hours. It's not like her to leave him alone for so long without asking me to walk and feed him. She gave me the key to her apartment months ago, but I can't find it or I wouldn't have bothered you."

Casey's chest tightened. Something wasn't right. "I'm on my way. Glad you called." She jumped in her car and headed south to the Ventura Freeway.

A part-time science teacher at Santa Monica High and a PhD student in Marine Biology at the University of California, Santa Barbara, or UCSB, Isabelle lived in a small condo in Agoura Hills, halfway between Santa Monica and Santa Barbara. When Casey pulled up to Izzy's apartment building just off Kanan Road, she immediately noticed that her sister's silver Kia SUV was not in its usual parking spot. She edged her own decade-old Camry into the narrow space.

Barely avoiding a collision with a fast-moving skateboarder, Casey dashed for the steps to her sister's second-floor unit. The unpretentious building was salmon-colored stucco with a well-maintained garden of hot pink bougainvillea and birds of paradise. She could hear Booker barking his lungs out. Casey swallowed down a stab of panic. When she opened the door would she find her sister dead? She berated herself for the ridiculous thought, but it had her in its cold-fingered grip.

Titus stood at Isabelle's door, waiting with a leash and poop bag in hand.

"Hi, Titus," Casey said. They exchanged a quick hug before she jammed the key into the door lock. Her hands shook and were moist with perspiration. The door opened and Booker, a rescue pup suspected to be a Yorkie-beagle mix, came bounding out the door and into Casey's arms. Then he wagged his entire body over to Titus, who gave him several doggie treats. They launched down the stairs and into the garden.

Casey scanned her sister's immaculate, one-bedroom apartment. Black-and-white photographs of sea life, carefully matted and framed, full bookshelves, exotic seashells, dog stuff and a blood red Hawaiian protea in a glass vase. Her bicycle leaned against the living room wall. The apartment looked perfect, normal, disturbingly normal. No dead bodies, no sign of struggle or theft. *Why didn't she feel a bit relieved?*

Casey sat down at her sister's laptop next to a photo of the two sisters at the top of Pikes Peak in Colorado. Both tall and pretty with lean runner's legs, Izzy's long sun-streaked hair blazed in the wind, Casey's short do was contained beneath what her angler dad would call a fishing hat.

The computer was still on and ready. She hit *enter* and scrolled through the calendar and the browser history. Koi—every recent article and site was about koi. Izzy had mentioned that her landlady had recently restored the ancient, dried-up fish pond in the courtyard, and evidently her sister had decided to help out with some research. An exotic fish emporium called Nemo's Submarine on 16th Street in Ventura with a note in Latin, *piscem auratus,* had been bookmarked.

Casey jotted down the store information on a Post-it. Maybe Agnes had seen her leave and would know something more about Izzy's plans.

The building's owner, Agnes Melby, a seventy-something sprite of a woman who lived on-site and owned the property, sat in a white Adirondack chair on her first-floor porch overlooking the courtyard. The once-abandoned water feature bubbled a few yards away. Several gold, black, and white-spotted fish lurked below the surface amidst pots of water lilies.

"Casey, hello, dear. So pretty, isn't it?" She nodded toward the pond. "I finally had enough money to do it right. So peaceful, I love it." She took a long swig of bottled iced tea.

"It's wonderful." It really was. "My sister give you a hand with any of this?"

"Oh, sure. I mean she's an expert in marine biology. I gave her half off this month's rent for helping out. The koi are great little creatures, real personalities, like pups with scales. I've got Lucy, Ricky, Little Ricky, and Ethyl. Izzy's finding me a Fred."

Casey smiled, remembering the classic *I Love Lucy* TV show. She was not a fish-person herself but was sure that every kind of animal was much smarter and more remarkable than most humans gave them credit for. "Did Izzy say anything about going up to Ventura to check out a potential Fred? She seems to have been gone since yesterday and I can't contact her. Quite honestly, I'm getting scared."

Agnes put down her tea, concern furrowing her wrinkled forehead. "Yeah, she was off to a pet store of some kind yesterday, looking for a rare koi that was particularly translucent with extra-long whiskers. Sounded pretty. Izzy never goes for just the usual, always wants something special. I like that about her."

"Me too." But over the years, her sister's quest for the beautiful and rare had sometimes led her into very ugly situations. Casey could never forget how Isabelle, on a marine science internship, with eyes only for a brilliant tropical fish that caught her attention, ventured into a remote coral cave off the Great Barrier Reef in Australia. She was almost killed by moray eels. Casey pressed her fingers to her temples.

"Maybe you should call the police," Agnes said.

"I thought about it, but a grad student gone for less than twenty-four hours? They'll assume she's sleeping it off with some weekend hook-up."

"That's not our Isabelle." Agnes looked out across her courtyard garden. Booker was doing his business in a bed of petunias.

Casey agreed. Izzy'd had relationships, but was still an innocent, seldom aware of the effect she could have on those who might desire her. Or want to harm her.

Pushing her shaggy, dark bangs away from her face, Casey sighed heavily. "I guess I'll head back toward home and check out the store she was going to visit."

"Good idea. Keep me posted, okay, honey? Now I'm worrying too." Agnes stepped off the porch and gave Casey a hug before wandering toward her lovely, refurbished pond with a bag of fish food.

Casey returned to close up the apartment, grab her sister's laptop, and make arrangements for Booker to stay with Titus. Then, she jumped into her Camry for the return trip home along the Pacific. The low sun dazzled against the dark water. A serious headache was building. Casey adjusted her shades and grabbed an energy bar from the glove box for a little protein and sugar boost.

Forty-five minutes later, she turned into an industrial area just beyond downtown Ventura. A two-block-long retail strip edged a residential neighborhood and an office park filled with mom-and-pop businesses. All the shops were closed and eerily quiet. Zero foot traffic. Casey parked on the empty street and checked the address on her sticky note.

What was supposed to be Nemo's Submarine was an abandoned storefront that looked like it might once have been a resale shop. She cupped her hands around her eyes to cut the glare and pressed against the window to peer through the smudged glass. Racks with wire hangers spilled onto the dusty floor. A small, cracked plaster version of the Little Mermaid from Hans Christian Anderson's tales sat next to a *For Lease* sign in the front window.

WTF? Casey checked the Post-it again for the phone number. She called the store.

Disconnected.

She chewed at her lip. Trying not to freak out, she dialed the number on the lease sign. After a dozen rings, a woman finally picked up, her voice old and coarse.

"Sea Star Realty—this is Marjorie Ortiz. Can I help you?"

"Yes, uh, Ms. Ortiz, I was told that a shop called Nemo's was located at the address of your property on 16th Street here in Ventura. Do you know if it may have closed recently, or moved?"

"Nemo's? Like in the Disney movie?"

Like in the Jules Verne book, actually. "Yes, a store that sells exotic fish."

"Never heard of that one, lady. No pet stores ever in that location or even in the neighborhood. You interested in renting the shop? Looks a tad downscale, but a good cleaning and a little TLC'll make it shine right up."

"No, sorry to bother you." Casey ended the call, huddled in the empty entryway to the abandoned shop and stifled a scream. She could hardly breathe. Something was horribly wrong.

Casey crawled into her car, pressed her forehead against the steering wheel and tried to stop shaking. She was hyperventilating and becoming seriously light-headed. Although barely two years older than Izzy, she always felt such responsibility for her younger sister. Early on, she became Izzy's parent, by default. Their father had died of a heart attack when they were in middle school. Their mother succumbed to breast cancer six years later. With no other family to turn to for help, finding Isabelle was up to Casey. She'd go to the police and convince them that this disappearance had to be taken seriously, not in thirty-six or forty-eight hours. Now.

She turned on the ignition and sped toward Ventura Metro PD headquarters.

Chapter 4

Dusk was beginning to fill the shadows beneath palm trees and bushy tangles of oleander along the highway as Casey pulled off the 101 onto Telegraph Road. She glanced at her watch and her heart sank. It was past six in the evening and all city offices would be closed to walk-in business, including the police department. If she called 9-1-1, they'd probably insist that she file a missing person report on their website. Nothing felt more hopeless than typing sheer panic for your loved-one's well-being onto a mundane online form. It was as bloodless and lacking in desperation as buying a box of pens at Best Buy.

She pulled into the near-empty parking lot across from the faux Mediterranean-style law enforcement building. Casey grabbed her purse and slammed the car door hard behind her. To hell with phoning and online forms, there had to be someone still around who could help save Isabelle.

She tried the front doors but found them locked. A janitor ignored her calls for help, then finally looked up and pointed toward the rear of the building. A law-abiding citizen up until this point in her life, she'd never had the occasion to visit a police department. Circling the building, Casey spotted an adjacent parking area dotted with cop cruisers near an after-hours entry.

She pounded on the glass door. It was embedded with cross-threads of wire. Inside, a long, wooden counter beneath irritating fluorescent lights was empty. Behind it, a wall of warnings, notices, and FBI wanted posters was unwelcoming.

When Casey realized there was a push button next to the door, she pressed it hard, several times. A distant buzzing sounded. Finally, a hefty, gel-haired officer in his early fifties lumbered in from a hallway and moved behind the desk.

He glanced at her then spoke into a microphone mounted on his computer screen. "Can I help you?" His voice was tinny as it emerged from a speaker next to the door jamb.

Before she could reply, a tall, good-looking Asian man, mid-thirties in jeans and a pale blue T-shirt materialized from behind her in the parking lot. He carded himself in. Casey followed on his heels through the door.

"Closed to the public at 5:30, miss," the desk officer said gruffly.

"It's my sister," she blurted, moving fast toward the counter. "She disappeared and I think something bad has happened to her. She never takes off without telling me. And she didn't even leave food for her dog! You have to help me!"

"Slow down now, ma'am." The desk officer's name tag read Sgt. Wiznewski. He held up a finger to stop Casey from talking for a moment, then turned to his colleague. "Hey, Mac." He addressed the man Casey had slipped in behind. "Get that file on the Gomez case I left for you?"

"Yup, thanks, Wiz." He bent over a pile of paperwork waiting in a wire basket.

Casey grabbed the edge of the counter so hard her knuckles turned white.

Sgt. Wiznewski finally shifted his attention back to her. "So, ma'am, when did your sister disappear?" He clicked away on the computer keyboard in front of him.

Her breathing came in little gasps, like heartbeats. "I know it's not enough time, it hasn't been two days, but this is so out of character and I know in any crime the first twenty-four hours are critical—"

"Whoa, there," the sergeant said. He stopped typing. "This isn't a TV cop show; we don't have a hard and fast time requirement. Just settle down and tell me what happened."

"Okay, I'm sorry. It's just that I know something is wrong, way wrong. And I need help. I'm afraid I'm going to lose her." Tears tightened her voice.

"Take a breath and start from the beginning. Your sister is missing," he prompted. The phone on the desk rang. Wiznewski offered a little shrug of apology and picked up. There was a quick conversation about an incoming drunk and disorderly.

Casey wiped perspiration from her forehead with the back of her hand. Every second felt like an eternity. She glanced over at the tall Asian guy. He'd stopped what he was doing and was looking at her. His intense, almond-shaped eyes were brownish-green, the color of drying scrub grass in the Santa Monica mountains where she often hiked. She felt a strange connection. He gave her a faint smile, grabbed his papers, and disappeared down a hallway.

"Alright, ma'am." The sergeant was back. "Name, address, phone number, please."

Casey tore her attention from the detective called Mac and recited the mundane data of her existence in Ventura and the specifics on Isabelle. Then the dam broke and the story came spilling out. She'd gone to a tropical fish store called Nemo's Submarine.

Wiznewski stopped short and peered at her. "Nemo's Sub?" A new attentiveness straightened his shoulders.

She held up the wrinkled Post-it with the address on it. "But it doesn't exist." She gulped. "That name mean something to you?"

The sergeant nodded and focused back on his computer, typing slowly with only his pointer fingers. "Was a code name for a sex-trafficking outfit active here about ten years ago. Long gone. Dumb of me to have mentioned it. Guess I'm getting tired, pulled a double shift." He yawned. "Short on staff, damn tax cuts."

"You think she's been trafficked?" Casey's vision began to pop with dark explosions. *Settle down, girl.*

"Naw, huh-uh. She doesn't even come close to the profile—too old, too educated, a good job, somebody who cares about her." He asked for a photo which Casey immediately texted him from her iPhone.

Finally, he assured her they would do all they could and would be in touch. Then he was on to the next crisis as two officers came roaring in with a delirious, wine-soaked older woman. She was ripping off her clothes and screaming about a stalker who was stealing her mind. Casey slipped out the door, barely missing being clobbered by the woman's flying purse.

The air was cool as darkness floated down like a veil across the beach town. Streetlights flickered on. Casey crossed the parking lot and walked slowly to a bench on the edge of a small green space between the police station and a residential area of modest houses and businesses. She put her head in her hands and could no longer hold back the tears. She had never felt so alone in her life. Her sister Isabelle had gone out in search of a rare koi at a store that never existed, and now she was gone.

Strong gusty winds rustled the fronds of Mexican fan palms lining the sidewalk. A bicyclist rode slowly by and the music of a Spanish pop song swelled and then disappeared.

"Excuse me, ma'am." A man's voice sounded behind her, low and too close for comfort.

Casey jumped up from the bench. She wanted to scream but her throat constricted.

"I'm so sorry, I didn't mean to alarm you," the officer said.

Casey backed away and wiped her eyes.

It was the young cop from the police station. "You freaked the hell out of me and I'm already scared to death."

"Please accept my apology, but I overheard what you were saying back in the station. If there is anything I can do, well, here's my card."

Casey hesitated then accepted the card. She squinted to see the words in the dim light—it read: *Detective MacIntosh Wu, Ventura Metro Police Department, Crimes Against Persons Division.* She took a deep breath and nodded. "Thank you, Detective Wu. I know I'm losing it right now, but I'll be okay."

"I have some sense of what you must be feeling." His features darkened in the gloom. He paused and looked away, then sighed. "My sister disappeared a dozen years ago, and I guess I'm always looking for a chance to find the lost."

"You never found her?" Tears sprang again to Casey's eyes.

"We did, we found her. And your sister, she'll probably show up soon, most missing persons usually do. Call me if you need to."

He turned to go and she stepped forward. "I'm Casey Abbott." She reached to shake his hand in both of hers. The touch of his skin was comforting. "Thank you, Detective."

"No problem. Goodnight, ma'am."

She watched him jog over to a silver Ford 150 pickup, then checked her texts, hoping for a message from Izzy. Nothing.

Casey waved as Wu drove away, then she headed home, wondering if the handsome detective had found his sister alive or dead.

Chapter 5

Bea stood just outside the doorway and watched her six-foot-four son Dexter try to coil himself onto the barstool at the kitchen island. A wistful smile flickered on her lips then disappeared. At seventeen and still growing, he was all arms and legs topped by a high, lawn-mown hedge of dark Afro with side fenders shaved close that added another few inches.

Next to him at half the size, sat his closest friend, Sean Hayes. A skinny blond with scraggly surfer hair and huarache sandals held together with duct tape. The dude's fellow students often called him "Spicoli," the stoner character from the movie *Fast Times at Ridgemont High*. Bea had long-ago figured out that Hayes, despite being an occasional slacker who probably smoked weed now and then, was a good student who'd been the bookkeeper for his dad's long-haul trucking company since he was twelve. The two kids were in the process of decimating a jumbo pizza and talking about their AP Marine Biology class when she walked in.

"Miss Bea," the little dude's eyes lit up.

"Hey, mom," Dexter said. "Hayes brought pizza."

"I can see that." She gave Dexter a peck on the cheek and did the same to Hayes. Hayes grinned—he'd lost his mom before he was old enough to know her and appreciated any maternal attention. Bea's family had quasi-adopted a similar orphan when she was growing up in Savannah, Georgia, so affection toward the motherless was second nature.

"Help yourself." Hayes pushed the box in Bea's direction.

"Thanks, sweetie, but I'm on some stupid diet, again. And it doesn't include Domino's." She went to the refrigerator and pulled out a container of salad and poured herself a big glass of sweet tea. She pulled up a stool across from the two boys. "So, heard you telling Dex something about your bio teacher?"

Hayes leaned toward Bea, a big, drooping slice in his hand. Mozzarella hung like strands of thread. "Yeah, I was in the office, lost my student ID again, but anyhow, I heard Principal Pritkow tell Mrs. Winkler that our AP Bio teacher is missing."

"Missing? What does that mean?" Bea's eyes slid to her son. She could see a fine slick of perspiration begin to dampen his forehead. She knew the word *missing* could trigger traumatic feelings for Dex from when he was abducted by an insane maniac just over a year-and-a-half ago.

He hated when his mother reached out to comfort him, so she held back and struggled to look like she wasn't continuing to stress out over his experience. Their experience.

"Ms. Abbott went to buy this fish up in Ventura, a fancy koi or something. They're like big goldfish, not the dollar-and-a-baggie kind, real expensive. But she never came back."

"Jesus." Dexter fidgeted in his seat, looking like a slinky constricted in a small box, ready to spring.

"Sorry, man. Forgot how this shit gets to you. Sorry, Miss Bea.".

She took a forkful of salad and chewed, despite feeling ready to gag.

"It's cool." Dexter readjusted his long legs. "I gotta deal with it." He wiped his forehead. "Supposed to get easier. What else did Pritkow say?"

"She said, 'Mr. Hayes, this is the third ID you've lost this year, so this time it's a twenty-five-dollar replacement fee. And you can't graduate without paying it.'"

Dexter groaned. "No, man, what else about Ms. Abbott? She cool. Best science teacher ever."

"I remember her from parents night." Bea said. "She impressed me-smart, enthusiastic, loves you kids."

"Yeah. Pritkow said cops're coming to talk with the staff tomorrow after school," Hayes said. He turned to Dexter. "We should find out what's goin' down. My friend Lulu operates the copy machine in the office after hours. We can hang with her and check things out."

The guys fist-bumped to seal the deal.

Bea's *Big Momma* radar began to hum, painfully. She pushed the salad aside. "Sean, Dexter, you may not get involved with this. Remember what happened last time?"

"We each made a hundred bucks when the network bought our footage of the apartment fire." Hayes beamed with satisfaction.

Bea bristled. "Dammit, Sean. You both could've been killed."

His expression became marginally remorseful behind his lank bangs.

Bea knew she had to intervene. "Maybe I'll stop over and talk to Principal Pritkow, see what I can find out. Likely, Ms. Abbott's turned up already."

Hayes's eyes widened. "You can't tell Pritkow I was, uh, spying. I kinda walked in at the right, I mean wrong, time. They weren't whispering, just talking, uh, low."

"Heck with this salad. For a piece of pizza, I'll keep your name out of the conversation," Bea said.

Hayes handed her a gooey slice.

Chapter 6

After clearing security near the high, blue-and-gold-painted, concrete SAMOHI wall, Bea walked onto the Santa Monica High grounds just off Lincoln and Pico. The 1920s vintage public school sat on a nearly thirty-acre fenced property on million dollar real estate. It was in the midst of renovations. An abandoned backhoe, piles of concrete chunks, orange caution cones, and other signs of construction were evident.

Four blocks from the Pacific, seagulls squawked overhead, diving for discarded breakfast crumbs. A spilled pile of Cheetos was causing mayhem. A diverse array of students sat in chatty groups beneath huge ficus trees. A few slumped in isolation, eyes glued to their devices.

Bea glanced at her watch—twenty minutes before the first bell. She had talked herself into a before-school appointment with Dean Margaret Pritkow. The dean let it be known that she was less than excited about a visit from the media, especially when the journalist was a parent who'd likely be prone to emotionally-biased coverage when it came to their oh-so-very-special children. Maybe all concerns would soon be moot. Hopefully, good news had arrived that Isabelle Abbott was unharmed and back in the classroom.

Bea quickened her pace and scurried up the steps to the administration building behind an Asian man, probably Chinese, mid-thirties, wearing pressed khakis and a black nylon windbreaker. A cop? The guy definitely gave that vibe. He turned and held the door open for Bea, and they both headed in the same direction.

"You with LAPD?" Bea asked. She held the next door open for him and they both entered the dean's reception area. A half-dozen students crowded the front counter, handing in forms of some kind.

"Ventura Metro." He offered a faint smile.

Bea smiled back. The guy was good looking, intense, and reminded her of L.A. Sheriff's Department Major Narcotics detective, Pete Anthony, her on-and-off lover. "Here to meet with Dean Pritkow about Isabelle Abbott?"

"Lots of questions, ma'am. You a reporter?"

Before Bea could respond, the dean, a substantial fifty-something woman of color with short gray hair and clear plastic-rimmed glasses, stepped from her office to the front desk. "Ah, you're here together. I didn't realize you knew each other."

"We don't," Bea and the cop responded in unison.

"Ms. Middleton, Detective Wu, come on in. I only have about ten minutes, then I've got to get to a meeting with the parent council." She led them into her sunny, highly organized office. "Coffee?" She gestured to a half-filled pot on top of a bookshelf.

"No, thanks," they responded in unison again. Bea rolled her eyes.

"You two a Greek chorus?" the dean asked, chuckling.

Neither Bea nor the detective risked answering.

Pritkow motioned Bea and Wu toward a well-worn leather sofa across from her busy desk. The in-and-out boxes both towered with folders and papers. "Have a seat, folks." She slid into a high-backed, ergonomic office chair and adjusted her specs. "This is all so upsetting. Isabelle Abbott's a gifted teacher. We've been blessed to have her, even part-time. Anything we can do at SAMOHI to help find her, we're all over it."

Bea pulled out her notebook.

The dean eyed it with concern. "Ms. Middleton, we agreed that this is all off the record for now, correct?"

"Yes, ma'am," Bea said, "of course."

Detective Wu jumped right in. "Thanks for meeting with me, Dean Pritkow."

"With us," Bea piped in. Damn cop was already trying to shut her down. That wasn't going to happen.

"Yes, with us," he relented. "I know our time is limited this morning so, tell *us* about Ms. Abbott. Could there be anyone—a colleague, student, parent——who'd had a run-in with her? Even an argument over a grade, or plagiarism, detention. Any bad blood?"

"Not that I'm aware of. Ms. Abbott was well-respected, smart, had a very upbeat personality."

"I can vouch that the kids really seemed to connect with her. She's my son's AP Marine Biology teacher."

Pritkow's brows furrowed, trying to conjure up the right name.

"Dexter Jackson," Bea reminded her.

"Of course, I'm sorry. Lovely young man. I knew you were a parent of one of our students." The dean smiled at Bea, then shifted focus back to the police officer. "We offered Ms. Abbott a regular staff position but she's trying to complete her PhD and needs the time flexibility to finish her dissertation. She did her job admirably, but I never saw her hang out or get particularly chummy with anyone. Although, this past winter, she did work on a new curriculum proposal with our science department chair, Dr. Halliburton Jones."

Wu's eyes narrowed. "I'd like to talk to Dr. Jones." He shot a glance Bea's way. "And to Dexter."

"Dexter doesn't know anything about his teacher's disappearance," Bea assured him, aware that her voice was a touch strident. The last thing she wanted to do was get her son involved in anything else traumatic or disturbing. *I will not allow it.*

They spent a few more minutes with Pritkow but learned little else. She texted them Dr. Jones's email address, then rose and began to collect materials for the upcoming meeting. Bea and Detective Wu thanked her and were on their way.

To ditch Wu, whom Bea didn't trust to leave her son alone, she excused herself and ducked into a nearby restroom. Several minutes later, Bea re-emerged and hurried across the steps, skirting the Greek amphitheater that expanded down the hillside. She headed toward the newly completed Innovation Building where science and technology were housed. Wu was suddenly at her heels.

"Off to the science department to see if Doc Jones is in?" He drew up next to her and matched strides.

The move was irritating. "Yep. You, too?"

He scratched at his clean-shaven chin. "I'm not your enemy, Ms. Middleton."

She walked a little faster, then quickly realized she had to settle down. This was not about protecting Dexter. In that, she'd already miserably failed. This was about finding the missing teacher. The possibility of abduction pushed too many of her most vulnerable buttons. Wu had every right to be here, it was his job. She was the interloper.

She slowed her pace and took a deep breath. "Sorry. I, uh, sometimes assume cops won't play well with others."

"You know what they say about assuming stuff," he said.

She huffed. "The assumption has served me well on numerous occasions." Bea turned and stopped as they approached the plaza in front of an industrial-looking modernistic structure. "You have kids, Detective?"

"Not yet. Someday."

"It's one helluva trip." Her big brown eyes searched his greenish-caramel ones. "Listen, sorry if I seem a little impatient." *Downright bitchy? Yup.* "My son was abducted a year ago, and this thing with his teacher really scares me."

He returned her hard gaze. "I have a sister who disappeared when she was twelve. This scares me, too."

Bea's chest tightened with painful empathy.

Wu continued. "But we're going to find Ms. Abbott. I promised her sister. And I keep my promises. Enough said, ma'am?"

"Okay, 'nuff said." Bea pressed her lips into a grim line. Her journalistic instincts buzzed with curiosity. *What had happened with his sister?* Now was not the time to open that box. "Come on, let's go see what Jones knows. I did a little background before showing up this morning, and as department chair, he teaches only two classes. Should be in his office."

They turned again toward the Innovation Building. Students had already filed into their classrooms and the campus was relatively quiet. Bea and the detective entered the airy atrium which was filled with planters of drought-resistant grasses and succulents. The space was just dog-eared enough to say high school rather than high-tech corporate. Posters pocked the walls, a ratty gray hoodie was trapped in a bed of cacti, and fast-food wrappers overflowed a recycling bin. A directory of offices, classrooms, and labs was affixed to a glass showcase at the base of an expansive staircase. Science Department, second floor.

Bea and the detective briskly climbed the stairs. Down the wide hallway and to the right, the science department front counter was staffed by an Abby Sciuto look-alike from the NCIS TV show, right down to the raven-black pigtails, straight-cut bangs, and dog collar. Behind her, faculty members toiled away in a warren of cubicles. Several big-windowed offices and a conference room edged the perimeter.

Bea spotted a nameplate, Dr. Halliburton Jones, etched in plastic next to the closest open door. A full-body human skeleton hung from a stand just outside the portal. Bea gulped and tamped down a grisly memory from another time.

"May I help you?" doppelganger Abby asked, as bright and perky as the original.

"We'd like a few minutes with Dr. Jones," Bea announced.

"He's quite busy. May I tell him who's calling?"

Wu presented his credentials. Bea kept hers in check. A media visit was usually more worrisome than having to deal with the police.

Abbyette slid off her high stool and abandoned her laptop. "One moment, please." She bustled into Jones's office. Seconds later she returned to the counter, opened the gate into the department and ushered the visitors to the Chair's cluttered office.

Like a scene from a Hogwarts's magical sciences lab—books, bones, beakers, and a collection of strange taxidermy fish on stands, covered every surface. Bottles of greenish liquid containing dark murky specimens looked ready to pop back to life and cause mayhem with the tap of a wand.

Round-faced, with a graying ginger beard and unusually small dark eyes, Dr. Hal Jones greeted them with a quick, damp handshake each. His skin was the color of skim milk, except for cheeks that flushed with Santa-Claus-like rosacea. He wore a rumpled corduroy sport coat over a greyish shirt and an aqua, fish-themed bow tie.

"Please, have a seat." He removed a pile of academic journals from one black plastic chair and his briefcase from the other.

"Hard to believe Miss Abbott is truly missing. Awful, so awful, terrible." He ensconced himself behind the desk where a shark's jaw with rows of razor-sharp teeth grinned at Bea and the detective. When seated, they practically had to look through the gullet to get a full view of the professor.

Wu lifted the distracting jaws and placed them on a nearby credenza. Jones stifled a modest gasp.

Bea contained a snicker. The shark chops were probably

great for intimidating kids, but the detective was no high school student.

Dr. Jones rubbed his balding pate. "*Isurus Lamnidae,* commonly known as the Mako shark. Was a gift from my dear mother when I was in middle school. Supported my early interest in marine biology, she did. Forever grateful to her, yes indeedy." He pushed a well-tended bowl of fancy neon minnows circling a Little Mermaid statuette out of Wu's potential grasp.

After formal introductions, and without being asked, Jones launched into his impressions of Isabelle Abbott. "She's a smart, capable woman, helped me a bit on some curriculum work. I have no knowledge of her personal life. I do recall that she'd done scuba diving around the world. Loved the ocean, of course. Very enthusiastic on that count."

Bea flashed on a watery death scene. "You think scuba could have played any part in her disappearance?"

"You mean like drowning?" He shook his head. "No, no, divers go as a group, always a buddy. Equipment meticulously inspected." He drummed his fingers on his desk. "Maybe she got an opportunity to go somewhere exotic. Young, single, and unfettered. Why not?" His eyebrows hiked up and his beady eyes gleamed for an instant. He stopped the drumming. "Wish I'd been a little more spontaneous in my younger years. But alas, I'm an old fuddy-duddy, always have been." His brief smile pinched into a round wet bow. "But she left me having to teach another Marine Bio section, and I'm already impossibly busy."

Bea's gaze darted around the office—it seemed more disorganized than busy. "It's my understanding," she continued, "from various students, along with the dean, that Ms. Abbott was highly conscientious about her teaching and her commitment to the students. Not the irresponsible type."

"Her sister, Casey, would agree." Wu nailed the professor with a hard, skeptical look. "Isabelle Abbott was not a woman who would randomly disappear and disappoint a classroom of pupils."

Jones nodded enthusiastically. His already pink cheeks further colored. "Yes, well, you're right, of course. I'm sorry, Detective, and Miss Middlemarch——I wish I could help you."

"Middleton," Bea corrected. The squirrely dude was irritating as hell.

"Of course." He stood, indicating a dismissal. "But I really must get back to work. Leave your cards with my receptionist, and I'll be sure to call if I think of anything that could help."

Bea was about to rise, but Wu wasn't ready to let the department chair off the hook. Remaining seated, he pulled out his iPhone for a quick glance. "We got forensics back on Abbott's home laptop yesterday and she'd been nosing around the dark net looking for a particular exotic golden koi. She found an address in Ventura for a place called Nemo's that doesn't exist. You know anything about that, Doctor?"

Jones's mouth popped open and moved like one of his stuffed fish trying to intake oxygen. "Oh, Lordy, no. I would certainly not attempt to go on the deep net or encourage anyone else to do so, for any reason. Anyway, it's illegal, isn't it? Full of people wanting despicable things." He wrung his pudgy hands. "Oh, Lordy, I hope she didn't try that. Such a sweet girl, can't imagine her getting into something nasty. But, do we really ever know people?" His shoulders sagged.

"There's a huge exotic fish and animal trafficking industry that moves through the Port of Long Beach," Wu continued. "All navigated via the dark web. Heard anything about that through the scientific grapevine? I'm sure people in your field are aware of this problem."

Jones glanced at his chair, perhaps deliberating whether to sit back down. He remained standing. Wu was making it clear that there was potentially much more at play here than a part-time instructor bailing on a job and sneaking off for a Caribbean dive trip.

"Well, of course we know about the black market trade but we're leaders here in promoting conservation and we're totally against trafficking of any kind. Lordy be, everyone knows Santa Monica is an ethical and sustainable community." Looking a little green around the gills, he placed his hand on his chest.

Bea wondered, was he having a heart attack? Or pledging allegiance?

"I would never have hired Ms. Abbott, and Dean Pritkow never would have approved, if we'd known she was a purveyor of any nefarious means of, uh, research."

"We don't know that she was doing anything illegal," Bea reminded him.

"Yes, very true. Her references were stellar. A nice girl, very nice. Not a dark-web-troller type. Oh, no, huh-uh." He shook his head, grabbed a tattered Manilla file folder from his desk and fanned himself. Finally, the professor acquiesced and sat back down.

The detective checked his phone again, then stood, visually poking around Dr. Jones's office, pausing to take a comprehensive look at each stuffed animal, mostly shark species, of which there were close to a dozen on display.

Bea could sense Jones's anxiety. Would Wu move another one of his sacred scientific objects? The professor wiped his brow then drummed his fingers again on his desk.

"Each specimen was lawfully obtained, I assure you," he blurted.

Wu nodded. "Of course. You have provenance papers on everything?"

"Yes, yes, you bet, all on the up-and-up, Officer. No dark net, no black market."

Bea noted that Hal Jones had that overwhelmed, confused look that made her wonder if he'd forget his own name if they pressed him much harder. "What's Abbott's dissertation topic?" she asked.

Wu sat back down.

"Uh, uh, something about vocalization and newborn gray whales, *Eschrichtius robustus*. Let me call a colleague who knows Ms. Abbott better than I do, probably better than anyone at SAMOHI. He's in the same doctoral program, I believe." The professor pressed a button on his desk phone.

"Yes, Dr. Jones." The voice not only echoed through the speakerphone, but also from the nearby faculty cubicle area.

"Matthew, could you come in here, please?"

In seconds, a tall, skinny, dreadlock-haired man stood in the doorway. With shoulders like door knobs above long, twig-like arms, his facial bones, sharp as fan blades, made him almost handsome. He was likely in his late twenties.

"This is Matthew Corcoran," Jones said. "Matthew, meet Detective Wu and Ms. Middlebury."

"Middleton." Bea took out her business card and pushed it in his direction.

Jones made the suffocating fish move with his mouth again, then turned to his colleague. "Uh, yes, Matthew, these people want to know more about Isabelle Abbott. Told them all I can, and now I must run." He took quick glance at the big clock above his desk and feigned lateness. He'd been with them barely ten minutes. "Use the conference room. Please, be my guest. There's usually some pastries in there."

Matthew looked confused. He pressed the screen of his Apple watch. "Okay, sir, but the staff meeting isn't until—"

"Preparation! There's preparation I have to finish. Must hurry, hurry. Nice to meet you, Ms. Middle, uh, Middleburg and Detective. Thank you, Matthew."

Jones held on to the file he'd been fanning himself with, grabbed his briefcase and practically knocked minion Abby off her stool as he sprinted out the door.

Matthew chuckled. "Not much of a people person but knows shark genetics like nobody else. Follow me—the conference room is right next door."

They slid into slate-colored Herman Miller Aeron chairs and made themselves comfortable around one end of an oval, stainless-steel-topped table that could accommodate several dozen. Large-screen TVs lined the wall.

"Nice digs," Bea said.

"All second-hand, donated by a scientific animation and game company down the street. Too shabby for them." He grinned. "What the hell am I doing in academia, huh?"

Bea let go of her office furniture envy. "Dr. Jones indicated that you knew Isabelle Abbott fairly well. You date her?"

"Naw, I'm gay. Been with a wonderful partner for three years. Izzy and me, we're in the same PhD Marine Bio program at UCSB. I actually helped her get this gig when the part-time job opened up. Good lady." He chewed at his lip. "I can tell you for sure, something bad's happened. She wouldn't walk away from her students."

Wu rested his elbows on the table and steepled his fingers. "We did some forensics on her laptop. She was nosing around the dark web."

"Shit," Matthew said. "Looking for that damn glow-in-the-dark gold koi?"

"That's the one." Wu's jaw visibly tightened.

Matthew Corcoran continued. "Izzy said some dude she'd met on a scuba trip out of Ventura Harbor a few weeks ago told her about a dark site that sold exotic fish. Said she'd be okay checking it out. I told her she was crazy to mess around with the Tor browser and dark web market stuff, but the woman's got a mind of her own. And she's too damn trusting."

"She say anything else about this man from the dive trip?" Wu leaned toward the teacher. "Appearance? Profession? Where he lives?"

"Let me think." Matthew shut his eyes for a moment and pressed the bridge of his nose. "He wasn't from near the beach. Maybe lived out toward the desert. She said he was good looking but kind of a macho asshole. Wouldn't shut up about spear-fishing with these exploding charges. Sick."

"Anything else?" Wu asked.

The teacher narrowed his eyes. "She said he was a cop."

Chapter 7

A cop. Bea felt her skin crawl and couldn't help thinking of the Golden State Killer. The illusion of safety. The betrayal of public trust. Why did her brain always leap to the extreme example?

She exchanged a quick look with the detective. Despite an inscrutable expression, maybe he was in the same awful place.

"Did Ms. Abbott mention what department this man worked for? LAPD? Ventura Metro?" Wu's voice was quiet and controlled.

"Like I said, not a beach city, maybe high desert, like Lancaster or Palmdale. Heck, maybe she said Palm Springs. Not sure. Dude asked her out for drinks after the dive, but she turned him down." Matthew shrugged. "That's all I got."

A pissed-off suitor? Bea turned to Wu. "We better start looking for scuba-certified cops who were on one of those trips."

"I'll call the harbor division right now." Wu stepped out of the conference room, phone to his ear.

Returning her attention to Matthew, Bea asked, "What else

can you think of that might help us find your friend?"

"Let me check my Outlook calendar."

She watched him scroll through several weeks' worth of activities.

His mouth drooping in a bleak frown, Matthew swallowed hard and shook his head. "I'm just about positive her latest dive trip happened three weeks ago this past Saturday, out of Ventura. My partner's parents were in town from Michigan, that's how I remember." Then he paused and sniffed, wiped damp eyes with the back of his hand. "Shit! Sorry. Talking with you guys has made this all very real."

Bea sighed and pushed a half-empty box of tissues his way. *Reality's a bitch.* A knot of pain twisted in her stomach. "Call us if you think of anything else, no matter how seemingly minor."

She gave Matthew a little hug, said goodbye to Abby 2.0, and joined Wu in the atrium where he paced and talked on his phone.

When he disconnected, Bea filled him in on the possible date of the dive trip. He texted the information to VMPD.

"I'd like to see Abbott's laptop," Bea announced before he could make another call.

Wu looked at her like she'd said, *I'd like to see your naked ass.* She couldn't contain a smirk. "I'm not sure what your resources are up in Ventura, but my office has deep pockets, and I've got an indie contractor who's a savant. Digital forensics. There may be more to Isabelle Abbott's searches than your people can identify. For now, how about we work at my office over in Hollywood for a couple hours and see what we can find on Isabelle's police-officer-scuba guy."

Wu frowned. "We're not sharing crime scene information with any news organization. I guarantee you that."

"All off the record until you give me the go-ahead." She squared up her shoulders. "And I don't do fake news. Ever."

"I wasn't implying you did." He toed the polished concrete floor of the atrium and gazed out across campus. "I'll see what

I can do. No guarantees. And Ms. Middleton, I still want to talk to your son."

Pain twisted her intestines again with a deep ache that antacids could never touch.

—

Wu parked at his laptop on the end of Bea's wide desk at CNN's West Coast building, looking for a scuba-diving cop from one of the desert communities. He saw Bea glance across the cube farm outside the office door.

"Action in the newsroom's thin this time of day." She sipped from a Lakers coffee mug. "Most staffers are out in the field."

"Was a good idea to set up shop here," he said. "The drive back to Ventura kills an hour and a half, easy." He'd have to keep her involvement on the down-low with his department, but he had to admit, she knew her stuff and had some awesome databases.

Bea nodded. *"Mi casa es su casa.* As long as you keep me in the loop. Plus, my boss is in Atlanta 'til Monday."

Wu smiled and scanned the customer lists that had just come in from the local businesses providing scuba trips in and around Channel Islands National Park. The four hundred square-mile area featured five primary islands and a dazzling array of sea life. Hundreds of clients had been exploring the underwater wonders over the past several months.

"Her sister, Casey, said Isabelle dove with a couple different outfitters, but couldn't remember their names." Bea poured them both another round of coffee from an almost-empty pot on her credenza, then picked up the pages of customer names and contact information spewing from the printer.

Wu took a swig of the tepid brew, eyes locked on his monitor. "Sweet. A buddy of mine from the police union emailed me staff lists for Palmdale, Lancaster, and Victorville. Here they come." He pressed the send button. "But remember, Isabelle's so-called admirer could also be state, federal, military, even a security guard."

"Yeah, I know, but let's not get ahead of ourselves. We'll begin with what we have and cross-match—see what we come up with."

"Agreed. How about I start with the Palmdale list and you take Victorville? We'll find the sucker."

"Sounds like a plan. Thanks for letting me in on this, Mac. I know you could get pushback."

He was both surprised and grateful to hear her acknowledge the line he was walking. "If I always waited for the department to free up somebody for online support, days could be lost with *nada*. Plus, you're better at this research stuff than anybody we have at HQ."

"Not sure if that's a compliment." Bea smiled.

"It is, and again, I appreciate your help but it can only go so far. First and foremost, this is a missing persons investigation; second, until I give you the okay, it's a not a news story. *Capiche?*"

"I understand." she said.

Wu was sure she didn't. He was also pretty sure she saw him as *her* helper, not the other way around.

Several hours, a bowl of trail mix and a pizza later, they'd compiled an initial list with social media profiles of cops who'd been on recent dive trips with Isabelle.

"We got six guys from five excursions." Wu studied the names. "This one, Preston Hicks, stands out." He tapped on his screen. "Single, good looking, former actor. Pictures of him with bodybuilder men and overly-sexy women with those pumped-up lips. He looks like a player."

"He may be a player but he also works with Habitat for Humanity, is a member of the LA Gay Men's Chorus—they're really good. Claims to have been in a relationship with the same guy for ten years."

"Really? Guess I missed that."

Bea chuckled. "That's why you need me."

"And vice versa," Wu winced at the defensive tone in

his voice. Bea seemed not to have noticed. No, she noticed everything, just chose to ignore it.

"Makes us a good team," she said. "How about we put Hicks and the other three officers who appear to have stable family lives aside for now."

Wu frowned. "Happy photos can cover up all sorts of shit."

"I'm not saying toss them, but move them further down on the priority roll. I'll see what I can find on their financial situations later. I have a contact who might be able to help with that if we need a deep dive, so to speak."

Wu let out a long breath. "Okay, so in our initial group of suspects we have two—Detective Cole Hobbs of Palmdale PD, and Hiram Lewis of Victorville's Domestic Violence Unit."

Bea frowned, wrinkled her nose, and adjusted reading glasses she clearly resented having to use. "Just emailed you California State records on Hobbs. He's been with the department for twelve years, worked his way up the ranks. Lots of nice citations but a couple excessive-use-of-force complaints. None amounted to anything. Been married and divorced four times and has five kids—three under eighteen he's gotta pay child support for. All are in a Catholic school. More cha-ching."

"Money could be a huge motivator," Wu said. "He's gotta be one angry dude after a bunch of fizzled relationships and kids sucking him dry financially, maybe the exes too."

He switched screens. "Okay, I got Hiram Lewis's info. Been with Victorville for five years, came over from LAPD. Not married but has one ten-year-old boy. Hiram used to play semi-pro baseball and now coaches the kid's Little League team. Placed third in last year's regionals. That takes a shitload of time."

"Kid's sports can cost a pile of money, too." Bea remained intent on her typing. "I have someone at LAPD who might be able to give us the scoop on Hiram. I'll email him."

"The fact that he works in the domestic violence area tells me the guy has access to kids who are runaways or trafficked.

Move him up the list."

Bea nodded. "And once we get our people flagged, we need to compare faces to the dive trip photos we have from Isabelle's social media pages. She took lots of underwater shots, but not many of the folks onboard the boat."

They worked in silence, then Bea stopped typing and glanced over at Wu, a Cheshire cat smile on her lips. "Hobbs owns a 2016 Maserati Levante S. My ex, my first ex, had one of those pricey toys."

"You're talking funds way beyond a detective's salary." Wu felt himself begin to get a warm fuzzy feeling about this dude. He stood and stretched his cramped muscles.

"Let's move Hobbs to the top for now," Bea said. "Next, I'm starting on the Lancaster posse. I already see a rookie named Bruno Diaz who moonlights as a bouncer at a strip club."

"Another position of opportunity to pimp messed-up girls looking to be loved." Wu sat back across from her and picked at a leftover pizza crust. "Let's see if that bouncer punk has a sheet."

"As a police officer, could he get a job in law enforcement with a record?"

"Probably not, but it depends on the severity of the offense and how old it is." Ten minutes later, "Diaz had a domestic assault charge against him that was withdrawn before prosecution. He killed his girlfriend's dog and cooked her parakeet in the microwave."

Bea gasped. Wu could see her jaw clench.

"Ho-lee-shit. Top of the list for this asshole." She wiped moisture from her tired brown eyes. "Nobody messes with kids or animals on my watch."

Wu saw her gaze cut to framed pictures at the far edge of her desk—a beautiful young girl in a pink tutu, and a tall skinny boy in a basketball uniform. This was becoming personal for her, as it was for him. "We gotta stay objective, Bea. Too much at stake to get all emotional about this one."

"Emotion drives everything, Detective, everything." The haunted look in her eyes raised goosebumps on Wu's arms. They turned back to their laptops, that great tool of both information and avoidance.

—

Lucy lay on a chaise lounge Elsa had recently purchased from Costco, sipping lemonade beneath an ancient fire-scarred olive tree. She tied her wavy dark hair into a ponytail and stared at the modest twenty-eight-week-old baby bump beneath her baggy white T-shirt. Big shirts, leggings, and flip-flops seemed to be her go-to wardrobe these days. A little foot kicked a field goal under her skin. She massaged the impact point, knowing that every pain and cramp could signal her uterus beginning to rupture. The next month would be particularly critical for both of their survival.

"The massive scar tissue from your childhood accident doesn't stretch, it tears," Dr. Carole Blanchard had said. "Your chances of maintaining this pregnancy are slim and become more dangerous as your womb expands. Bed rest, gentle stretching exercises, expert deep-tissue massage, constant monitoring, and prayer—those are the best prescriptions I can offer. We'll keep the baby in *utero* as long as we can, but you'll never get this cutie to term."

That report, which would have devastated most pregnant women, was actually better than Lucy had expected. She'd been told since puberty that she could never become pregnant. It was her punishment for surviving the car accident that killed her family. She'd seen a gravel truck about to pull out from the side road, but she couldn't yell to warn her father. The sound had stuck in her throat like cement. And then last year, her uncle had been murdered—driven off a mountain pass in a terrible storm. Why would she expect this baby to live? Or even herself? Maybe it was poetic justice taking its time with her.

The phone buzzed on the coffee table. It was Bea.

"Beebs, what's up?" Lucy's voice, rather than the upbeat tone she'd hoped for, sounded shrill to her ears. Lucy hadn't confided the details of her dangerous condition to anyone, even Bea. Her friend had enough of her own family issues to handle.

"How're you feeling, girlfriend?" Bea asked.

"Pretty good, all is well." *Other than the fact that my uterus could break open like an over-filled water balloon at any moment.* Lucy shuddered.

"Glad to hear that. Your aunt arrives from Mexico on Friday, right? You ready? Will be her first time out of the boonies in, what? Fifty years?"

"Yup. All under control. Elsa hardly lets me do anything."

"Good. So, who's bunking where? Not exactly the Four Seasons up at Casa de la Vega with no *casa*."

"Ha! My aunt and I'll be sharing the yurt. I've made it very cozy. Cheyney has a nice executive-style porta potty hooked up, and the water well is back in action. We're in good shape."

"Talk to your baby daddy lately? How's Burleson doing?"

Lucy flicked off a dusty gray olive leaf that had fallen onto her lap. "He's busy up north. Mending fences with his family."

"You're his family now, too—you and your jellybean."

Lucy gulped down a wave of sadness and loss. "We're talking. It's cool. He'll be down to visit. Might even have a job possibility."

A long silence hung between the friends.

"So, what aren't you telling me?" Bea finally asked.

"I'm okay, I'm fine, truly, just bored out of my mind, Beebs. You working on anything interesting? Need a photog for an easy assignment?"

"Well actually," Bea said, "that's one of the reasons I called. I've got a guy in Malibu about two miles from your place that I want to interview. An expert in illegal fish and reptile trafficking, a former federal agent named Bartlett who's now a consultant— whatever that entails. Thought you might want to tag along."

"Huh, fish and reptiles? Wasn't expecting Flounder and

Kaa."

"Who?"

"*Little Mermaid* and *Jungle Book*—they're characters."

"Yeah, okaaaaay. Lucy, have you been binge-watching Disney videos?"

"All but *Bambi,* can't handle that one. I told you, I'm bored out of my skull. Bless you for the diversion. Can't wait to meet this fed. Ha! Never thought I'd say *that*."

Bea filled Lucy in on the missing SAMOHI bio teacher, the woman's foraging on the dark net, and the overall investigation with Detective Macintosh Wu from Ventura Metro. "Pete just delivered Isabelle Abbott's laptop to our dear friend Bijan Rachmaji. He's looking into her Tor activity. In the meantime, we have to move fast on Bartlett, see what he knows. The chances of Abbott's survival go down by the hour."

Lucy felt her pulse begin to accelerate. Finally, some action. "When do you need me?"

"In an hour. PCH and Cross Creek, the Arroyo Building."

"Perfecto."

"Are you sure the doc says this kind of thing is okay for you to do?" Bea asked.

Lucy could hear her friend's concern. "As long as I'm not moving hay bales or climbing rock walls, I'm good to go."

Lucy ended the phone call and rolled off the chaise. A nail gun rat-a-tat-tatted from across the driveway as the walls of the barn went up. The sound was unnerving. Lucy flashed on a terrible moment of gunfire and blood in Mexico a year ago. *Stay in the present, Lucy,* she commanded. *Don't go there.*

Holding her budding belly, she trudged toward the yurt to retrieve her car keys and camera. Recording an interview wasn't exactly bed rest but was no more stressful than an easy walk down the road. She ignored the butterfly protests deep in her abdomen.

Chapter 8

There was no sense of day or night, only of the piranha's feeding cycle. Frenzy, gobble, then lethargically swim around and around like tigers pacing in a zoo, slowly losing their minds.

Isabelle was no longer handcuffed to the bed but was still locked in the small dorm-type room with a four-by-four-foot window looking into a deep blue aquarium that offered the only light. Tears dripped slowly down her cheeks as she thought about Casey and how worried she'd be. About her dog—please, God, have somebody find Booker and feed him. About her students. About her life. Was anyone looking for her? Looking for Celeste?

Izzy's roommate had disappeared hours ago, after the delivery of their twice-a-day plate of apples, carrots, and string cheese. Celeste reported having had some almonds included on the tray before the last "performance." Their tormenters must figure the women needed the extra protein when they entertained the sicko predators. Entertained? What a benign description for being raped and murdered by the next tour group of perverted monsters.

Izzy shuddered. There was no way five days had already passed—maybe two. Or three. Since the bastard had tased the girl, they'd been pretty much left alone. There was little sense of activity other than someone feeding the fish in the aquarium and the arrival of the meager meals for the mer-victims trapped in their cell. Izzy wondered how many other women were locked away in the aquarium from hell.

She pressed her fingers to her temples then pushed back her lank hair. No, she could not begin to think of herself as a victim. She was a mermaid. Not *their* mermaid but her own creation. Hans Christian Andersen's Little Mermaid takes charge of her destiny and finds her own salvation. Other mermaids drown their mortal lovers. Yes, she and Celeste were little mermaids in a different story—they were smart, plotting, and ruthless, with shiny tails as sharp as knives.

After some minutes of yoga stretching to ease the weary tension in her body, Izzy plunked down on her rubber air mattress. Without warning, the door to the room flew open, then slammed shut behind Celeste. She stumbled in, landing hard on the floor. She didn't attempt to rise but lay quietly sobbing. The girl was no longer wearing the canvas straight-jacket but pink scrubs streaked with shiny gold paint.

Isabelle crouched next to her and stroked her damp forehead. Celeste shivered and reached out. With help, she crawled to her bed and slumped against the wall, still shaking. Her eyes were sunken holes of terror.

Minutes later, the door opened again, and strong, bluish light filled the room. Taser man cocked his chin toward Isabelle. "You, follow me."

Heart hammering, she rose obediently and trailed him down a long, dark hall, planning his murder as she went.

—

Pete Anthony stepped into Bijan Rachmanji's dim, monitor-filled office. Air conditioning thrummed through the silvery ducts in the open, loft-like ceiling above. Bijan was the lead digital engineer at WarChallengeWorld game company in Santa Monica, and also an indie contractor for both the LAPD and the LA County Sheriff's Deputies digital crime units. His unmatched expertise was in forensic accounting—following the money and other illicit trails and transactions into remote digital backwaters. Tracking the Isabelle Abbott breadcrumbs into the dark net was right up his alley.

He pushed the remains of a Thai chicken bowl to the side of his sprawling, action-figure-packed desk. The smell of peppers and soy sauce spiced the atmosphere. "Hey, Pete." Bijan wiped his mouth with a napkin, then threw the crumpled paper toward the garbage can. It joined the pile of misses. Oh, well. He had other skills. "Come on in, just finishing lunch. You got the laptop?"

Pete, tall and broad-shouldered with dark hair and dark complexion, wore a hefty gold Saint Christopher's medal around his neck and a black leather bomber jacket despite the warm weather. He handed over the computer. "Thanks for doing this on short notice, man. Ventura Metro was a real pain in the ass about chain of custody. I promised to stay with it while you work, so I hope you can track down whatever you're looking for real fast."

Bijan's round, babyface lit up like a jack o' lantern. "You must be doing this for Bea. Either she or Lucy. Those two can drag any red-blooded man into almost anything their devious little minds conjure up."

"You got it, bro. Not exactly what I wanna be doing today, babysitting a laptop." He rummaged in his pocket, came up with a thumb drive and gave it to Bijan. "All the Abbott woman's passwords are on this. Ventura PD traced her last digital activity. I'm told there's stuff that can stick to her deep search like digital Post-its, and that shit's almost impossible to track."

Bijan grinned. "The operative word is *almost*. You been on Tor?"

Pete scratched at his bristly GQ chin stubble. "Huh-uh. I leave that crap to the geeks. No offense."

"None taken. Bea calls me 'geek-a-licious.'" Bijan chuckled and picked up a glow-in-the-dark keyboard that resembled a Frisbee. He ensconced himself in an oversized leather desk chair that had programmed massage functions built in. "Why don't you grab a seat, Detective—watch and wonder. You'll find all this disgustingly fascinating. And, you'll get a better sense of what you're up against these days."

Pete pulled over a nearby director's chair and slid in next to the computer wizard. "Hang on a sec. Got a text from the hot woman of color we were just dissing. She wants you to take a quick look at the finances of three cops who might have some connection to Abbott. I'm forwarding you her message. Doesn't need it until later today."

"She forgets I also have a day job."

Pete laughed. "I know what you mean, man. Anyhow, on to the darkness."

Bijan nodded, popped a handful of peanuts into his mouth, offered them to Pete, then began. "For your background info, researchers say only about 4 percent of the internet is visible to the general public on the clear net. The remaining 96 percent is made up of the deep web." Bijan typed at warp speed and in seconds a cartoon of a creepy-looking dude in a black hoodie and soul patch appeared center screen, beckoning them to follow. "It's a little confusing but the dark net's a subset of the deep web where there are sites that sell everything from drugs, 747s, and counterfeit money, to exotic animals and human beings. You can even hire a frickin' hitman. You pick the tool to be used— bat, awl, gun, boa constrictor, whatever."

"All the happy shit," Pete said, his face grim. "A lot of sick assholes out there."

Bijan nodded. "Okay, now we're on the extreme black market

of the twenty-first century. Was first called the Silk Road, but the name changes constantly to avoid detection. A very effective moving target."

Both quietly studied the list of services and products.

Pete cleared his throat, then asked, "maybe I'm a nutcase and wanna off my ex. Do I pay with Mastercard? Or PayPal? Or maybe our first-born child?"

"If you can dream it, it's probably an option. But actually, transactions are in Bitcoin or similar digital forms of currency. I'll give you an overview of the crap that's on here and then we'll follow the Abbott woman's search for this fishie that got her into so much trouble."

If Pete had had a seatbelt, he would have fastened it. Drugs— everything and anything. Instructions on how to cook and season a woman on the Cafeteria *Cannibale,* bizarre game sites, fetishes, child porn, hawkers selling every kind of degeneracy. Need a passport or any kind of ID? All available. Want to kill someone and put it on video? In the red room you can direct your own show featuring a hapless homeless person or a psycho who volunteered online to be tortured and murdered. Real? Fake? Who the hell knew. And then there were benign organic farm sites featuring produce and eggs from happy suburban chickens. Huh? Even perverts needed to eat.

Pete sat back in the gloom, mildly nauseous, as Bijan finished up the grand tour of vice and depravity. The detective had seen some hideous stuff in his job, but he never quite got used to any of it. He sat quietly, feeling intense shame at being a member of the human race. Vipers were kinder to each other. He closed his eyes for a moment and listened to the sound of Bijan clicking deeper into the slime.

Just as he dragged his attention back to the monitor, a graphic of a black hole in outer space appeared—letters and numbers swirled and the program sucked their information into darkness. "Whoa, what was that?" Pete asked.

Bijan didn't have an immediate answer. In about ten

seconds, the blank screen turned yellow and *voilà*, they were on a browser called The Yelluh Brick Rogue.

Bijan sat up straighter. "L. Frank Baum and his Oz books were about adventure and fantasy, but I think the ol' dude would roll over in his grave if he saw this shit."

"We ain't in Oz anymore, Frankie," Pete said.

"This should get interesting." Bijan pounded away on the keys. A munchkin popped up and something akin to a travel brochure skittered by so fast it was just an impression of exotic locations interspersed with blood and graphic sex. "I think Abbott's information was captured by some kind of international sex tourism site. I've stumbled onto this shit before, even mentioned it to Lucy, who told Bea. Thought she could use it as an angle on a trafficking story she has to produce. Let me figure out the precise key-in."

Pete and Bijan leaned toward the screen. Bijan's thick fingers again stabbed at the glowing Frisbee-esque keyboard. Code scrolled. A list of names appeared.

Before Bijan could continue, the detective grabbed his hand. "Stop!"

"What? These names mean something to you?"

Pete felt cold sweat dampen his neck. "Simpson Bartlett. Bea and Lucy are on their way to chat with the guy up in Malibu. He's a former federal agent who worked in exotic animal recovery for a decade, out of Long Beach. You think he could be involved in this crap?"

"Wouldn't be the first time an agent went bad. Must be a shitload of money involved. Beyond bizarre that he'd use his own name, though." Bijan grabbed another handful of peanuts. "Maybe he's being setup or framed, maybe he's been hacked, or maybe he's a master predator who doesn't know what the fuck he's doing in the digital sphere. Anybody's guess."

Bijan brought up a promotional video from a place called Piscem Auratus—Fish of Gold. What they saw was horrifying. Stunning, naked-breasted mermaids danced beneath the water until jaws packed with razor-sharp teeth ripped the women to bloody shark chum. The aquamarine water swirled with scarlet clouds and bits of gold from glittering costumes. Men's faces flashed orgasmic—then, fade to black.

Pete grabbed his cell phone and texted Bea and Lucy, *"Tell Bartlett NOTHING and get the hell out of there, NOW."*

Chapter 9

Lucy pulled her new top safety-rated, hybrid SUV into the visitor spot. Safety—what a cosmic joke. The image of her father's totaled '67 Mustang convertible, the bright color of spilled blood, circled her brain's periphery, then vanished like her family had disappeared on that golden afternoon. She would never put her child into an unsafe car. Just an unsafe womb. Lucy swallowed hard, burdened by her own form of recklessness.

She saw Bea's ride parked a couple spaces down. A silvery white BMW—the replacement car she'd finally purchased after a major brushfire had consumed the Vega ranch and destroyed their vehicles. Lucy spotted her friend waiting outside the glass doors to the Mediterranean-style, two-story Arroyo Building. A high-end women's clothing store and a dance school took up most of the first floor. Lucy paused to peep into the glass-walled studio. A well-known actress waited for her kid to finish a tap class. Mama looked to be swooning at her offspring's amazing talent. Click-click-click went the little girl's patent leather shoes.

Lucy wondered if she'd ever have a tap dancer to admire.

Bea appeared and slipped her arm though Lucy's. "Seems like just yesterday that was my Alyssa."

They hugged and headed up the wide steps to the second-floor offices, still arm in arm.

"Surprised that the doc okayed you to drive," Bea shot Lucy a suspicious glance.

"Got the ultra-safe car. No problem." She was not without guilt at stretching the truth.

"What if somebody crashes into you and the airbag explodes, and, and—"

"Bea, please, stop. Shit happens. If I get hit, I get hit. I'll be super careful." She hated thinking about her vulnerability and glanced at her watch. "Come on, we're late."

Bea scowled and held on to Lucy tighter, only letting her go as they entered the office.

Simpson "Sonny" Bartlett's place of work opened into a small, unstaffed reception area furnished with two peach-colored armchairs and a Formica coffee table circa 1980s Holiday Inn. A struggling ficus slumped in the corner, barely clinging to life. Enlarged photos of fishing trips and dive expeditions hung from the wall behind a matching Formica desk. The door opened into an expansive corner office where the former agent quietly conversed with someone on the phone.

"Agent Bartlett," Bea called, to let him know they'd arrived.

She heard him sign off from the call. A very fit, square-jawed man in his mid-fifties stepped through the door into the reception area and offered his hand. Introductions were made.

"Thanks for agreeing to see us so last minute," Bea said.

"My pleasure. Have a seat."

Rather than inviting them into his inner sanctum, he motioned them to the peachy arm chairs. Odd. Bea's phone buzzed, low but persistent. She ignored it and sat down next to Lucy. Bartlett perched on the edge of the desk like a coach surveying his lackluster players.

Bea took a quick glance at her notebook, then jumped in. "So, Agent Bartlett, we have a case that might involve exotic fish, likely koi. A woman disappeared up in Ventura while in search of a special golden variety. She'd been poking around on the dark web trying to find this particular species."

Bea's cell buzzed again. Then again. She gritted her teeth. "I'm so sorry. Let me grab this. Maybe there's an emergency with the kiddos." She checked her messages. Paused, then texted a quick response before silencing her phone.

"All okay?" Bartlett asked.

"Missing jazz shoes. Children sometimes think the smallest thing's a major crisis," she said with the barest of a smile.

Lucy cocked her head and looked quizzically at Bea. Something was going on. Bea didn't acknowledge her.

"So, again, Agent Bartlett—"

"Call me Sonny," he said.

Bea's eyes narrowed. "Sonny. You have impressive credentials in the exotic animal apprehension arena. As a federal agent talking to a layperson, if I wanted to get involved and score some big bucks trafficking, say, in rare fish—how would I get started?"

His lips pursed for a thoughtful moment and he steepled his fingers like he was shooting a gun. Lucy was afraid he was off-put by the query, but he took to the subject.

"Interesting question. Trading in exotic and endangered animals is a multi-billion-dollar business but it pales next to good old drugs, sex, and weaponry." He looked into middle distance, then back at Bea. "Combining that triad with a little deep-sea fishing kicker on the side would be lucrative."

Lucy's always vivid imagination percolated fast. "You mean like killing sharks with an AR—that's the weaponry. Then making an aphrodisiac out of their fins—that's the drugs and sex. With a Grateful Dead cover band playing in the background."

He laughed out loud revealing perfectly sculpted, arcti-white teeth. "Yeah, okay. That could work. Want to partner up and get rich?"

Bea didn't join in the gaslighting game. "Agent Bartlett, Sonny, anyone you've come across over the years who might be involved in trafficking rare fish? I understand you're following this stuff, still consulting with law enforcement."

He fidgeted in his seat. The pearlies disappeared. "Yes, I'm still involved, but very part-time. You said you're looking for a young woman who disappeared while hunting for a rare species in Onionland."

"Onionland?" Bea asked.

"Tor—The Onion Router—lets you browse the net anonymously. The deep web can be a dangerous place. Not at all unusual for random people to call you or show up at your house after you've been online."

"Guess it's not as anonymous as you'd think." Lucy fingered her camera. Was like a pup on her lap—warm and comforting.

"Anything could have happened to this woman," Bartlett continued. "If you're thinking sex trafficking, most traffickers look for younger girls—vulnerable, immature, without family support. As you described her, your gal doesn't fit the profile."

"Why do think someone would snatch her instead of a younger girl who'd be an easier victim?"

Sonny shrugged. "It's not exactly my area of expertise. But maybe she appeared more vulnerable than she really was—like she looked younger. Could be whoever took her liked how the dive suit fit her. Or somebody wanted her gone for their own illicit reasons. Or hell, maybe she randomly fell off the dock, hit her head and sank to the bottom. Could be anything." He threw up his hands and shrugged.

Bea nodded. "About the rare koi she was after, who can we talk with to shed some light on that?"

"You're talking to him." He preened for an instant. "Koi, rare or not, are a man-made breed of fish. Not much black market demand. I'd say the koi thing's a dead end."

Lucy watched the agent's body language as he spoke.

It seemed more rigid and controlled once talk shifted from ideas for making money on the dark web to Isabelle Abbott's disappearance. There was also one angle he hadn't mentioned.

Lucy shot Bea a quick glance then addressed Bartlett. "Could someone have come after her for her knowledge base, her research? She's finishing her doctorate in Marine Biology. I got a hold of a paper she wrote last year on genetics and communication among shark species. Way out-there stuff, borderline sci-fi, but compelling."

"I don't have the foggiest idea on that one, sorry. Miss, uh, Vega, is it?"

Lucy nodded, suddenly dismayed that he remembered her name. There was a creepiness factor emanating from the guy that was unnerving.

Bea shuffled some notes on her lap. "Do you know a police officer named Cole Hobbs? Works out of Palmdale. Big into the scuba scene. Does lots of spearfishing off the Channel Islands."

Lucy added, "We think he might be the one who referred Isabelle Abbott to animal procurement sites on the dark net."

Agent Bartlett rubbed his chin and squinted. "Hobbs, like Luke Hobbs in *The Fast and the Furious?*" He chuckled. "Never heard of him. But lots of cops and fire fighters dive. If I was working up in the high desert, I'd be down here every minute I had off."

His enthusiastic smile was porcelain ready to crack.

Bea continued. "How about Hiram Lewis or Bruno Diaz? Heard those names?"

"No, can't say that I have, but I can check my records. Will email you if I find anything."

The phone rang in Bartlett's inner office. He glanced at his Apple Watch. "I'm sorry, ladies, but I've been expecting this call. Gotta grab it. Maybe we can do the taped interview another time. Will get back with you on any information I come across on the men you mentioned."

He rose, signaling his request for their immediate departure.

Lucy went over to the dying ficus and dumped the contents of her water bottle into the pot. "You need to take better care of this plant."

Bartlett looked at her as if she was out of her mind. "Uh, okay."

"Thank you for your time, Agent." Bea smiled and handed him her business card. "I'll be in touch."

"Would be my pleasure," he said like a Maserati salesman who suddenly realized you were on a Camry budget.

Lucy grabbed her camera and followed Bea out the door. It shut with a solid click behind them, followed by the twist of a lock.

"Guy's lying his ass off," Lucy whispered.

Bea nodded. "Sonny pulled the plug on his light and bright sunshine-boy demeanor the minute I said 'Hobbs.'"

Chapter 10

Lucy led Bea into a coffee shop across from the Arroyo Building for a quick caffeinated pick-me-up. The informal country-store vibe was calming as they compared impressions of Agent Bartlett. Patsy Cline sang the classic, "I Fall to Pieces" in the background.

"I've got a smarmy feeling about this guy," Lucy said, slowly drinking pregnancy-correct chamomile tea.

"He's a piece of work." Bea poured a few packs of stevia sweetener into her steaming brew and frowned. "His flashy dentition alone reminded me of the shark teeth in Halliburton Jones's office at SAMOHI."

Lucy smiled. "I ran the camera's audio for most of the discussion. So, we've got a little something recorded for future reference. I'll transfer it to a file and email it to you."

"Excellent, you wonderfully sneaky woman." Bea's dark eyebrows drew together. "Not sure why Pete was so freaked out about us meeting with Sonny-boy."

"Was that Pete on the phone?"

"Yup. Said Bartlett was bad news and doesn't want us near him. Did my sweet detective think the guy was gonna wrestle us both to the floor and sell us into sex slavery? Not on my watch."

"Maybe it's worse than we think," Lucy said. "We should call Pete right now."

Bea nodded. She had her honey on speed dial.

He picked up immediately. From across the table Lucy could hear him yelling.

"Calm down, darlin,' I'm putting you on speaker phone so Lucy can hear. We're in a public place, so chill," Bea said.

Silence from the detective's end of the connection.

She placed her cell on the table and glanced around. Bea and Lucy were the only customers inside. The other patrons lounged on the patio. "What's with this former agent?" Her voice was low. "He practically threw us out of the office when we started talking about Isabelle Abbott and the dark web. We mentioned Cole Hobbs and the discussion was over." Bea took a sip of her steamy hot coffee.

"Ah, shit, ladies. I'm here with Bijan. Bartlett's name came up in conjunction with an international sex tourism site where you get to fuck a mermaid."

"Language, Sarge," Bea reminded him.

"You pay extra," his voice lowered then shot back up, "and you can watch a shark or a piranha or some freako monster tear her the fuck apart. Like a snuff thing. Looked authentic as hell."

Bea gulped, her face tinged gray. She took the phone off speaker and sidled closer to Lucy so they could both hear Pete. "You think Abbott was kidnapped so she could be one of their prey?"

"Very likely. The pictures were bad, really bad. Worst I've seen outside of pedophile shit. We took a break from the horror show to puke, then went back online a minute ago. The site is *gone*. Even Bijan can't trace it."

"Can't trace it—*yet*," the digital marvel called from the background. "Gonna nail those sumbitches. Count on it."

Lucy glanced across the parking lot and noticed Agent Bartlett jogging toward a shiny black Range Rover. "Looks like Sonny Boy's fleeing the scene." She pointed out the window then looked over at Bea. "Should we follow him?"

"No! NOT a good idea." Pete's voice was borderline shrill, drowning out Patsy Cline. "You have no idea what he could be leading you into. Get his license plate and text it to me."

Lucy ran to the window. Recorded the plate number on her phone as the car sped by. She returned to the table and sent the image to Pete.

"Sorry we gave you a scare, sweet pea," Bea said to Pete, "but we can handle ourselves just fine."

The discussion stopped for a moment, then the detective continued, "You two would look pretty hot in mermaid tails, so yes, I was scared shitless for your lives. You would've been, too, if you'd seen those videos. And with Lucy pregnant and all. I'm just so damn relieved you're both okay."

The detective muttered several undecipherable curses under his breath. Then he paused. Lucy could hear his breathing.

"And I'm still pissed that you went through with that interview. These people gotta be stone cold psychopaths."

Bea pressed her thumbs to her temples and closed her eyes. "We appreciate your concern, sweet men, both you and Bijan. But all is well. The girls are all right."

"But Isabelle Abbott is *not* all right," Lucy added. "Three days and nothing. I hope this info about Bartlett's possible involvement will give us some momentum."

"Arranging for a BOLO as we speak," Pete said.

Bea finished the call after scheduling an early evening meeting to update Mac Wu on their latest grim discoveries.

—

Izzy followed taser-man through a maze of dark passages running between huge aquarium tanks. They were very commercial-looking—maybe holding 50,000 gallons or more. Through narrow, slot-like windows slashing the hall, she glimpsed hammerhead sharks, and something mammoth, golden, and nearly transparent. It moved like a dirigible. The sad whale song recordings she'd heard days earlier echoed through hidden loudspeakers.

Eventually, they came to a small corridor opening into a wider hallway. Taser-man marched ahead toward an open door, then stood like a sentry beside it, motioning for Izzy to enter.

She hesitated. The bright light in what appeared to be a design studio was blinding to eyes now used to darkness.

"Come in, sweetheart. Don't be afraid. This is the fun part." The voice crackled like a vintage radio that wasn't quite tuned in.

A wizened old woman, her face a dried apple beneath a purple beret, stood in the center of a costume shop, arms outstretched as if claiming her world. She wore a black silk sheath dress which made her look like a shiny crow amid racks of glittery apparel. A sewing machine, poised for action on a work table, was ready to piece together uncut swaths of golden cloth. Isabelle stepped through the door.

Over a large white desk hung an array of framed pictures of a slim, pretty woman in a bathing suit, caught in synchronized swimming poses, meeting with Hollywood glitterati, and diving into a pool of mermaids. Below them were what appeared to be framed medals from competitions.

"Esther Williams had nothing on me, Cloris-Edna Jones. Oh, yes. Do you remember her? Silly me. You're too young, but you can Google her."

You going to give me access to a computer, old woman? I'll Google 9-1-1.

"'America's Mermaid,' they called her. Couldn't act her way out of an inner tube but came alive the minute she hit the water. Oh, those were the days. And I was right by her side. Technically, I was a much better swimmer, better figure, too, if I dare say." She struck a pose as if ready for the paparazzi. "But it was all stupidly political. Couldn't drown her, now could I? Can't say I hadn't thought about it though." Her bitter laugh turned into a coughing spell.

She sounded to Lucy like the swimming pool version of the insane fading film star, Norma Desmond, in the classic movie, *Sunset Boulevard.*

"Okay, dear," she chirped, "let's get you measured up and off to water ballet practice."

"Water ballet practice?" Izzy was not the toe-pointing type, but she'd do anything to stay alive.

"Oh, yes. It's a combination of synchronized aquatics and waterboarding. You'll be wonderful, dear." She laughed again, this time daintily into a lace handkerchief. "Hop up on the riser and off with the clothing. Chop-chop. Don't have all day." She picked at a puffy pink pincushion affixed to her wrist by an elastic band.

Izzy hesitated and looked over her shoulder at taser-man. He stood planted at the door, arms across his chest, ready for the show.

"Come, come, child." As she guided her unwilling model onto a riser the old lady squeezed Izzy's elbow hard and dug long, red fingernails into her flesh. The crooked old digits still had impressive strength.

Burning with humiliation, Izzy dropped her clothes, the woman whipped out a measuring tape as if ready to start flogging. "Lovely form, dear—breasts a bit modest, but perky."

In minutes the crone finished her task, entered the numbers on a small legal pad and tossed it onto her desk. "I think I have just the thing for you. We work with a seamstress up in Montreal and she has sent me several brilliant costumes. But for now, something more practical." The woman shuffled over to a gym-type locker and pulled out a nylon racing Speedo in bright blue.

"Put it on, dear. Off to your practice. Have fun and don't forget to hold your breath."

Izzy stepped into the suit then taser-man approached and

yanked her down from the dais. His touch was tepid and wet like a dead fish. She tensed with repulsion.

The old lady laughed again. "Don't worry, dear. Oscar will take good care of you."

Izzy gulped and struggled not to throw up as he dragged her away.

Chapter 11

Agent Bartlett suppressed a sneer as off-duty detective Cole Hobbs sauntered past the bar in his direction, Corona in hand. If macho arrogance had a magazine face, it would be this high desert cop. Tall and ruddy-faced with windblown auburn hair, an array of shark tats interspersed with Bible quotations decorated his arms. The man made most people want to simultaneously stand and gawk and run for their lives. Bartlett figured the dude was every chick's fantasy bad boy. Hobbs slid into the booth.

Across the table, Sonny Bartlett downed a shot of tequila and wiped perspiration from his neck with a Francisco's Taqueria paper napkin. He fantasized about running Hobbs over with his car.

"What the fuck were you thinking?" Bartlett's jaw tightened. "The bitch you dumped on us is a PhD candidate and a school teacher. You thought she'd just disappear without anyone noticing? She's friends with a nosy TV reporter and a bunch of cops."

Hobbs took a swig of beer then polished his Ray-Bans. "Not my bad, man. Said her parents were dead, and it was just she and her sister. Thought she was like, um, sixteen. When she talked about school, I figured she was a goddamned high school cheerleader."

"Due diligence. Vetting. Heard of that shit? Isn't that what detectives do?" Bartlett felt his face flush. "Your reckless, poor judgement is going to bring this truly amazing enterprise down. We'll never find another setup like it."

Hobbs scowled. "I've been risking my ass to provide a hundred percent of the product. And where's the gratitude, man? Fuck, I'm not being paid enough to put up with this bullshit." He studied his reflection in his sunglasses then put them on, even though the bar was dim.

"You're being paid plenty." Bartlett squeezed a fat lime into his tequila then leaned back and watched the detective stuff a fistful of mini pretzels into his mouth. Hobbs had zero class and shit for brains, but up until now, he'd been an effective procurer of talent. "Stay the fuck away from Ventura for a while. Your buddies at Metro PD are all over this disappearance."

Hobbs shrugged. "Shit, interest'll pass soon as the next shiny object comes along." He downed his beer and held up the empty bottle to signal for another. He wiped his hand across his mouth and turned to Bartlett. "I want a boat."

"Huh?"

"I said, I want a boat."

The agent rolled his eyes. "So, buy one. You've been whining about sea kayaking for years."

"No, I mean I want a real boat." Hobbs leaned forward. "Got my eye on a nice pre-owned Aquariva 33."

"You're delusional. A fucking quarter-of-a-million-dollar wet dream. No chance."

"I'm sick to death of these crummy dive trips full of amateurs with rented wetsuits. If I had a nice-looking rig, I'd be able to pick up baby bitches left and right. Float 'em right up the river and into Piscem. You're raking in the cash. I need a better cut."

Was this a shakedown? Fuckin' blackmail? Bartlett felt his asshole pucker big time. He started to respond but the cop's attention was now on the bartender and her low-cut T-shirt as she shook a mixed drink to a Jimmy Buffet song.

Bartlett knew how this would end if he didn't put a stop to Hobb's demands, ASAP. He slid from his chair, threw down some bills and turned toward the door. He growled over his shoulder, "We're all meeting at Piscem tonight, nine o'clock sharp. Going over our new strategy. No excuses, be there."

"Roger that, sunshine," Cole Hobbs called. "See y'all at Piss-cum and we'll talk more about my boat."

A fresh plate of taquitos was placed before Hobbs and he dug right in. The waitress flipped her platinum hair and giggled.

Bartlett felt ready to hurl.

When the agent hit the sidewalk outside the restaurant, the temperature on the bank's sign across the street read 118 degrees. *I hate the fucking desert.*

His black Rover sat at the curb, shimmering in the heat. After remotely opening the windows, starting the ignition, and activating the air conditioning, Bartlett stepped back into the relative shade of the building, pulled out his phone and punched in a number. Cloris-Edna picked up after five rings.

"We're getting rid of Hobbs," Bartlett said.

"You'd better clear it with our benefactors, Barahona and the Hondurans. They'll want to be consulted."

"Fuck them. I know what we need better than they do."

"I hope it doesn't come back to bite us," she said.

"If they give us any shit, I'll take care of it." Bartlett disconnected and reluctantly crawled into his supposedly cooling vehicle. The thermometer on the dash read 121.

—

Isabelle Abbott stood on the side of a turquoise-colored holding pool chewing on her lip. A collection of stainless-steel equipment, a microscope bay, and an array of supply racks around the room's perimeter gave her the serious creeps. The area appeared to be set up for veterinary research purposes and she prayed that she wasn't going to be the next lab rat, or whatever the finned equivalent was.

Roughly twenty-five yards square, the tank before her could be twenty or thirty feet deep, but was hard to tell. The water smelled salty, not chlorinated. It was a pond compared to the huge aquariums Izzy had hustled by, intent on staying well ahead of Oscar and that hundred-thousand-volt stun gun he wielded like a cattle prod. The terrifying weapon emitted a shrill, bone-chilling whine as it powered up. The sound itself was enough to lay a victim flat.

Two other young women in their teens, stood beside her, all in blue nylon swimsuits. A short, busty gal wore a curly ginger wig secured to her head with stringy fake seaweed. The other woman, dark-skinned and slim, had long dreads threaded with gold beads and tied back in a pony tail. They each stared ahead through vacant, hopeless eyes, suggesting that they'd been through the mermaid experience more than once. Izzy shuddered.

The fast click-clack of heels reverberated from a hallway behind them. Izzy turned to see the nasty old woman from the costume studio mince through the doorway with short staccato steps like Bette Midler on the runway. Her gold turban was the size of a small life raft.

"Okay, darlings, we have two days of rehearsal and you won't get out of this pool until your routine is nailed down tight." She removed her diamond-studded eyeglasses, held them up to the light, and cleaned them with her sleeve. "Two more performers, rookies, will be joining us tomorrow so I'll expect you to lend a hand in their training. Black Pearl," she said to the dark-skinned woman, "and Sea Star," she nodded to ginger-wig, "this new entertainer with us today is Coral."

Sea Star? Wasn't that the name of the Ventura Realty

Company whose sign was in the window of the supposed koi shop? *Assholes.* Izzy sneered and hoped to catch the other water ballerinas' attention for a quick side-eye glance. No response.

"As a reminder," the old woman continued, "your breathing tubes hang into the water from the compressor above. You may take oxygen only at the allotted times in the routine. Any violation and your regulator will be turned off until you decide to behave. Oscar is here to ensure that you don't break the surface without my say-so." She winked at him with her heavy false lashes. "I'm sure you'll all fully cooperate, my dears, and we'll have a lovely time." She slapped her hands together for two sharp claps. "Let's get into our wetsuits now, shall we?"

Izzy followed Black Pearl and Sea Star's mute, robotic lead. They sat down on the edge of the pool and Oscar tossed them each a black neoprene wetsuit with short sleeves, zip-up backs and rather than legs, a tightly-fitting mermaid tail, perhaps six feet long.

"You'll wear goggles for training, but not for the performances. It's hard to see in the saltwater, so know where your air hose is and practice finding it. Each is cleverly disguised as a kelp strand."

Cloris-Edna smiled and made a floating seaweed move with her skinny arms.

"You'll get used to the tails soon. Thirty pounds of mermaid appendage ready to dazzle."

The women struggled into their rehearsal garb, adjusted their masks, and slipped into the water. The initial plunge was a cold one, but Izzy welcomed the rush. It sharpened her brain and invigorated her body. The water indeed was salty to the taste. They were surrounded by real marine creatures—languid yellow tangs, stingrays, nurse sharks, and an enormous grouper. The lighting was dim and moody. Bubbles fizzed up from below like champagne in a flute. Had it been different circumstances, the experience could have been quite magical. Instead, it was a nightmare.

Swimming with the mermaid tail proved ridiculously cumbersome. The movement was made possible from the knees and thighs using core strength. Izzy followed Sea Star and Pearl's sequence as they swam to high-energy, water-distorted, misogynistic pop music. *Bam-bam-thank-you-ma'am. Perfect for jerking off.* The deep, throbbing bass chords never let up, and Izzy's head began to pound along with it.

The women moved in circles, dragging the arduous tails. They dolphin-dove, twisted, turned, and shimmied. Primped their flowing hair and practiced teasing the assholes who'd be their audience. The old woman studied their every move through a large subaquatic porthole. She resembled a moray eel Izzy'd encountered at the Great Barrier Reef. It had almost killed her. The woman, the Esther Williams wannabe, shouted out directions through a staticky loudspeaker.

After what seemed like hours, Izzy was exhausted. Her muscles were beginning to cramp and her lungs were on fire. The time between each allowed gulp of air was wearing her down. Why weren't they at least provided with small oxygen tanks?

Control. It was all about controlling their victims.

She tried not to panic but knew she couldn't hold her breath long enough between O2 hits anymore. Izzy was too winded, too spent—and she was a certified diver in good shape. Miss Cloris-Edna peered through the dark window and smirked. Her face was skeletal in the flickering water, like pictures of the Grim Reaper. Maybe this was what the old bitch had meant by mermaid practice being part synchronized swimming and part waterboarding.

Izzy struggled to her tube and tried once more to suck in air through the regulator. Nothing. Her heart begged for oxygen and her chest wanted to rip open. Alarm tightened its noose around her neck. *God, don't let me die. My sister, my dog, my students. No!*

She realized that Pearl and Coral were no longer in the

pool. It must be her turn to get out of the tank—she'd somehow missed the old woman's cue. Flailing toward the light above, Izzy broke the surface and gasped. Oscar brutally pounded her head and shoulders with a wooden oar, driving her back under. Sparks shot through her vision. She tasted blood in the water.

Wait! You don't understand, it's my turn to get out!

Madly propelling herself over to the other women's air tubes—she sucked in nothing but despair. The mermaid tail dragged her down as if she were attached to a skidding boat trailer.

She was going to die.

In horror, Izzy once more clawed toward the surface with all she had toward Oscar's distorted face. Instead of helping her out, he again crushed her down. The blows were dizzying.

There must be some misunderstanding—it's my turn to get out. God, no! She breathed in the water, gagging, suffocating, dying.

There was no misunderstanding.

—

The white-tiled room took hazy form. As she regained consciousness, Izzy felt the hardness of the cold pool deck beneath her body. She shivered violently. Twisting onto her side, she vomited a stomach full of salty brine into a puddle of water. Her lungs ached and her head spun.

"Get her right back in," the wicked raspy voice ordered. "She stays at it until I say she's done. Unpleasant little attitude she has. Gotta nip that in the bud."

Cruel hands grabbed Izzy by the hair and shoved her back into the pool. Thrashing, she was barely able to function. Fear began a full-out assault on her senses. Maybe there was no escape. No, she would not go there.

"Okay, Coral, let's start once more from the top," Cloris-Edna clucked. "A one, a two . . ."

The pounding music began to scream again.

Chapter 12

When Lucy arrived back at the ranch, the sun was beginning to melt into dusk like a big yolk on the gray pan of the horizon. As she drove up the gravel road, the Santa Ana winds scraped their hot, dry tongues across the chaparral, sucking up any moisture that could be had from the already dried-out yuccas and prickly grasses.

This weather always gave her the heebie-jeebies. It was the harbinger of restless nights, of urban legends of murder and mania, and of fires like the one that had burned her home to the ground. Walls of flame high as tidal waves, panicked wildlife, every breath toxic and agonizing. She and her friends had barely escaped with their lives.

Her inner voice chastised—*Focus on the good stuff, not the horror, the loss.* After the disastrous burn, Lucy and Elsa were now living in a small yurt and an old supply shed, but they had survived and had a roof over their heads. It was a helluva lot more than many people had.

Refusing to be further unsettled, Lucy said a prayer of

gratitude and then turned her attention to the new barn, a phoenix rising above the cinder-scarred concrete pad it sat on. She pulled her car up next to it. The ranch was indeed coming alive again. She knew her Uncle Henry, who had left her *Rancho de la Vega,* would be proud.

Elsa waved from the porch of her tiny shed-house then ducked back inside. Dinner prep was likely underway. Howard the cat sat on the windowsill, and Bugle and Maddie came galloping up from somewhere behind the yurt.

Suddenly exhausted, Lucy collapsed onto her lounge chair beneath the olive tree. The pregnancy was taking its toll on her endurance. Light, fluttery contractions, hopefully benign, tightened her belly. In seconds, the dogs were all over her with kisses and whines. She welcomed the happy distraction, scratched their ears and rubbed her face into their warm fur. Maddie dropped the gift of a long, slimy stick onto her lap. Lucy grabbed it and stood, ready for a quick game of throw and fetch, but there was something about the stick that was not stick-like. It was rubbery, pliant, and felt very wrong. She paused, looked more carefully. "What in the . . ."

Like ridding herself of a hot coal, Lucy dropped the object to the ground and frantically wiped her hands on her jeans. "Shit, no way." Her abdomen tightened more severely.

Maddie's 'stick' was a human arm.

From the ragged elbow down to where the fingers had been gnawed off, bits of gold glitter were embedded in the tattered, bloodless flesh. Lucy swallowed hard, willed herself into news reporter mode and took several photos with her phone.

Ready to play, Maddie attempted to grab the prize, but Lucy shooed her off. Lifting the side table next to her chaise, she set it down over the limb to help protect it from the pups. Crime scene folks would have to come and do their assessment. Accident? Suicide? Or murder? What was going on?

Hands shaking, Lucy dialed Pete. He'd put an investigation in motion.

The call went to voicemail. *Damn.* Lucy texted him the photographs.

"Pete, phone me back immediately. The dogs just brought in a body part from the field. I think it's a chewed-up forearm. Definitely human. And pretty fresh." She disconnected and gazed out over the ranchland. Her one hundred fifty acres were bisected by the LA County/Ventura County line. Bea's acquaintance, Detective Wu from Ventura Metro, would want in on this, depending on what side of the boundary the body was discovered—if a body was still around. Insects, coyotes, hawks, and Maddie, may have already trashed the remains.

Elsa toddled across the drive toward the picnic table carrying a tray with plates and iced tea. Lucy washed the touch of dead flesh from her hands with hand sanitizer from the bottle left over from Covid days they always kept near the picnic table. Then she jumped up to help Elsa. The canine kids trailed excitedly, as if they hadn't been fed in days.

"I saw you moving that table over something the dogs dragged in. What is it? Roadkill?"

"You don't want to know, sweetheart. This dinner's too great-looking to spoil." Bile rose in Lucy's throat. A gust of hot wind blew the paper napkins into the sky. They fluttered upward like white moths. Lucy picked them up as they landed, even grabbing one in mid-air. She returned them to the table, adhering to the one-minute contamination rule.

Elsa narrowed her watery eyes. "Gotta be a bunny if Maddie retrieved it. Am I right?"

I wish it were a bunny, Lucy said to herself.

"Cute creatures," Elsa continued, "but back on the farm in Norway, my mother did occasionally cook a lovely rabbit stew with boiled potatoes and leeks."

The thought of heavy, gamey food made Lucy further nauseous.

Elsa put two beautifully prepared plates of baked salmon and artichoke hearts in wild rice on the blue-and-white cloth-topped picnic table. She slid onto the bench.

Lucy's phone rang. She checked caller ID—it was Pete. "Excuse me for a sec, Elsa." She stood and walked away from the table.

After quick hellos, Lucy whispered, "Looks like a woman's arm. I need Crime Scene, Homicide, and whoever else you send for something like this. There's a Ventura Metro detective at a meeting with Bea, he should probably be notified, too. She's got his contact information. The county line runs right down the middle of the ranch and I know some of you folks take those territorial lines seriously."

"Pissing Contests R Us. I'll get it set up. Think you'll need a tracker dog? One of Sherlock's hounds?" he asked.

"Maybe, but Maddie might be able to lead us to where she found it. She's not a tracker by any means but likes a good game of find-the-treat."

After they disconnected, Elsa said, "Not rabbit. I guess you warned me but I couldn't help overhearing. Shall I cover the meal and we'll heat it up later?"

Lucy nodded and squeezed one of Elsa's dear, strong hands.

—

The forensic unit's long white CSU van was the first to arrive. The dark blue Los Angeles County Department of Medical Examiner-Coroner's logo was plastered across the side of the vehicle. Maddie and Bugle greeted the head criminalist, Demetrius Brown, like he was a long-lost friend. Mid-fifties, African American with close-cropped gray hair and a goatee, Lucy had worked with him on various cases over the years and had been impressed with his professionalism.

Detective Anthony told us to haul ass over here, ASAP." He smiled at Lucy and began to unpack his gear.

Accompanying Brown was a young Asian woman introduced as Meghan Li, an assistant forensic investigator. Her eyes radiated joyous enthusiasm for the work most would find repugnant.

"This is her first week on the job, but she was five years in Tucson," Brown said. "I'm going to let her take the lead."

Lucy nodded. "As long as you're here to supervise. Nice to see you, Demi." They exchanged a hug.

Elsa called the pups to her cabin, luring them inside with marrow bones. Howard still sat on the sill, eyeing the human activity with the barest of interest. He was more intent on the shiny green-necked hummingbirds thrumming around a feeder.

Lucy led Demetrius and Meghan to the olive tree. "It's under that table to keep the dogs away," she told them.

A great blast of wind sent a dust devil across the yard. Lucy covered her face and grimaced. The Santa Anas always seemed angriest at sunset. Grit coated her skin. Meghan and Demi already had on masks, booties, and eye protectors. Standing aside, she let the crime scene investigators have at it.

Within the hour, Pete arrived from the County Sheriff's Department. He wore a navy blue LACSD golf shirt, jeans, and hiking boots. A Glock was holstered on his belt.

Minutes later, Macintosh Wu showed up. He pulled his non-descript silver Chevy next to Pete's ride. Bea, last in, parked near Lucy under the rafters of the new barn.

Demi gave the crew a wave of acknowledgment, then resumed taking careful photos while his assistant measured, prodded, and examined the specimen. Lucy stood nearby.

Meghan shook her head, face pinched with confusion. "See these marks? Looks like a shark attack. I did an internship in Australia and saw this kind of injury a few times."

"A shark?" Lucy's brows rose in stunned disbelief. "My dog retrieved it from the far side of that meadow." She pointed across a browning field dotted with several fire-scarred mountain oaks, rocky outcroppings, and thatches of coarse grass. "That's pretty much the edge of Maddie's range, she doesn't go far. But another critter could have hauled it up the hill from the beach, I guess."

"The only other marks look like dog." Meghan gazed across the open space then turned her attention back to the arm. "As for the appendage, I'd say female, late teens or early twenties, and not long dead—less than twelve hours. The skin is still intact and relatively firm but not in rigor. This gold stuff in the abrasions," she took out a magnifier, "might be glass bead chips. There are fibers, too. And, oh, wow." she flashed a quizzical glance at her boss. "Looks like a shark tooth broke off just above the subject's wrist."

"What in hell?" Lucy stepped in closer.

Meghan looked up at Demi again. "We should get this to the lab right away and start running the DNA."

He turned to Lucy. "Can you give us a minute here to finish our initial work? Then y'all can come over and take a look-see before we bag and tag."

Lucy nodded. While the two criminalists spoke in quiet tones, she walked over to Bea's car where her friend was in discussion with Wu and Pete.

Lucy gave Pete a quick hug then asked the group, "What are your thoughts on tracking the remains now before it gets dark?"

Wu removed his Los Angeles Dodgers cap and wiped his forehead. "Bea says your dog might be able to lead us to where she found the arm." He ran his fingers though his damp, black hair then replaced the hat, this time with the brim to the back.

Pete looked over toward the criminalists. "As soon as the crime scene folks finish their prelim, we'll take a good look at the limb before they wrap it up, then we'll try your pups, Luce."

Lucy nodded. "I think we should use both of the dogs—the beagle has a great nose, too. And he can be loud and obnoxious when left behind."

"Sounds like a plan," Bea said.

Lucy continued. "Could amount to zilch."

"Worth a shot," Pete replied. "Ain't got shit else."

"If it's our geographical jurisdiction," Wu said," I'll call in backup as soon as I can. Sorry folks, but I need to focus on the

Abbott case."

Lucy folded her arms across her chest, sadly confident that the chewed-up arm had something to do with that very case. She'd leave it to Demi and Meghan to reveal the shark attack details, and Mac and Pete could fight out jurisdictional issues.

Demi soon joined the group. "Okay, folks, we're done with our initial field assessment. Take a look, then we'll transport the remains back to the lab."

"If you guys can stay with us for a bit longer, that would be great," Pete said. "We're going to hike over to the area where the arm might have been picked up by the pooch. Could be more to bag."

Demi's face was grim. "How 'bout Meg and I drive over to Mulholland and pull off above the gulch Lucy talked about. We'll write up our reports while we wait for you and be on scene to process anything you might find."

Lucy nodded. "Sounds like a plan. The hike should take us maybe twenty minutes."

"Boot up, people." Bea went to her trunk and pulled out a pair of purple Merrell hikers.

The crew grabbed their water bottles, miscellaneous clothing, and gear, then gathered around the grisly specimen displayed on a plastic tarp. Meghan stood beside it like a watchdog. She gave a concise summary of their findings.

Wu edged close to the body part, bent down and examined it from various angles. He snapped images with his cell phone. Shadows were growing long and somewhat disorienting. Lucy moved to give him better light.

"May I borrow your magnifying glass?" He turned to Meghan.

She pulled it from her bag, handed it over and knelt protectively next to the fleshy object. Wu took his time then finally spoke. "Those embedded teeth have an unusual luminous quality, don't they?"

"We'll have to call an expert in the field," Demi said. "With the current *El Niño* conditions in the Pacific, weird creatures show up from the tropics that we don't usually see in our waters."

Demi and Meghan loaded the specimen and their field equipment back into their van.

Bea said to Wu, "You starting to think that the,

uh, arm has some connection to the sex tourism/mermaid snuff site Bijan ran across on the dark web?" Her eyes lingered on the spot where the appendage had been.

Wu nodded. "Maybe. But why the hell would we find something like this here at your place? Doesn't make any sense."

Another blast of hot air tore at Lucy's hair. Her deep blue eyes were stormy pools. "Maybe it's a sign of some kind, a warning. Am I sounding paranoid?"

"We need someone with you from now on. You and Elsa are too vulnerable alone." Pete pushed his hands deep into the pockets of his cargo pants. For a moment, the blustery wind provided the only soundtrack.

Feeling unsettled, Lucy rubbed her modest baby bump. "I'll get with Cheyney Hitchcock, our dear retired stuntman across the road, for some backup later. He's been our guardian angel more than once."

Bea nodded. "When the ranch burned down, we would have lost all the animals and maybe our own lives without his help."

"In the meantime," Lucy said, repressing a growing wave of vulnerability, "we gotta track this thing down before our light's completely gone." It was the golden hour—just before sunset when the atmosphere was warm and soft as a kiss, the time of day when her family had met their fate. As a photographer the illumination was exquisite, as an orphan, it was hell. She turned briskly and called the dogs.

0-0-0

Maddie and Bugle had been given a good sniff of the gnarled arm before Meghan stashed it away in a plastic cooler for safekeeping. Then, the lab on wheels disappeared down the drive toward Kanan Road and on to Mulholland.

Purple shadows lengthened as the searchers began their trek across the quarter-mile meadow to the gulch where Lucy thought Maddie's plaything had likely been retrieved. The pups pranced and yipped with enthusiasm. Insects rose and fled as the hikers crunched through the chaparral. Walking in intervals several yards apart, they scanned the landscape for anything that appeared out of the ordinary.

Light-headed and slightly nauseated, Lucy unwrapped an energy bar and munched it down. When she missed a meal or snacks, the voracious little passenger in her belly made her pay.

Maddie danced around Lucy, following a game trail toward the far edge of the field where sycamores and scrub willows gathered along a seasonal creek bed. Bugle lagged behind, nose to the ground.

"Find it!" Lucy called. Thoughts of what obscenity they might actually discover made Lucy want to vomit what she'd just eaten.

Maddie ran out a hundred yards then scampered back for a treat. Then forward, and back again to Lucy for another piece of kibble. That playful sequence would, hopefully, keep the dog moving onward to where they'd discovered the abomination. Bugle, less food-driven, trotted barely ahead of Lucy, probably snuffling out the coyote pup he'd once befriended.

Chapter 13

The old woman, posing as if for Vogue in a black chapeau tipped at a jaunty angle, snarled at her nephew, Dr. Halliburton Jones. Sour resentment rose in his throat.

She stretched her slim body into her signature tall, black-sheathed exclamation point. "Where have you been, Halliburton? You haven't taken the aquarium readings for days. Oscar had to clean up the hammerhead tank this morning. Not his job. We must be meticulous, and you've been sloppy, sloppy, sloppy! I expected you hours ago. Did you get the leftover bits to the incinerator in the Valley?"

Her sharp, narrow teeth reminded Jones of a chihuahua he'd once ran over with his car on a day when his patience had snapped. Unfortunately, this woman was his Aunt Cloris-Edna, and he continued to have an obligated attachment to her, despite their contentious, toxic, relationship.

"Yes, dear Aunt. No need to get snippy. I finished the aquarium maintenance, so all is taken care of." He neglected to mention that rather than making the tedious drive to the Sylmar crematorium, he'd thrown the bag of "leftovers" out the window off Mulholland. Maybe it was his passive-aggressive way of dealing with a situation he found degrading and beneath him. They needed to make big bucks to sustain his genetic research, but Auntie funneled significantly more money into costumes and production design than into his scientific work.

"Did you check the mermaid viewing lounge? Everything in place for our next guests?" Aunt Cloris-Edna demanded.

He scowled. "I'm a scientist and curator of this, this . . ." Dr. Jones looked out the studio door into the deep blue tank where his golden shark circled. "This world-class aquarium and research center. I'm not a Jiffy Maid or a damn caterer." His teeth ground so hard he thought his jaw would dislocate.

Jones took a deep breath and struggled to calm himself. The smell of Auntie's vintage European perfume was further irritating. His mother and grandmother had worn it, too. Dark Water. The fragrance portended incoming criticism and pickiness. Pick, pick, pick. Thousands of little injuries.

The old woman studied him for a long moment, her pencil-thin black eyebrows rose almost to the widow's peak at her hairline. "Perhaps you're not getting enough lab time. I know how that can feel. Must follow our passions, mustn't we, little minnow? After this weekend, I'll have the funds. A nice deposit from the Saudis. You can start on that translucent hammerhead variety if you'd like. I want you to be happy, dear minnow. I know you adore your research."

His heartbeat accelerated. He pressed his hand to his chest. "Thank you, Aunt. That's music to my ears. So happy. Yes, yes indeedy."

This was what he'd been waiting for. This was why he still endured her. Overcome with excitement, he slumped onto her black velvet fainting couch. A bolt of shimmery cloth fell to the floor.

"I shall leave you alone now," she said. "I'm getting ready for a photoshoot with our newest starlet. A little older than most of our performers, but quite a pretty girl." Pensively, she pressed a red-painted fingernail to her chin. "Halliburton, dear, too bad you never found a lover."

"You forget, Auntie, my only love was the first woman you tossed to the horde."

Her eyes narrowed. "Just an experiment, sweet minnow. They barely nibbled her. She wasn't eaten, she accidently drowned."

"She told you she couldn't swim."

"Everybody knows how to swim." Cloris-Edna glided from the room.

The man's moment of pleasure at the research funding sputtered and extinguished. The scent of Dark Water lingered like blood on guilty hands.

Dr. Jones's shoulders sagged while he reflected on his situation at Piscem Auratus. Once a state-of-the-art research facility created for ultra-secret cold war marine mammal research, his scientist father had high hopes of developing the use of dolphins for government projects. His dreams died with him a decade later when one of his own genetically altered creations mauled him to death. Jones shuddered, recalling the brutal mayhem he witnessed at age six. With his mother long-gone, Cloris-Edna had become his guardian.

Jones heard his aunt conferring with Oscar in the hallway, then her heels tap-tap-tapped his way. He gripped his hands into tight fists. When she poked her head back into the studio, he imagined her scrawny neck snapping like a dry wishbone in his grasp.

"Darling minnow. Would you like to watch the photoshoot? Always so much fun. The model is a bit, uh, unruly, but Oscar is locked and loaded." She chuckled. "How he loves that electric magic wand of his."

Jones frowned, stretched out his fingers. "That asshole had better keep his fucking cattle prod clear of my fish."

"Language, dear, language." She made little *tsk, tsk* sounds with her slit of red lips.

Dr. Jones despised Oscar, with his pretentious swagger and his domination fantasies. One day, the jerk would slip and fall into Big Goldie's snapping jaws. He smiled and ground his shoe into the expensive cloth unraveling on the floor. Then he followed his aunt down the dark hall to the production studio where she and a void-brain named Standish made little marketing videos and took pictures for brochures.

Stan-bitch, with his sniveling, effete demeanor, was a perfect match for Auntie. Another wannabe who had never quite made it in a way he thought he deserved.

An unsettling thought struck Jones hard. His head began to throb. Was he, the brilliant doctor Halliburton Jones, becoming one of the resentful losers? He must stop the slide into bitterness and disillusion by recommitting himself to his work, to creating an even larger, more intelligent, and beautiful shark of gold. He would let nothing get in his way.

—

Lucy tailed Maddie down a narrow dirt path that led to a seasonal stream at the bottom of an oak-shrouded gulch. They skidded in the loose gravel and Lucy fell on her rear end. She winced as Pete grabbed her hand to help her up and steady her. Lucy gently pressed on her cramping belly—the passenger was not happy.

Maddie bounded forward joyously into the stream with Bugle at her heels. They splashed among the creek willows. The sweet fragrance hid any whiff of decomp. "I'm going to leash the pups now," Lucy said. "If we find remains ahead, I don't want them to further contaminate the scene."

"Good thought. Let me help you. I'll take Bugle," Bea gave Lucy a suspicious look. "You feeling okay?."

"I'm fine. Let's get moving. It's practically dark out here."

The dogs were put on their leads and continued along the stream. Wu pulled out a flashlight and cast the beam ahead.

And then, there it was.

Perhaps a hundred yards below the oak-shaded Mulholland turnout, a black plastic garbage bag had been ripped to shreds.

Maddie yipped and Bugle did his beagle wail. Wu and Pete stepped forward. Lucy took both dogs while Bea called the investigative team on her cell.

Lucy could see the crime scene van high above the big granite boulders and tangled underbrush.

"Demi, I'm afraid we got something," Bea said. "Be careful coming down."

Lucy swallowed hard. The garbage bag's bright yellow drawstring flapped in the breeze. The bag undulated in the stream and gold dust sparkled. Shards of desiccated flesh and bone were caught on twigs nearby. Sitting down on the bank, Lucy pulled Maddie and Bugle tight and gave them treats for being such good search dogs.

The sound of the van doors opening and closing snapped like gunshots from Mulholland. Wu, Pete, and Bea began climbing through the brush to help carry equipment and secure the scene. Lucy rose to follow.

"Don't even think about it, sister," Bea ordered.

Lucy slumped down on a flat, cool rock, overcome with a hot flash that soaked her clothing. Straining at the end of her lead, Maddie whined and paced in front of the garbage bag. Bugle settled onto a mossy spot at Lucy's feet and nuzzled her ankle. That was the last thing she remembered.

Chapter 14

Dr. Jones leaned against the wall across from the darkly-illuminated diorama of an ocean cave that lapped with water from a magnificent aqua pool below a white sand spit of beach. Dried kelp and conch, driftwood and pale blue glass orbs from old fishing nets created a sensual, otherworldly environment. He had to admit, Auntie's extravagant production design budget had yielded some pretty nice work.

Cloris-Edna appeared from behind a black duvetyn drape leading a procession of her minions. Enya sang the evocative 'Orinoco Flow' from a hidden speaker. Naked except for a barely-there black thong displaying his formidable package, Oscar carried a semi-conscious, masked mermaid to a golden chaise. As he bent down to lay her on a bed of satiny aqua coverlets, Jones spotted a mermaid tattoo on the creep's rock- hard ass cheek. Repulsed by the tacky marking, Jones was beginning to realize how sick he was getting of the compromises he had to make to get what he wanted. He had to start thinking about his options.

Together, Oscar and Auntie positioned the body and primped the model's lush hair woven with bits of seaweed and seashell fragments. Stan-bitch shouted directions, scurrying between klieg lights and scrims, like the rat he was. As the photog, he acted like he was directing some epic superhero movie, not a sad trailer of a tased girl in a pricey fish suit.

"More glitter on the tits," Stan whined. He adjusted the model's shiny silvery-blue half-mask. It was a style right out of a lush Italian opera.

Cloris-Edna pulled a spray can from a black apron around her narrow waist. Pockets galore, she was a walking beauty salon. Soon, the model's lovely breasts glittered like twin suns. Jones felt like he should be getting excited. The show usually turned him on, but today, it seemed like an insipid game.

Cloris-Edna, Oscar, and Standish huddled at the edge of the set, talking strategy. All seemed ready for the first take, until the girl sat up and ripped off her face covering. In a blink, she rolled from the chaise and began to crawl toward the door—toward Jones, struggling for breath, moaning. She reached out with desperate fingers.

He gasped, couldn't believe what he was seeing. Isabelle Abbott, his bright, talented colleague from Santa Monica High School, was begging for help at his feet.

—

Lucy awoke in the back of the forensics van amid shelving packed with an array of plastic tool boxes and other unidentified gear. The smell in the vehicle was a cross between a hospital and a gardening shed. Inches from her nose, she stared into a container labeled *Biohazard Bags-10 Gallon*.

She sat up and immediately the world spun.

Demi's strong arm provided support. A stethoscope hung around his neck.

"I thought you only worked on dead people." Lucy pressed her thumbs against her eye sockets, then rubbed her temples.

"I keep my medical bag with me 24/7. I *am* a licensed physician, you know. Police officers are always getting hurt or passing out at the crime scene, particularly the rookies." He removed his scope and tucked it into his pocket. "Your heart's loud and strong, the baby's, too, but the paramedics are on their way."

Bea handed her pregnant friend a bottle of water. "Drink up, don't need to have you and jellybean dehydrated."

Lucy obeyed and took a long drink. She slowly stood up, accepting Demi's assistance. "Hey, I'm fine, just got a little queasy there for a sec." She handed the water bottle back to Bea. Lucy tried to smile but her face wouldn't cooperate.

Demi patted her shoulder. "Bea says this pregnancy is high risk. You could use some fluids and a night in the hospital for observation. Gotta be cautious."

"I'll be fine." Lucy felt her lip quiver. "It's gonna be what it's gonna be, right? Life's all a crap-shoot."

"Wrong." Bea wore her lemon-eater expression. "Don't give he that hapless victim shit. You need to be monitored closely."

Lucy winced. "No hospital. You know how creeped out I get. My aunt is coming from Mexico tomorrow. She'll keep an eye on me."

"She's a doc?" Demi asked.

Bea stepped up. "She's a *curandera*."

Demi's dark brows furrowed. "A what?"

Lucy bristled. "You say that like she's some kind of witch doctor, Bea. Aunt Catherine Lucia's a nun and a highly skilled medical professional. Went to nursing school in Guadalajara."

"Fifty years ago," Bea whispered to Demi.

Tears welled in Lucy's eyes. "Fifty years of healing and saving lives, relying on her courage and wits. She's a hero." Hating how this discussion stirred up such intense emotions, Lucy dabbed her eyes on her sleeve and looked away. Hell, these days, even passing roadkill could bring her to tears, let alone a mangled human body. "She was even invited to a conference on indigenous medicine in Santa Barbara last year. And she knows medicinal herbs like nobody else."

Demi squeezed her shoulders. "Sounds like a very special lady."

"Yes, she is." Lucy's knees were beginning to dissolve as the paramedics pulled up behind the crime scene van. She clutched the van's door jamb, refusing to sink to the ground. Any display of weakness and Bea'd have her hauled off to the damn ER.

Two emergency medical techs hopped from their ambulance and moved toward Lucy, Bea, and Demi. Meghan and the detectives had set up a spotlight down in the gulch and were processing body parts. Lucy could hear their distant conversation.

"Hey, Doc. What do we have here?" the EMT asked. A young man in his mid-thirties, his head was shaved bald and a wispy blonde mustache shadowed his lip. Beneath the LA County paramedic arm patch was an Army Combat Medic badge. His partner, a slim African American woman with short natural hair, opened the back door to the ambulance, pulled out an equipment kit, and removed a blood pressure monitor.

"Hello Brian, Mimi." Demi shook hands with both techs. "This is Lucy Vega and Bea Middleton. Lucy's about twenty-eight weeks pregnant, and she passed out about ten minutes ago. Heart rate is a bit accelerated, baby's sounds normal, maybe a little fast."

Mimi indicated for Lucy to sit on the camp chair Brian had set up. She wrapped the patient's arm in a blood pressure cuff and pumped in the air, listening carefully with her stethoscope as the cuff deflated. Next, she took out another piece of equipment and wrapped its two straps, attached to an electronic display, across Lucy's belly.

"Fetal monitor," Mimi said. Then she was quiet long enough to make Lucy more nervous than she already was. "Little pumpkin's sounding good," she finally reported. "Let's get mama here hooked up to a drip and then we'll take her into

Santa Monica for bloodwork and a full assessment."

"Fluids are okay, I might have gotten a little dehydrated, didn't really eat enough either. But no hospital—way too stressful. I want to go home and rest. I'll be fine. Just got a little careless—it won't happen again."

Bea groaned. "Please, Lucy, you need to be checked out, thoroughly."

"I saw the doctor a couple days ago and she said I, we, were fine."

"You of all people know things can change with the blink of an eye." Bea crossed her arms on her chest, eyes narrow.

Lucy burst into tears. "Why are you saying that to me? Why do you want to scare me into doing something I don't want to do?"

"You're so stubborn, sometimes you have to be reminded that you're not superwoman, you're a vulnerable human with a kiddo onboard."

"You are so damn bossy." Lucy coughed and sniffled.

"And you are such a pain."

Lucy allowed Mimi to help her onto the gurney, then the medic hooked up an IV.

Lucy noted that Demi and Brian stood off from the scene with body language that said, *better stay the hell out of this little drama.*

Bea stomped around, took a deep breath, then grasped Lucy's hand in hers. "It's gonna be okay, sweet pea."

"I can't go to the hospital, I hate them," Lucy insisted. "I'll have a panic attack. I'll die, the baby will die."

"You're not going to die, and neither is that tyke of yours. If they give you the green light at the hospital, you can go home and know you're okay." Bea looked beseechingly at the paramedic then stepped away and dialed a number.

Mimi placed her hands on her trim hips, looked down at Lucy, prone on the gurney. "I got four kids ma'am, so believe me, I've been through it. Fatigue, lack of food, and an upsetting event like this body-part thing y'all have goin' on—it all messes up the system. Let's get you over to St. John's and have your levels checked, just as a smart precaution."

Bea handed Lucy her phone. "Got your OB on the line. She wants to talk to you."

Lucy's mouth dropped open and she shot Bea an angry look. "Oh, no, you didn't."

"I did." Bea ventured a quick glance at Demi and he nodded agreement.

Lucy took the phone and quietly listened as the no-nonsense Dr. Blanchard ordered her to get her ass into the hospital, ASAP. Lucy meekly agreed.

She handed the cell back to Bea. "Okay, you got me. I'm going."

Bea sighed and nodded to Mimi.

"Sorry to be such a bitch," Lucy whispered. "I'm not coping well with all this."

"You're doing fine, sweetheart." Bea gave her a reassuring hug. "My first pregnancy, I walked into the Beverly Center, practically my second home, and couldn't find Nordstrom. Now *that* is a true emergency."

Lucy couldn't restrain a smile. Then a few more tears.

Wu emerged from the underbrush among the oak trees, leaves and twigs in his hair, hat askew. He pulled biohazard bags on a sled behind him. "Lucy okay?" he asked.

"All good," Bea responded.

Lucy gave him a thumbs-up.

Demi scuttled up to the detective and began to move the evidence from the sled into the van. Seconds later, Pete emerged toting additional bags, followed by Meghan with her backpack CSI kit. It was almost dark. They moved quickly in the gloom. Bats flitted in the sky above, darting for insects.

A half-dozen Harleys rumbled past on their way down Mulholland to PCH, their headlights zooming by like big fireflies. The bit of traffic on this remote stretch reminded Lucy of something, but what? She watched the others finish loading the evidence. Meghan took notes and logged in each item on an iPad.

Then, recollection dawned. Lucy called over to the group. Bea and the detectives gathered around the gurney as Mimi adjusted the IV drip line.

"When Maddie brought me the arm, I was thinking the location of the body dump was some kind of warning, but in reality, this is the only turnoff up here that's hidden by oak trees with easy access to a deep ravine. It's the perfect drop spot. Think about it—plenty of predators, can't see anything from the road, and you could pull something nasty out of your car and send it over the edge without other drivers seeing you, especially at night."

"Maybe it was no coincidence and the perp knew exactly where he, or she, wanted to ditch the remains," Bea said.

Wu nodded. "Also, it might say that the site of the murder isn't far from here."

Lucy smiled and whispered to Bea. "See, I'm not completely in a hormonal funk."

Before Bea could respond, Wu's phone dinged. He checked the text, then looked around at the investigators, eyes hooded in the darkness. "We've found a cop who might have recruited Isabelle Abbott. Out near the California aqueduct in Palmdale." His focus returned to his cell phone, then he looked up again. "Bullet to the head."

Chapter 15

She was smaller than Lucy remembered. A petite older woman with a long gray braid. She wore dark, simple clothing and wire-rimmed glasses. A colorful straw purse was slung on her shoulder and around her neck hung a silver crucifix on a leather cord.

Lucy swallowed, her throat dry. She was both thrilled and terrified about the reunion.

Sister Catherine Lucia de la Vega waited amid the throng at the luggage carousel, her eyes bright and curious. Lucy knew that she'd taken several long, grueling bus rides to get to Guerrero's capital of Chilpancingo, then a van to Acapulco where she'd boarded a flight to LAX. Having done the trip in the opposite direction a year ago, Lucy recalled the exhaustion, even though she was a good forty years younger than her aunt.

Her pulse quickened as she approached her only living blood relative.

The old woman glanced Lucy's way and recognition sparked in her eyes immediately. She waved excitedly. The two women pressed their way through the crowd where arriving passengers stalked bags shuffling by on conveyers.

"Lucia, *mija!* Sweet child!" The little woman caught Lucy in her bird-like arms, kissed her on both cheeks and embraced her fiercely. "*Alabado sea al señor*. Praise the Lord."

"*Mi querida tia!* I can't believe you're here!" Lucy felt the lump of her baby belly snug and safe between them. Tears rolled down her face.

They remained glued to each other, eyes watery, until an annoying baggage attendant asked them to save the hugging until they retrieved their luggage and cleared the area.

Lucy laughed out loud and wiped her damp eyes. "Your first minutes in Los Angeles, and you're yelled at for hugging too long. What a world."

"*Es magnífico,*" Sister Catherine Lucia said, glowing with joy and awe. "The airplane ride was terrifying *y mágico*. I never been on plane, now I think I like to be pilot in next life. And the—what you call them—the pretzel snacks were free, too."

Smiling broadly, Lucy hugged her aunt one more time, not ready to admit her own phobic fear of flying. "Let's grab your stuff and get out of here."

Catherine Lucia turned and pointed to an ancient, avocado-green, plastic Samsonite suitcase sliding down the luggage ramp. A dolly-like contraption was tied to it with bungee cords. "That's mine. Borrowed it from nurse at *Clínica de Tingo Tia*."

Lucy squeezed to the edge of the conveyor and nabbed the bag.

"No, you mustn't lift!" Sister's voice was high and anxious.

"It's okay, I've got it." The suitcase dragged Lucy a few feet before a young man with a bushy beard hoisted it off the carousel and dropped it onto the floor beside her.

"Thank you, sir." Lucy guiltily avoided eye contact with her aunt.

"It *muy pesado* for one in your condition."

Sister Catherine Lucia's voice was stern. The woman would

have made a good Catholic school principal.

"Was heavier than it looked. What did you pack? Rocks?" Lucy untangled the cords and readied the huge bag to roll.

"I have my herbs, books, laptop, my portable ultrasound *máquina,* clothing and—" She tapped a finger to her chin, as if trying to remember something else. "Oh yes, *el té especial—*tea, and very good tortilla flour, too. And, uh, what you call it—*papel higiénico,* uh, toilet paper. Not sure you had it on the burned-down *rancho.*"

"Yep, we have it." Lucy chuckled. "Quite the list. And you've been practicing your English. Very impressive. *He estado practicando mi español también.*"

"*Muy bueno,* we both been practicing. I use online program. We do great together, sí?"

"*Sí!* Follow me. The car's right outside in short-term parking."

After loading the baggage into the SUV's cargo space with help from a passing security guard, they escaped from the parking lot. Lucy pulled onto Century Boulevard then onto the 405 north to the 101. She wanted to get her aunt home to the ranch and settled as soon as possible after the woman's long journey. Elsa was waiting excitedly to meet Uncle Henry's sister.

The freeway traffic was uncharacteristically decent—no accidents, no SIG alerts shutting down lanes, no car chases. They chatted about the city sites. Lucy pointed out landmarks as they drove through the Sepulveda Pass beneath the Getty Center where she and the father of her child, Michael Burleson, had enjoyed strolling through the galleries. Sister met him in Mexico when Lucy had gone after Uncle Henry's murderer and Michael had saved her life. And, they'd fallen in love.

She pushed aside painful recollections of their breakup as the two women drove further into the San Fernando Valley. She glanced over at her tia's face, dazzled with the urban density. Welcome to Mars.

It was not the Mexican way to jump right into conversation

about important topics. Talk started slowly, politely, and eased into addressing whatever elephant was in the room. Lucy finally exited the freeway and turned her trusty SUV onto Las Virgenes Road. As they climbed into the hills toward Malibu Canyon, Sister brought up the inevitable.

"Lucia, *mija,* how are you and the little one doing?"

Lucy chewed at her lip. "So far, so good. All is fine."

"Señora Beatrice say you have a—what you call it—a tendency to overdo."

Lucy's face warmed. She glanced at Sister. "You've spoken with Bea?"

Sister nodded. "We email. The local men put up a satellite tower outside of Tingo Tia. We are somehow tied into Acapulco. I think it is what you call . . . pirated." Her eyes flashed heavenward. "Lord forgive me, but I use it."

The old woman continued, "Señora Beatrice is a true friend to you, Lucia. I understand that you might be a little *imprudente.* I, too, am like that. Sometimes good, sometimes not so good."

Lucy gulped to fight the tightness in her throat. The truth hurt.

She slowed as a pickup stuffed with alfalfa bales veered onto a side road.

"How does the father feel about what you are going through? señor Burleson, *sí?* He very kind, a good man. He very handsome, too, like Roberto Redford. I watch *Butch Cassidy y Sundance Kid* on Netflix."

Lucy couldn't help but smile. "My aunt now watches Netflix in the hinterlands of central Mexico?"

"*Sí,* very interesting show, but it's Miguel Burleson I want to know of."

Lucy's chest constricted at the mention of the tiny passenger's father. She was seized by lightheadedness. A panic attack? She turned from Kanan onto Triunfo Canyon Road and into the gravel parking area of a summer camp, empty this time of year. She turned off the ignition. Then, *wham*—tears Lucy'd long held back flowed so powerfully she could hardly breathe. Sister's arms were soon around her, comforting like little else could.

"*Mi cariño,*" she said, "you have not told him, have you?"

Lucy flushed with guilt. "It's probably going to die anyway. Or be horribly handicapped. I've been warned about all the possibilities. Why put Michael through this pain? I'm used to loss. I can deal with it."

"And Miguel, Michael, cannot deal with it?" Sister gently turned her niece's face toward hers. "I think he can. He strong as you, Lucia, *mija*. That why you found each other. You must tell him."

Her aunt was right. Lucy'd somehow known this day, this moment, would come with Catherine Lucia's arrival. She would call Michael tonight and tell him the impossible had happened. After being told by experts she could never conceive as a result of the childhood car wreck that killed her family, the impossible had become reality. *Oh God.* What would Michael's reaction be? He already had two young adult children to cope with—one with a serious drug problem.

Sister Catherine Lucia asked, "*Es una niña o un niño?*"

"It's a boy, *un niño.*" Lucy grabbed a wad of tissues from the center console and wiped her eyes. "It's a bad omen. Uncle Henry was killed during an *El Niño* storm. It's that season now."

"Maybe Henry's spirit returns with this little *tormenta* of a boy-child." She smiled and sat back in her seat. "We are together now, Lucia. I do everything I can to help you, but you must want this with all your heart. No reckless doings, must think good thoughts of healthy *bambino.*"

Lucy nodded and watched two young girls on horseback galloping fearlessly across a field on the edge of the camp. To want this child with all her heart was terrifying. What if her heart was crushed again? Could she survive? Did she deserve to?

"Let me tell you of something, my niece." Sister fingered

her silver crucifix. "I, too, know suffering and survival. You may know some of this history from Henry, but many year ago near Chiapas, my brother, your Uncle Timóteo, was murdered. My sister-nuns, too." Catherine Lucia took a deep breath. Her eyes followed the children on horseback. Lucy squeezed her hand.

"Was during brutal government purge. *Activistas* of the church who support rights of poor were target. Bad men attack our convent with guns, machetes. Rape, unspeakable brutality, *y asesinato.*" She removed her glasses as if that act would dim her recollection.

The darkest of images bled into Lucy's consciousness. "Oh, Lord. I am so, so sorry."

"At twenty year old," Sister continued, "I the only one who lived." She crossed herself. "Could I have save the others? Hide them from guerillas? But no. I ask Lord, *Why me?* Why I survive? The stain of living was *todo consumiendo.*"

"I disappear into jungle, work among dangerous people, took foolish risks, hoped He would strike me down. He did not."

Lucy shuddered. *Why did I survive that collision that took my entire family from this Earth? I saw the gravel truck coming, I couldn't cry out. No sound would come.* She felt the shame of not being able to warn her family, down to her core and into her bones. They called it survivor's guilt. But like her aunt, she knew there would never be an answer to the question of why one person lived and another died.

Sister patted Lucy's hand. The children on horseback disappeared over a ridge.

"As healer, I save many lives, but many I have not been able to help. I now celebrate every day and live it in honor of those who are gone. You will find that place of peace, Lucia. And, however pregnancy go, *el niño* will help get you there. So will I. De la Vegas—we strong women, Lucia. And you have Viking on papa's side, too. Lagertha, shield-maiden." She raised her arm, hand in a fist. "I watch that, too. History Channel."

A pale smile flickered on Lucy's lips. She nodded and

released the grip she had on her aunt. "I'm so sorry, tia. I knew bad things had happened to you, but I've been so fixed on my own feelings I haven't been thinking of others. Thank you for telling me of your life. It helps me understand who I am, who we are. I am de la Vega and Viking—strong, resilient, and loving." She stared out across the parched chaparral.

The little man, her son, kicked hard as she backed the SUV out of the parking lot and turned onto Kanan Road toward Rancho de la Vega. It was the first time she'd thought of it, of him, as something other than *the passenger*.

Chapter 16

At Tatiana's Coffee & Tea, a few blocks from her house in Ventura, Casey Abbott scrubbed at her short spiky hair, her deep blue eyes narrow with frustration. Wu couldn't help notice that she was a beautiful woman whose rare, quick smiles revealed dimples to die for. But today, there were no smiles.

"I'm her sister, her frickin' sister, and I want to know exactly what's happening. How dare you withhold anything? You have to realize what this secrecy shit is doing to me.

You had a sister who disappeared. Did you sit around passively waiting for answers?"

Wu caught his breath. That statement got his attention like a slap to the head. He sucked up the pain. "I'm truly sorry, Casey, but this is an ongoing police investigation and I can't discuss specifics."

"You know what I say to that? To hell with the police investigation. What's happening? Something? Nothing? I have to be involved whether you like it or not. I'm going to sign up for every dive trip out of the harbor and be the shark chum. I'll dangle myself out there and see if I can get abducted. Then at least Izzy and I can be together. You can back me up, or, or . . ." She bit hard on her quivering lip.

He shifted in his seat. "Okay, okay. I get it." Wu stared at his untouched coffee. The whip had melted into chalky flat scum.

"No, you don't. If you did, you'd let me know what is happening."

She was right, he had to share something or Casey could potentially cause real problems. Wu took in a deep breath and slowly let it out. He made direct, intense eye contact. "First of all, anything I tell you is completely off the record, no blogging, no telling a friend, no nothing."

Casey frowned across the table. "Of course. If you think I'd do anything to jeopardize the investigation, then you're crazy." She slumped back in her seat, clenched and unclenched her fists. "Listen, I'm sorry, Detective. I'm . . . desperate." Her eyes welled with tears.

Wu sighed. "All right, I'll share what I can." He took a quick glance around the near empty coffee shop.

Life sparked back into Casey's wan face. She took his hand and squeezed it, then quickly withdrew.

He took a sip of his lukewarm brew and leaned toward her, elbows on the tabletop. "This isn't going to be easy to hear. But I'll put it right out there."

"I'd appreciate that. Nothing could be more frightening than my imagination."

Wu was not at all sure about that. "Your sister met a guy on that dive trip out to the Channel Islands last week. He was a cop from Palmdale. We think he drugged and kidnapped her."

Her damp eyes popped open wide. "Was she roofied?"

Wu nodded. "Very likely."

"Oh my God. Have you arrested him?"

"Before we could catch up with the piece of shit, he was shot dead, murdered yesterday. Dirt bikers found the body out by the California Aqueduct near Sylmar. No idea who did it."

Casey hugged herself and swayed back and forth.

"After doing some research on the dark web, we're pretty sure Izzy's been taken by an international sex tourism ring that sells a mermaid fantasy to wealthy foreigners."

A shiver rocked Casey further. "Oh God."

Wu continued. "There seems to be saltwater fish, maybe sharks, and a there might be an aquarium of some type involved. We're fairly certain that it's based here in Southern California." He'd leave out the snuff part of the story and the recovered female body parts.

"Who's it run by?"

"Very likely by a former federal agent who was in charge of investigating exotic animal trafficking out of the Port of Long Beach for many years. Just retired. Knows we have a bead on him and he rabbited."

"Disappeared?"

"Correct."

She nodded and continued to chew at her lip. "So, it's a swim with the exotic fish then screw a mermaid kind of thing?"

Wu nodded. "That's what we think."

"What do they do with the women when they've, uh, served their purpose?"

Wu was silent. Casey nodded and looked out the window as shoppers passed on the street. She turned back to the detective, expression grim, tears dripping down her cheeks. "How can I help?"

—

Back at the Ventura Metro PD headquarters, Detective Wu picked up the phone receiver on his very organized desk. He sneered at the neighboring workspaces cluttered with empty coffee cups, food wrappers and messy piles of paperwork.

CSI Agent Demetrius Brown came on the line, hopefully with news on the ID of the remains.

"Demi, what've you got?"

"Hiya, Detective. Was just handed the report. Based on the DNA that the sister, Casey Abbott, provided," the CSI said in his sonorous James-Earl-Jones voice, "the remains don't belong to Isabelle Abbott."

Wu felt the tension in his body uncoil the tiniest bit. *She might still be alive.* He rubbed his neck.

"We matched it to a young woman who'd been reported by her family as missing two weeks ago. A Celeste Kaufman, seventeen, quit high school last year and worked in a tourist shop at Ventura Harbor. Lived above her folk's garage in Camarillo."

"That poor family." Wu knew to his core what toll this loss would take. "Can you send me the file on Kaufman?"

"On its way, check your email. And get this, the flesh was saturated with saltwater, but not directly from the Pacific, more like from an aquarium with high quality filtration. I contacted our friends at Sea World and the chemistry, the pH, GH, water hardness, nitrate content, and all that stuff, were almost identical to their own readings."

"Interesting," Wu began listing Southern California aquariums on a post-it—Aquarium of the Pacific, Cabrillo, UCSB, Santa Monica Pier. "Sounds like we've got some kind of water specialist, like an aquarist, involved."

"Agreed. And the two teeth found embedded in the subject's forearm are similar to those of a great white shark, but not a great white. This thing's a species our expert ichthyologist from UCLA couldn't ID."

"Holy shit. Sounds like mad-scientist stuff."

"Yeah, right. The choppers are big and have this glow-in-the-dark quality. Bioluminescence. Could be some kind of genetic aberration."

"Pretty damn freaky." Wu scratched his head then reached for the Advil in his desk drawer. Swallowed two pills dry. The sour aftertaste irritated the back of his throat.

"So, that's what we got," Demi continued. "You wanna do the girl's next-of-kin notification?"

"Yeah, I'll take it. I want to talk with the family anyway."

Wu hated this part of the job. It transported him back to the horrible moment in his childhood when an officer had come to his parents' door to let them know their daughter had been abducted and was likely dead. He quickly banished that memory and compartmentalized, like he always did. Popped one more pain med. "Thanks for your help, Demi. Keep me updated if anything else breaks."

"Will do, Detective. Take care, bro." The connection clicked off.

Wu let out a long exhale. Time was ticking for Isabelle Abbott. The only real lead they had was an aquarium somewhere with a glow-stick killer shark and the former fed, Bartlett on the lam. But where was that son-of-a-bitch and how could they make him slither out of his slimehole?

His cell lit up and "Wipe Out," a 1960s surf-rock classic by The Ventures, played. Caller ID showed Beatrice Middleton.

"Hey, Bea."

"Mac, I just got a call from that teacher we spoke to at SAMOHI."

"The strange, shark-obsessed, department chair?"

"No, not Jones, it's the young guy in Isabelle Abbott's PhD program—Matthew Corcoran."

"Oh, yeah. What did he have to say?" Wu doodled shark images in the margin of his yellow pad.

"Just wants a quick meet. Wouldn't say anything more. Dogtown Coffee in Santa Monica, 5:00 tonight. Can you make it?"

"I'll be there. Anything new from your pal, Bijan?"

"*Nada*. The info on the sex tourism site was deleted, and even the code he'd been able to salvage wasn't enough to bring it back online. Poof. Into the ether."

"Damn, something else we can't quite get a handle on. I contacted the feds about our Bartlett suspicions, but we don't have enough evidence for anything actionable—like a search warrant or even a BOLO. As expected, they're nervous as shit about pushing up against one of their own."

"What's new on the executed Palmdale cop, Hobbs?"

"His department's investigating. Nothing on the slug that was recovered in our databases."

"Have you heard back from Demi yet?" Bea asked.

"Just hung up." Wu filled her in.

"The teeth belong to some unidentifiable glow-in-the-dark killer shark species? Oh, Sweet Jesus." Bea's voice lowered. "Sounds like these poor mermaids leave this world in a bloody feeding frenzy. Shit, Wu, we have to move faster."

"I put two of my people on investigating local aquarium staffers. We need to narrow the search. Even a crazy fish freak at a local pet store might be able to pull off water chemistry in a big system. Maybe Hal Jones could give us some leads. He seems to know the field exceedingly well."

Wu heard a busy office and someone calling Bea's name in the background.

"Okay, I gotta run," she said. "My boss is breathing down my neck for an update. If I can't come up with at least a convincing broad-brush summary he'll give this to somebody else. Or deep-six it completely. Can't let that happen. I'll see you with Corcoran at five."

"I trust you to keep the investigation under wraps. If—I mean when—we find her, the details are all yours."

She disconnected before he could finish his sentence.

Chapter 17

The air conditioning pumped out a continual arctic blast. Former federal agent Sonny Bartlett slumped in the seat of his rented gunmetal gray sedan, a car too common to draw attention. The AC had only two settings: sweat-your-ass-off or freeze-your-ass-off. He went for frost. Zipping his hoodie all the way up, he adjusted his ballcap while shivering and watching girls come and go from a safehouse for female runaways. Recruitment at the Harbor was out for now. Kidnapping the school teacher had totally screwed that source.

Trolling for teenagers was the work Cole Hobbs got off on. Pimping was not Bartlett's strong suit. He wracked his mind for someone he could enlist to take the asshole's place. All Bartlett really cared about was the money, and lately it had been rolling in big time. He'd almost paid off the debts he owed his two vengeful exes.

He scratched his armpit and gulped down a watery, high-protein smoothie. Nothing was happening on this bland, faceless street where every 1950s ranch house looked the same. Maybe he'd have to cruise the mall again. Piscem Auratus needed two attractive, healthy girls today or there'd be no way they could possibly be ready for the Saudis by the weekend. Putting off world-class clients was not an option—he refused to let that happen—even if he had to kidnap his own mother. He smiled to himself. That was a sight he'd like to see—the bulbous old crone torn up by razor-sharp piranha teeth, the fish viciously picking her tendons like guitar strings.

He was still lost in the fantasy when the front door to the women's shelter across the street opened. Two girlss walked down the steps and crossed the sidewalk past his car. *Twins? Be still my heart! And hot twins, shit! What were the odds?* It was a sign from heaven. Cha-ching. He could hear the price of the mermaid experience rise.

In the innocuous gray ride, Bartlett followed the attractive duo at a distance down Petit Road across Telephone and into a busy strip mall. A portly middle-aged man in a greasy white apron struggled to take down a *Now Hiring* sign in front of Tony's Breakfast-at-the-Beach. It was nowhere near the beach, however. Could be in Kansas for all the personality the restaurant projected.

The girls entered, blonde ponytails swinging behind them, their asses packed into tight, cut-off jeans. Were they having coffee and waffles, or did they work there?

The former agent parked his car several stores away in front of a Massage Envy, and walked slowly toward Tony's. Twins. He still couldn't get over his luck. He picked up a local newspaper outside the restaurant door and tucked it under his arm.

As Bartlett pulled open the heavy glass door, he was immediately greeted by twin number one. Blonde with a purple streak in her hair, not beautiful, but good boobs. She was tall, maybe five-nine, and had nice facial bones. Old Cloris-Edna was a magician with makeup and lighting. The Saudis would be beating their black royal Visa cards against their dicks for a piece of these bitches.

The girl's name plate said Syd-nee. He followed her to a nearby booth, slid in. Her sister, Char-lee, blonde with a green streak, bounced by with a pot of fresh coffee, which he accepted with a wink. She blushed and deposited four small containers of cream next to his cup. Her nails were chewed to nubs.

Bartlett knew they might see him as an old lecher—he was fiftyish but in great shape for his age, maybe he might just be the type of kind, generous, semi-hot older man who'd appeal to the girls' neediness. Their father, or more likely mama's latest boyfriend, probably treated the kids like shit and molested the hell out of them. Bartlett knew how to spin this old, predictable story to his advantage.

Several minutes later, Char-lee returned to take his order.

"What can I get you today, sir?"

A nice smile. Lots of piercings in her ears—a walking tackle box. Kinda sexy. He returned her smile and ordered a big breakfast so he could hang around as long as possible. It wasn't the kind of place where people set up shop and worked on their laptops all day.

"I see you have a twin sister." Bartlett shut the menu and handed it over to her. "I'm a twin, too." He enjoyed lying, or as he liked to think of it, role-playing. "We were servers at an IHOP together in Northridge during college. I think everyone should work in the food industry before they head off to make the big bucks."

Her eyes widened and she stuffed the order pad into her apron. "Cool. We worked at Denny's back in Moab, that's in Utah, before we, uh, moved out. I'm like, so relieved to have a job. Crazy expensive here." She raised her bitten fingers to her mouth, then quickly pulled them away. "Your order will be up shortly. More coffee?"

He took a last swig and finished his cup, pushed it toward the edge of the table. "Please."

Syd-nee with the purple streak, grabbed a pot from the warmer at the server's station, poured a fill-up then scampered back to her twin. She whispered in her sister's ear, then glanced over her shoulder toward Bartlett. He opened up his newspaper, trying to project the appearance of a normal breakfaster, not that of a predator on the prowl. Can't seem too overly friendly, too anxious to help. The girls obviously needed money, were newbies living at a halfway house for troubled teens. They definitely scored pretty enough to be convincing mermaids.

The former federal agent felt a surge of confidence. He had the answer to Piscem's critical "staffing" problems: Syd-nee and Char-lee from Moab. *Damn! This was going to work.* He'd give the girls his theatrical agent business card with the link to his fabulous website touting clients he didn't have. His fake online profile was impressive, even if he did say so himself.

Sonny began to see why Hobbs found the trolling enticing— just a challenging form of deep-sea fishing. Select the right lure, set the hook, a little patience, then reel 'er in. He'd roll up at shift's end in his favorite chick bait—a kiss-kiss red Maserati.

They'd want to crawl in for a short ride. The ride of a lifetime. He chuckled to himself and winked at Char-lee as she served two gelatinous yellow-eyed eggs that stared at him from a bed of pancakes and sausages.

"You girls surf?"

"No opportunity—yet. But we're really good at waterskiing." She tossed her ponytail and moved on to the next table.

Waterskiing—the chicks must be good swimmers! Bartlett shoved his fork though the yolk, almost too excited to eat.

—

Their shift was over at 2:30 p.m. On cue, Sonny Bartlett sauntered out of the veterinary clinic next to the massage studio and took his time climbing into his black Land Rover. He'd dumped the rental, now was the time to be seen but not too in-your-face. He'd decided that the lipstick-red sports car was too ostentatious. He didn't need all that firepower to net these two back-water fishies. More importantly, he didn't need to be overly memorable to passers-by. He had to be smart and cautious. Recklessness had been Hobbs's downfall.

Syd-nee stepped out first with Char-lee at her heels, happy smiles on their faces. Good tips this shift? He'd left a nice pile of dollars on the table. Bartlett backed out of his parking space and caught Syd-nee's eye. He waved. Recognition dawned on the twin faces simultaneously.

Snagging a quick look at himself in the rearview mirror, he wore a sky-blue polo shirt that matched his eyes. Pushing the Ray-Bans up on his head, his Tag Heuer flashed on his wrist. He'd just had his dark blonde hair highlighted and perfectly tousled. Bartlett looked good, so did they.

The former federal agent pulled up beside where the two paused on the sidewalk and said, "What a coincidence, the best breakfast-serving duet in town."

Syd-nee laughed a cute little giggle and Char-lee grinned. They seemed to like what they saw. *Hoo-rah.* Bartlett's chest warmed with anticipation. So did his loins. These girls were his—just exude interest and concern. Crank the reel, pull 'em in.

"I was dropping my rescue pup at the vet to be spayed." He was proud of himself for coming up with the dog scheme.

"Aww, a rescue, nice. What kind of dog?" asked Char-lee. The twin with the purple streak in her light hair seemed to be the most outgoing. Both of their faces were suddenly sad, probably left a family pet back in Utah.

"She's a golden retriever mix. Ariel's her name, like from *The Little Mermaid.* I live on the beach, so I wanted something oceany. Dumb, but I'm an old softie at heart." He laughed at himself, maybe he was a natural pimp after all. "She's about two months old, a real sweetheart. I lost my dog this winter. She was fourteen."

Char-lee's lips blossomed into a plump pout. "Ohhh, I'm sorry. We have a Bernese mountain dog back home."

"He's the only thing I miss," Syd-nee added. She wiped the back of her hand across her forehead. Sweat filmed her face.

"Can't believe this weather," he said. "Never used to get this hot near the beach. Good old global warming. You girls need a ride home? I'll turn up the air."

They shot each other a quick look. "That would be nice, sir, thank you. We're less than a mile from here." Char-lee stepped off the curb and headed for the car.

Bartlett felt positively giddy. The trap was closing. "I'm Sam Weisberg. Sorry that I don't have my IHOP nameplate anymore."

Both girls laughed along with him. Char-lee slid into the front, Syd-nee climbed into the back. He was about to shut the door when a severe-looking woman, mid-forties, wearing a gray T-shirt dress and Birkenstocks, stepped up to the vehicle.

"Girls, out. I told you we'd pick you up."

Syd and Char seemed to shrink in their seats. Tears filled Syd-nee's eyes. Char-lee glowered at Nurse Ratchet.

"You want to stay with us, you follow the rules. You got jobs now, don't blow this opportunity."

The house mother at the shelter? Bartlett's prize was slipping away. Cut bait and move on? No way, huh-uh. The grip he had on the leather-laced steering wheel turned his knuckles white.

"He was only giving us a lift home. No biggie." Char-lee said, definite attitude in her voice. She seemed to be the rebellious one, Syd-nee the compliant sister.

"I didn't mean to upset anyone here," Bartlett said, feigning an apologetic demeanor. "Hot as Hades today." He wanted to fucking shoot the woman in the head. "Just being neighborly."

Mouth in a nasty line, Ratchet nodded her head toward the shelter's crummy van.

Syd-nee immediately scrambled out of the Rover and trudged over to a dated silver vehicle of indeterminate brand. She got in. Char-lee followed, looking pissed and resentful. She glanced back at Bartlett and shrugged her shoulders.

Bartlett's heart raced and his jaw locked as tight as a piranha on a mermaid's ass. *You can't take my twins, bitch.* But she could, and she did. He had no way to stop her without making a scene, but this wasn't over.

"Later, girls," he called as the van pulled out. Was the cunt taking a picture of his license plate? *Shit*. He'd been made.

Chapter 18

Bea found a spot in the public parking lot off Main Street, a block from the Santa Monica coffee house where they were to meet Matthew Corcoran. The late afternoon was uncomfortably hot—the usually crisp breeze off the bay felt halfhearted at best. She opened the sunroof a couple inches for ventilation and then slid from her seat, slammed and locked the door behind her.

Bea's sandals made a snicking noise as she walked across the soft blacktop. Even the seagulls seemed to have slowed down. Their usual fast swoops and glides through the nearby greenspace took on the labored appearance of winter flies trapped inside a window screen.

Crossing the street at the corner, she saw Wu in front of the whitewashed Dogtown Coffee chatting with the Santa Monica High School teacher. She approached the men and they exchanged greetings. Wu opened the shop door and they staked out a table by an open window before putting in their drink requests. Bea and Corcoran ordered the place's signature Salty Dog iced caramel coffee. Wu went for green iced tea. Niceties over and beverages in hand, they settled into their chairs.

Corcoran kicked off the conversation. "You guys come up with anything on Izzy yet?"

Wu sighed. "A few leads but we've stalled out, man. In an active case we can't go into details with you."

Corcoran nodded and gazed out across the street where a gaggle of bicyclists sped toward Palisades Park. "I have this terrible feeling she's dead." He shuddered. His coffee sloshed in the cup. "Most abductions don't end well."

Wu took a long drink of his tea. "You're right, they don't. But there's always the exception."

Bea fidgeted impatiently with her straw. "So, help us, Matt. What've you got?"

"I'm glad to see they use paper straws here. All that plastic, killing the wildlife, the oceans." His voice, low and tense, sounded like he was watching the horror take place in front of his face.

Bea tapped her fingers on the table top. The guy was clearly having a tough time dealing with the disappearance of his friend, but avoidance never helped. "Matt? Focus, sweetheart. What've you got that could help Isabelle?"

His attention returned to Bea and Wu. "I dunno, probably nothing, I don't want to get anyone in trouble, but Hal, Dr. Jones, our department chair, has been ordering some really expensive equipment online and it's not for the high school. Where does he come up with that kind of money? We almost never get awarded big grants, and when we do, everybody knows about it. Something's off. And he's been all nervous-like lately."

Wu glanced at Bea then back to Corcoran. "How do you know what he's been ordering online?"

"I came into his office looking for him the other day and the screen was still up on his personal laptop. The bottom line was more than a quarter mil. Gene splicers and shit, sophisticated lab equipment."

Corcoran pushed back a stray dreadlock, then continued.

"I didn't catch much more because he came fast-assing in and slammed the cover shut. Boom. Said he was putting together a wish list for fun. That's bull. The order had been placed. I pretended like I hadn't seen anything."

The teacher pulled a folded piece of notebook paper from the pocket of his khaki shirt and pushed it toward Wu.

"What's this?" The detective opened the paper.

"The invoice. Golden Gate Scientific Supply Company."

Bea choked on her coffee. "Whoa. How the hell did you get that?"

"I hit *Print* before he came back into the office. Made it by a millisecond." Corcoran's lips curled into a fleeting smile.

Wu studied the note. "Thank you for coming forward, Matthew. Who knows—maybe this'll give us the break we need." He took a photo of the number sequence on the billing with his phone. "I'm sending this off to a colleague to check out ASAP."

Wu fidgeted restlessly in his seat, looking anxious to be on his way.

"One more thing," Corcoran said. "You may find this interesting, too."

Wu settled back down.

"I did a Google search into Jones's research before I was first hired, so I'd, you know, have a topic for discussion that might impress him at my job interview. He was into bioluminescence in large ocean mammals. Doesn't really exist, according to the literature. I thought it was kind of a weird subject, but hey, we're all a bunch of geeks with our own esoteric interests. Anyhow, this week, I went back to my research notes and reviewed it all."

Bea nodded. "What did you find?" She finished her Salty Dog coffee. Her nerves buzzed, and a sugary, caffeine-induced hot flash began to percolate beneath her skin.

She glanced at Wu. He was reading a text message. Eyebrows squished together in a dark line. He avoided eye contact with Bea.

Corcoran paused for a moment as a rowdy group of high

schoolers walked past the cafe. Bea supposed he didn't want to be interrupted or overheard by nosey students—students like her son and his friend Hayes. Several called greetings his way. He lifted a hand with a quick wave.

The teacher let out a deep breath when the kids kept on going. He continued, "Halliburton Jones's father, Keaton Halliburton Jones, was a geneticist and an ocean biologist in the early sixties. Studied under the famous scientist Heinrich Orletti in Munich and at Stanford. They were working on bioluminescing dolphins for the military. Keaton Jones died in 1980. Some kind of boating accident."

Bea thought back to the shark teeth embedded in the girl's arm. Demi said they were golden, glow-in-the-dark—similar to those of a great white, but not. Mad scientist stuff.

"So, the father worked for the U.S. military?" Wu asked.

Matt nodded and finished his drink. "Had a contract with the U.S. Navy. Before Orletti died, which was well after Keaton's death, Keaton's kid, our very own Dr. Halliburton Jones, was one of Orletti's most promising acolytes."

"Jumped in to take his dead father's place?" Bea wondered if there had been bad blood between father and son.

"Hal Jones and Orletti co-authored several papers together. After Orletti was gone, Jones dropped off the radar. Showed up here at SAMOHI a decade later. Couldn't find anything much about what he'd been up to for those years. Maybe you'll have better luck."

"Can we turn Bijan loose on it?" Wu asked Bea.

She nodded.

"So, that's all I got," Corcoran said. "Hear anything that could be helpful?"

Wu nodded, angled out of his chair, and stood. The others followed suit. "Thank you, Matt. I appreciate your willingness to talk to us. You've got my contact information if anything else comes up."

Matthew bid them goodbye. Looking like one of his students,

he threw his backpack over his shoulder and jogged off down the sidewalk toward the high school.

"Thanks for setting this up, Bea." Wu turned in the direction of his parked vehicle a few spots from the café. "I'll be in touch soon."

"Detective, you're not going anywhere without telling me what that text was about." She waggled her head and put her hands on her hips, a heavy mustard-colored Dooney & Bourke bag hung from her broad, brown shoulder. "I can tell when a man's got information he should be telling me."

Wu stopped on the sidewalk, pushed his hands deep into his pockets and scoped the scene as if he were about to pass on some deep-state spy information. "Listen, I'm not trying to be secretive."

"Bullshit, *partner*." Bea was pissed. She folded her arms across her chest and watched his jaw clench and unclench.

"Okay, okay," he finally said. "We gave a heads-up to all Ventura metro women's shelters telling them that active trolling was likely going on. Asked them to contact us immediately with anything that looked suspicious. The director of a runaway girl's shelter called my captain and said a dude in a black Land Rover tried to pick up a couple of twins, sixteen-year-olds, both in recovery from heroin addiction. She snapped a photo of this asshole—can't see much—sunglasses and a baseball cap. But she got his license plate."

"And, who is this moron?"

Wu chewed at his lip for an instant. "Vehicle's registered to one Sandford Bartlett."

"Holy shit." Bea gasped. She could almost feel steam shooting out of her ears. "And you weren't going to tell me this?" She gripped her purse in her hand like she was about to smash him with it. "What is going on Mac? We might finally have a lead, and a suspect so stupid he drives a car around he knows we've seen, and you don't share it?"

The door to the café opened and the wafting scent of coffee, earlier so delectable, now made Bea queasy. The detective shuffled his feet like he was about to break into a run.

"Listed Bea, my cap asked me, ordered me, to keep this one under wraps. Made me swear I wouldn't tell you. He's really nervous about the press, been burned too many times. This info is too important to risk."

"You wouldn't have this Hal Jones stuff without me, Wu. You wouldn't have known about Bartlett in the first place, or had the chewed-up pieces of the girl."

He frowned and stopped moving. "We eventually would've gotten there."

"Maybe. Maybe not."

Silence hung between them. Bea heard only the sounds of automobile wheels stopping at the nearby light, the soft whirr of a skateboarder passing by, then the rumble of a garbage truck towing its rotting load. "Okay, Wu, here and now, we're either working completely together on this, or not. Your choice. I'm happy to do my own thing."

He tilted his head skyward. Looking for an answer? A blessing? For seagull shit to rain onto his face? Finally, he held out his hand. "Would you accept my apology?"

Bea shifted her purse back onto her shoulder and clasped his hand in hers, first tentatively, then with conviction. "Okay, *partner*. And for your information, my people located Bartlett's house in Manhattan Beach, but he hasn't lived there for over a year. It's leased to a screenwriter from Fresno under a private offshore corporation. Bijan's following the money. In fact, he's waiting for us at his office right now."

"Okay, let's go. And after we talk to Bijan, it's time to reconnect with our squirrely Dr. Jones."

Bea nodded agreement. The thought of this possible pervert leading a classroom of young teens was appalling. "Should we confront him right away? Threaten to take apart his workplace?" She smiled, remembering the look on the doc's face when Wu moved the shark jaws. "Cops messing with his precious specimens might put him right over the edge."

"Since we likely don't have enough for a search warrant, let's surveil the slime ball instead, see what rocks he crawls under. Could be as interesting as what's in his high school office."

Bea scanned a text that had just buzzed, then looked up at the detective. "Time to boogie. Bijan's got something."

Chapter 19

Casey Abbott felt like she was losing her mind. She brushed tears from her eyes with the back of her hand. Izzy was being held somewhere awful—dying, dead, or wishing she were. The images conjured in her imagination were crazy-making. She winced and picked up the phone to call Wu. Again. His response was always the same: we have a few leads, pursuing aggressively, be patient, we'll be in touch the minute something breaks. She put the phone back down. Making another call was worthless.

The detective was a conscientious officer, but Casey was done with being helplessly dependent on the police. She'd learned online that local malls were hot spots for sex traffickers aiming to hook up with victims. Made sense that scared, isolated kids would congregate somewhere with a familiar feel. Some would be desperate enough to fall for the empty promises of predators. So, that's where Casey was headed. She'd circulate, schmooze, photograph anyone who seemed too interested in her. Then she'd send the images to Wu. Maybe it could help.

He'd be pissed that she'd gone rogue, but tough shit. At least she was taking action.

Reaching into her closet, she pulled out an old Abercrombie T-shirt and a pair of skinny jeans that nicely highlighted her slim assets. Izzy had forced her to buy the jeans several years ago when she was attempting one of her irritating sisterly "makeovers." Grabbing her styling gel, she squirted a quarter-sized glob into her palm, then scrubbed it though her short hair until it stood on end. She ferreted a mostly-empty can of hairspray from beneath the bathroom sink and pressed the button. A weak stream of sticky spray coated the crown of her head before sputtering out. She stood back and admired her "I slept in the bus station" look.

Casey's spirits began to rise as she plucked long, gold chandelier earrings from a vintage cigar box containing her meager jewelry collection. Next, she added an assortment of rubber wristbands touting various causes and a couple woven bracelets she'd snagged in Mexico. Oooh, she found a press-on butterfly tattoo and applied it to peek from the neckline of her V-neck tee.

Now, the makeup. She didn't have much. Could sludgy, five-year-old mascara cause a serious infection? She'd take the chance. Added some shimmery pink eye shadow and dark plum-colored lipstick she'd used for a Vampira Halloween costume way back when. Could it have been from high school? Oh my God. Insane. It would make her lips rot. She couldn't find the blush, so she rubbed the lipstick onto her cheeks. Looked more like bruises but maybe that would enhance an image of vulnerability.

She slid her feet into a pair of purple flip-flops. She needed some tawdry nail polish. She'd buy something glittery at the drug store and apply it in front of Domino's at the mall. Nicely tacky.

Grabbing her fringed shoulder bag, Casey headed out the door, energized and relieved to be doing something, anything, to help find her sister. She felt safe—she was not naive enough to get sucked into a bullshit story of rescue from some lowlife.

—

Bijan looked like he hadn't moved a muscle from the last time Bea had seen him several days previously. The McDonald's bags had simply been switched out for Golden Dragon cartons and Taco Bell wrappers. The plastic Big Gulp cup from the gas station likely contained his usual disgusting mix of Dr. Pepper, diet cola, and Mountain Dew. Smelled like it also might include a shot of Jägermeister. The master hacker swore it was great for the digestion. With the crap he ate, he'd need something to keep his stomach from disintegrating.

Bea blinked her eyes as they adjusted from the dazzling sunlight outside. The dark office was illuminated only by monitors, a small desk lamp, and several strings of tiny orange lights.

"The beautiful and brilliant Beatrice Middleton and her Charlie-Chan-of-a-detective associate, Officer Macintosh Wu. So good to see you both."

Bea noted Wu's immediate frown.

Bijan noticed the reaction, too. "No offense intended, Wu. Detective Chan is one of my all-time oldie movie favorites from the thirties."

"And he was played by an American of European descent," Wu responded, expression dour.

Bea immediately recognized his unease. How many times had she experienced the same thing? Small, well-meant comments that stung like pinpricks. Micro-agressions—*We all do it, we're all human,* she reminded herself. *Just have to try and be better every day.*

"Sorry if I offended, man. Yellow peril, xenophobia, racism. Troubled times back then. We haven't come that far, have we?" Bijan gestured to canvas director's chairs and invited them to sit where they could see the big screen on his desk.

Wu's rigid shoulders seemed to loosen and he sat down next to Bea.

"Sheee-it, man, I'm Iranian—we're about as popular as head lice these days. And speaking of infestations, this Bartlett dude's a real disease."

"Fill us in, big guy." Bea's chair creaked as she leaned toward the monitor. Charts, graphs, scrolling numbers—what did it mean?

"Okey-dokey, kiddies. From what I can tell, Sandford Bartlett has been laundering millions through a company called Untamed Adventures. Hunting endangered species, exotic animal trafficking, kinky sexual adventures that pit girls against big cats. Really fucked-up stuff. Dude's been using his status as a Federal Fisheries and Wildlife agent to procure the animals, and probably the women—they seem to mostly come from Eastern Europe. No big surprise there. But he's not the main actor. There's some kind of Honduran cartel involved, headed by an accountant-type going by the code name *El Tiburón*."

Bea felt a shiver like melting ice run down her spine. "'Tiburon' means 'shark' in Spanish, doesn't it?"

Bijan grinned. "*Sí, sí,* my bilingual *señorita.*"

"Far from it, unfortunately. I've got a friend who lives in Tiberon up near Sausalito. Filled me in on their local fish lore."

"Well, the shark theme's pervasive with these A-holes. And, hey, check this out." He pointed to his monitor. "A quarter mil in American dollars showed up a few hours ago in one of Bartlett's offshore accounts. Was from a Saudi IP linked to a restaurant called Sharky's Cafe in Morocco, as in *Casablanca.* Very Humphrey Bogart."

"That's a lot of gin and falafels," Wu added.

Bijan continued. "Joint's probably a beard, likely one of many, for this fuck-a-chick-with-scales thing."

Bea glanced at Wu, his face shadowed in the darkness. "A quarter million. Payment from clients booking a mermaid experience? Where have we heard that number before?"

Wu rubbed the light stubble on his chin. "The bottom line for Hal Jones's equipment order."

"Bingo," Bea said. "Not sure what it means but it's no coincidence the sums seem to match."

Bijan took a noisy slurp of his drink. Ice rattled. "That sex tourism site I hit on when Pete was here, disappeared afterwards for a good twenty-four hours, but now it's back. It cycles at seemingly random intervals for twenty-second pop-ups, and then it's gone. I haven't been able to capture the sucker."

Bea felt a twinge of optimism, or was it the handful of Tums kicking in? "Think you can grab it at some point?"

"You betcha, baby girl." Bijan continued tapping the keyboard with his big fingers. Digits danced on a scrolling screen. "The sex tour biz looks lucrative as hell. Two money buckets seeing the most consistent action include one in the Caymans and one in Cyprus. Your dead cop, Hobbs, has also been receiving regular deposits of $20,000 a month for the last two years into an account out of Switzerland. All fairly sophisticated."

Wu leaned forward, studying the complicated numbers. "So, Untamed Adventures is definitely a multinational enterprise?"

Bijan turned the monitor so Bea and Wu could more easily check it out. "Yup. It's connected worldwide. Whatever nasty action's happening in or around Ventura's probably a drop in the ocean. And that's all I got, my friends. *No mas* for now."

Wu rose from his seat, looking ready to leave. Bea stayed put and chewed on her thumbnail. "Bijan, could you also check out real estate holdings that might come up linked to Bartlett? If we have sharks and fake mermaids, we gotta have some kind of facility that can accommodate this sicko untamed shit, right?"

"Correctimundo, my beauty. Will get to it later tonight."

"Thanks, Bijan. Very helpful stuff," Wu said. He held out his hand, and they shook.

Bea checked her watch. "I want to tail Jones, see where he lives." The school day was over, but Professor Halliburton Jones might still be in his office. She wanted to drive by and take a look-see, just in case. Otherwise, they were out of luck on a tail until end of school tomorrow. Little puzzle pieces were trickling in, but no big picture yet and the clock was ticking.

Chapter 20

Wu followed Bea to the high school where they staked out the faculty lot. At 5:45 p.m., it was still about a quarter full. The teachers were a dedicated bunch. Bea found a parking space half a block away, then joined the detective in his innocuous gray sedan directly across an alley from the lot. According to Ventura Metro, a 2015 black Honda Prius was registered to Jones. A car of choice in Santa Monica, there were two in clear sight. One with a license plate number matching the department chair's vehicle.

Bea felt a tinge of excitement. "He's still here."

Wu nodded and continued to edit a report on his tablet.

Twenty minutes later, Doctor Jones ambled toward his car, chatting with, of all people, Dexter and Hayes.

Bea's eyes popped wide. "What the . . ."

Wu closed the tablet and stashed it beneath the seat. "Isn't that your kid?" he asked.

"Used to be, until about one second ago. What are those delinquents up to?"

Wu's eyes narrowed. "Hold on, does Dexter know Jones is a suspect?"

"No. No way." *Does he?* "I've said *nothing* because I know what a damn snoop my son is. He and Hayes, his sidekick there, think they're the next Woodward and Bernstein. I can't begin to tell you how much trouble it's gotten them into." She mentally deleted frightening scenes threatening to play in the movie trailer of her brain.

Across the way, Jones opened the rear door to his Prius. Hayes slid the backpack from his shoulder. He looked about to crawl in. That's all it took.

Bea's blood pressure sky-rocketed. She jumped out of Wu's car and marched down the sidewalk toward the trio. She could hear the soundtrack to *Jurassic Park,* when the T. rex approached.

Calm down, she told herself.

Jones looked up at her, stunned, the proverbial deer in headlights. "Oh, hello, Miss, uh, Middlebury, isn't it?"

"Hello, Doctor Jones. It's Beatrice Middle-ton, ton." *Like a ton of shit about to drop on your ugly bald head.*

"Hi, Miz M." Hayes flashed his thousand-watt smile and ran up for a hug. Such a mama's boy—so sad he didn't have one. Bea gave him a loving squeeze instead of strangling him. *Eau de teen boy* wafted from his stringy hair.

"Hey, Mom. What're you doing here?" Dexter asked.

"Hey, baby boy." His embrace was more tentative. God, she loved her sweet and irritating little troublemaker. "What am I doing here? Uh, uh, a parent council meeting about Career Day." She pulled that one out of the air.

Dex raised a skeptical eyebrow.

"This is your, er, son?" Jones's cheeks took on the roundness of a puffer fish.

"Yes, these two hang with me."

After dropping the key fob and having to practically crawl under the car to retrieve it, Jones opened the driver's side door and tossed his briefcase across the Prius's center console onto the passenger seat. "I was chatting with the boys about helping me with a special research project." His eyes blinked nervously. "They seem very enthusiastic. Yes, indeedy."

Like how to commit murder by shark? "Oh, how interesting. I'd love to hear all about it soon, very soon. Maybe it's engaging enough for me to do a story on it for my show."

Jones paled and slumped against his car for an instant before recovering himself.

Bea struggled to be civil; Jones was definitely central to their investigation. She didn't want to scare him off. By the looks of him, she'd already kicked him in the nuts.

She turned to her two bad boys. "You guys need a ride home? My car's right down the block." Sweat dampened her neck.

"Got our bikes." Dexter adjusted the recently acquired lacrosse stick that threatened to fall from his backpack, then asked, "What's for dinner?"

Who the hell knew? A good mother would. "Burgers, salad and, uh, sweet potato fries." The pantry was empty—she had nothing. "From Holy Cow BBQ, we'll order in. And okay, Hayes, you're invited." She could never resist his lost-puppy expression.

"Yes!" Hayes let loose with a fist pump.

Shifting his weight from foot to foot, Dr. Jones peered at the detective's car across the street. Bea was relieved that Wu didn't seem to be in it. Smart.

"We'll talk another time, gentlemen," the professor said to Dexter and Hayes. "Gotta run now. Late for a date. Always something, indeedy. Bye now, nice to see you again, Miss Middle-*ton*." He smiled as though proud of himself for remembering some complicated scientific theorem. Then his mouth twisted into a lemon-eater frown and he hopped into his Prius.

"So nice to see you again, too, Doctor Jones," Bea called as the professor backed out of his parking spot, almost side-swiping a nearby van. Then he turned right and headed toward the Pico exit. Bea looked across the street to see Wu pulling out after him.

Wu! *Hell*. He'd dumped her.

Pissed off, Bea rushed to her car ready to follow, then stopped and breathed out a big sigh. *Let it go*. Getting upset was a total waste of energy. He was a smart cop and would handle the Jones pursuit just fine. He didn't need her breathing down his neck every minute.

Her son, however, could probably use a bit more scrutiny. She tried her best at single-mom-hood, and was damn good at it, but could never quite keep all the balls in the air at once. "Hop on those bikes, baby boys. See you at home in fifteen."

She'd pump the boys for anything they might know. Unless it was a woman who was a total hottie, they wouldn't be following a teacher out to the parking lot without an ulterior motive. Had Hayes overheard words in the copy room that could prove informative? She'd weasel info out of them both, between mouthfuls of sweet potato fries.

As Bea walked to her car, she texted Wu, filling him in and apologizing for her impulsive behavior in leaping out of his vehicle. At this point, even the Lord could come down and offer her kids a ride home and she'd throw herself in front of the chariot to stop it. Both her children had suffered badly from being hauled into the wrong ride. It would never happen again. Bea whispered a prayer for Isabelle Abbott and for all in jeopardy.

Wu texted right back. Said he was five cars behind Jones, motoring through Brentwood toward the 405 then to the 101. He'd be in touch.

Sliding into the front seat of her Beemer, Bea punched up the Holy Cow website and ordered dinner with extra fries. Then she called Lucy to check in. She wanted to give her a heads-up about an unexpected visitor.

Chapter 21

What heaven to have her aunt at Rancho de la Vega. Lucy marveled at the gift the universe had bestowed upon her in the guise of this kind, brilliant woman. She found herself continually touching her aunt's arm, just to make sure she was real.

After settling into the yurt, they enjoyed a light lunch of pasta and greens prepared by Elsa. Then, Sister Catherine Lucia lost no time unpacking and organizing her medicinal herbs and potions atop Lucy's small desk. Bugle and Maddie were immediate Sister fans. Howard, the feline, slinked off to watch from outside the door.

Lucy's cell sounded. It was Bea calling, but auntie requested the silencing of phones while they discussed high-risk pregnancy.

"I no have cell phone," she said, "but I read on internet about the buzzing, the flashing, and what you call it— vibrating. No good. You need peace, *mija, un útero calmo.*"

Lucy smiled. She followed the *curandera's* orders and stashed her device. She would call Beebs later.

While Sister explained the advantages of cramp bark and black haw, Lucy struggled for enough energy to listen.

"These fine herbs help stop contraction, bleeding, and tension *nervosa*. Really good in early months with child. Black haw also make weak cervix strong like superhero."

A smile again flickered on Lucy's lips. *Hell, yes, give me a powerful cervix, maybe like Wonder Woman's lasso of truth.*

The old woman's musical voice, combined with the unfamiliar soothing aromas of freshly dried herbs, filled their round, canvas hacienda. The tension in Lucy's muscles eased. She forced her eyes open and tried to concentrate, but could feel her body's need for rest overtaking her brain's desire for information, however fascinating. She moved onto the bed and fluffed the down pillows. Sister sat on a wooden rocker next to her, and the dogs fought for space at Lucy's feet.

Her aunt continued. "First, some things make contractions we no want: dehydration, stress, and too hard work." Sister held up a note card that spelled out the three threats in black marker. "Had to write down to remember English words." She pocketed the card and chuckled. "Next, I tell about special remedies I use for *muchos años*, sí?"

Lucy nodded. Her gaze caught Sister's fine gray braid and silver loop earrings that gleamed in sunlight filtering through the window. Her aunt was a magical, fairy godmother.

"I also want meet your *médico*, uh, doctor," Sister said. "We work close together, *no?*"

Lucy nodded, then felt herself begin to doze as Sister explained the finer points of a light massage technique called abdominal effleurage. She tried to stay present, but sleep demanded its way. Wasn't a thirty-something supposed to have more energy than a seventy-something? This baby was like an alien parasite, sucking her dry.

—

Dreams of dead infants and hacked body parts shimmering with crushed golden shards terrorized Lucy's slumber. Rest was just a passage from one tension-filled scene to another. How could she remain in a state of calm when a young woman's grisly remains were found in a nearby gulch? And when the munchkin inside her threatened to abandon her damaged body, which was incapable of properly nurturing a growing baby?

Lucy awoke and forced herself to turn her focus from dark negativity and tuned in to the comforting sound of birds chirping at the nearby feeder. Ravens ripping, cawing? No, merely sparrows and wrens.

She kicked off the sheet that covered her. Sweat cooled on her skin. Soft female voices floated from the direction of the barn. She let them wash over her. Gradually aware of the softening light behind her eyelids, she realized she'd probably dozed off for several hours. Lucy felt the dogs hop from the bed and heard their toenails clip-clip on the wood floor as they went out the door. Must be dinnertime at Elsa's cabin.

Slowly, Lucy opened her eyes expecting to see her aunt's concerned face, but the person sitting next to her holding her hand was not Sister Catherine Lucia. Long masculine legs in well-worn jeans, capped by cowboy boots that had seen even more mileage, rested on the rug next to the cat.

She gasped and clutched her swollen abdomen. "Michael, what in the hell are you doing here?" Her sense of *un utero calmo* was obliterated. "Sweet Jesus."

Michael Burleson's fingers intertwined with hers.

She ripped her hand away. Anger and desire exploded in her chest. "You can't just walk back in to my life, like boom, here I am."

"Lucia, I tried to contact you so many times after you threw me out but you completely blew me off."

The fine bones of his face were cut more sharply than she'd remembered. Pain etched the lines of his forehead.

"I needed to see you, Lucy. Everything ended in total chaos. All my fault. But I love you, deeply, and I need to make amends."

Lucy's laugh was harsh. "Amends? It's so much more than that. I'm not one of your 10-step assignments."

Burleson winced. ""Please don't think of it like that." He swallowed hard and continued. "When you wouldn't respond, I finally convinced Bea to give me some damn crumbs of information." His handsome face was sad and gentle but his eyes sparked hot. "I knew something was going on but I didn't expect this." He looked toward her belly. "So, when were you going to tell me, sweetheart?"

Lucy pushed herself up onto one elbow and struggled to contain tears. These days she was a wall-to-wall water fountain.

But guilt tightened her throat. She forced out the words. "I was going to tell you that last day, but when I walked into the apartment and saw you loaded after a year clean, I lost it. I had no idea what had just happened to your daughter, that she'd overdosed. I'm so sorry."

Burleson rubbed his face as if there was a stain he couldn't remove. "Drinking was the absolute last thing I should have done when I found out what she'd done. What a stupid asshole I am." He paused for a long moment then raised his eyes to meet hers. "But I was hoping that eventually, you might be able to forgive me. But Lucy, dammit, not sharing this pregnancy with me is really, just, cruel."

She felt her blood pressure skyrocket. "I was going to, but I was so unbelievably pissed. You, you, threw away what we had. "I was—I am—devastated." Her fists clenched. "You bastard, I never wanted to see you again." *If only that were true.* "And maybe I wanted to be cruel. Maybe I wanted to punish you. And, maybe, I figured the baby would be dead before it even got started."

"I know the doctors said you could never get pregnant. Your body was too . . ."

"Yes, too damaged." She mopped her eyes with the edge of her T-shirt.

Burleson gazed out into the dimming sunlight. His face was

drawn and pale. She loved the sonofabitch, but she fought tooth and nail the desire to welcome him back with open arms and trust him again. She'd been told by too many people, and had seen it herself, that with addiction, love was never enough.

"Look, I know I really fucked up and being sorry doesn't come close to cutting it." He stood and faced Lucy, his hands open in supplication. "But I swear, I've been sober ever since you found me laid out on the floor." He shuddered and knelt down on his knees. "I don't blame you for not wanting to share our child with an unfit parent, someone like me." His eyes brimmed with remorse. "But I *am* the father. Aren't I?"

"Of course, you are. I can't believe you need to ask." Lucy sat up on the edge of the bed and wrapped her arms around herself. *Our child.* What did that imply? "But I told you if you started drinking again, it was over between us." Every neuron in her brain vibrated with fear. Was he going to demand some kind of custody? She struggled every day to keep this kid alive, to

tamp down the terror as her fragile body threatened to betray her. If the infant survived, any custody discussions would be a long, long way off.

"I swear to God, a relapse will never, ever happen again. The booze is history." Burleson slid onto the mattress next to her. "I don't expect you to believe me, or let me jump right back into your life. But can we try? Take it slow?"

She had no doubt he meant it profoundly, but the usual results of that statement were an old cliché. Could he really make good on his word? Probably not. His illness was a sly and powerful succubus.

Reluctantly, despite knowing she shouldn't, Lucy let him reach out to her, draw her close. He was so beautiful, and had such a good heart—when he was sober. And she loved him, really loved him. He was, in fact, the love of her life.

Lucy slid her arms around his neck. "The docs can't believe I actually got pregnant, all that scar tissue, all that injury."

"We're a powerful force together, Lucy."

They were indeed. His embrace was numinous, healing, but she was nowhere near ready to have faith in it. Maybe it was too late.

After a long moment, he pulled back and grasped Lucy by the shoulders. He searched her eyes, seeking something she wasn't sure she had to give.

"Listen, sweetheart, I've got to go back to Santa Cruz for a few days, family stuff—I'm staying very connected to my daughters. Trying to step up and make things right."

"I'm glad to hear that," Lucy whispered.

"Then, let me come back here and be with you." With wary hesitation he continued, "Please, can we give it a try?"

Could she do it? Was it worth the risk, only to be devastated again? If the baby didn't survive, what would their relationship be? Would he demand any kind of custody if the child lived?

Lucy pushed away wild tendrils of her dark, wavy hair and retied her ponytail. Skeptical thoughts ran rampant. If they spun the coin, how would it land? Life was so often a God-damned crapshoot.

Burleson continued. "And I won't interfere with you and the child. I promise. I have no doubt that you'll be an awesome mom and God knows, I have shit skills in parenting. I want you to understand that I'm here if you need me."

Warily, Lucy felt the anxiety in her bones release a notch.

Either oblivious to the tension in the room, or because of it, Sister bustled through the door with a glass of pink liquid in hand. "Sorry to interrupt but Lucia need raspberry infusion four times a day. *Muy bueno* for hydration *y* relaxation." She smiled at Burleson, touched his shoulder, then handed the drink to Lucy. "Sip now, Lucia, *mija*. If we *mucho* careful for month or two, little Henry Michael be okay."

"*Gracias,* Tia. From your mouth to His ears." Obediently, she sipped the drink. Tasted nice.

Burleson's eyes thawed from hard, fiery sapphires to warm pools of sunlight on blue water. "A boy? Henry Michael—I'm deeply honored. That is, unless it's named after Michael Jordan or Michael Jackson or some other hot shot from your past."

"No, it's after his S.O.B. of a father." Lucy winced. "Excuse the language, Sister." Why did all her relationships with men have to do with trying to fix the broken? Or was she just trying to fix herself?

Sister smiled at them, then her eyes narrowed and she patted Lucy's cheek. "She an unruly one, like her mama. Elsa say she hunt murderers, hike canyons, no eat regular."

Burleson laughed quietly. "You got your hands full, Sister." He reached out and patted the old woman's arm. "With Lucy's blessing, I'd like to be around to help out. It will take all of us to keep this force of nature out of trouble and on her back."

"I'm certain you want to help with the back part, *señor*. But no, no, no." Sister waggled her finger. "*Utero calmo.*" She shot Lucy a stern look and disappeared out the door, closing it behind her.

Lucy flushed. The sound of her aunt's footsteps receded. Shadows gathered the room in a deep embrace. Michael reached for Lucy and pulled her down atop the rumpled sheets. Drawing her close, they lay together, savoring a quiet moment amidst the tempest of their relationship. The familiar scent of his skin, the feel of his heartbeat against hers, joined by the small, tender heart pulsing between them, was what life was about.

Day by day. Should she try? Lucy gritted her teeth. When he walked through the door again and took her hand, Lucy's world turned on its head. Everything was happening way too fast. But the horse was out of the barn, as dear Elsa would say.

Lucy lightly rubbed her belly. Felt a feathery kick. "Damn you, Burleson. This is probably going to be a disaster." They'd have to establish rules, boundaries. "Talk with Cheyney about bunking at his place across the road until we figure out what this is, and what we're doing, okay?"

"You won't regret it, Lucy." He nuzzled his warm face against her abdomen.

Yeah, right. I already do. Blast her impulsive nature, but she couldn't deny the father of her child a second chance.

He kissed her and the deal was sealed. God help them all.

Chapter 22

Traffic thinned as Wu pulled off Topanga Canyon Boulevard in Woodland Hills past the Westridge Village Mall. He steered left onto Sherman Way, then followed Jones through a labyrinth of side streets thick with lush trees, neat '70s vintage condo complexes, and small apartment buildings.

Turning into the parking area of the well-kept Wisteria House Condominium Community, Jones waved at a bent, carrot-haired older woman in a gauzy white muumuu. Her three Yorkies strained at their leashes, yipping and growling at Jones as he stepped out of his Prius, his briefcase clutched to his chest as if for protection.

Wu pulled his unmarked along the curb behind a thicket of oleander and rolled down the car windows so he could overhear their conversation.

"Hello, Mavis." Jones slammed the car door behind him. The lock beeped.

"Halliburton." A bit of disdain flavored her greeting. "How's your dear aunt doing these days?"

The professor has an aunt? Wu scribbled himself a note.

Jones edged down the sidewalk away from her. "Busy, busy, up at the house in Camarillo. Sends her best. Yes, she does."

Carrot-top woman sniffed as if offended. "We're missing her in the golden girls synchronized swim club. Tell Cloris-Edna she should never be too busy for old friends."

"Will do, Mavis. I'm, uh, sure she misses you, too. Terribly. Bye, now. Papers to grade." He dashed to the front door of his unit and let himself in.

Wu pulled away from the curb and maneuvered his vehicle into a guest parking spot. He slipped from the driver's seat and sprinted after the woman and her dogs. They turned down a shaded path marked *To Pool and Clubhouse.* Wu caught up and slowed, feigning nonchalance.

"Cute pups," he remarked, trying hard not to startle the woman. The dogs recommenced their bark-and-yip routine. He bent down and wondered if they'd chomp off his fingers. "May I pet them?"

"Of course. Lots of sound and fury but they're harmless," Carrot-top said, straightening what was obviously a wig. Her wrinkled lips were slathered in chalky, hot pink lipstick.

The Yorkies' pointy teeth didn't look harmless, but Wu decided to risk a dog bite in favor of bonding with the woman. To his relief, the pups licked his hands and were pretty darn cute.

"Tinker, Dilly, and Kujo." Mavis was clearly thrilled to find an admiring eye for her babies. She made little kissing noises.

Wu stood and joined her on the walk. An aquamarine pool shimmered ahead as the sun set behind the Santa Monica Mountains. The dogs danced and squirmed in anticipation of something significant. A dip in the pool? A pee in the garden?

"You swim?" he asked the old woman.

"Oh, sweetheart, all my life. Back in the day I was part of shows in Florida—Cyprus Gardens, and then one in Vegas. Been in the movies, too." She paused to turn and take a quick study of him. "You don't live here. Are you visiting someone?"

"No, just checking out condo communities in the valley. My mom's talking about moving out of her place in Ventura. Too big, too much to take care of. Think a seventy-something retired ER nurse would like the place?"

As Wu had hoped, it was the perfect topic to get the gal talking.

Mavis waxed on about the charms of the Wisteria House Community. She was a board member, of course. After ten endless minutes and multiple flashbacks to the old Seinfeld show and Jerry's parent's tribulations at *Boca del Vista,* Wu tried to steer the conversation to Jones's aunt.

"That man you were talking to looks familiar. Is he, by any chance, a teacher at Santa Monica High School?"

"Why, yes." She looked a bit stunned at being snapped away from her Wisteria House infomercial.

The smell of pool chlorine filled the air as they shuffled further down the walk. Mavis pulled off her coral-colored sunglasses, wiped her eyes, then put the specs back on. "That was Halliburton Jones, *Doctor* Halliburton Jones, as he still has the gall to remind me. Do you know him?" she asked.

"I went to SAMOHI eight, no, jeez, more than ten years ago. I think he taught biology back then."

"He still teaches there. He and his aunt moved to Wisteria twenty years ago, the same time I did. We used to be friends. Now they're both so *busy, busy,* as Halliburton always says."

While they chatted, the pups tugged her over to a grassy area and did their business.

"His aunt is a teacher, too?" Wu asked.

Mavis rolled her eyes. "A schoolteacher, no. But drama coach—oh, yes, *dahling.*" She paused to pull a lipstick-matching doggie poop bag from the pocket of her muumuu, then continued. "Cloris-Edna always had a coterie of young actors, mostly men, hanging around, reading lines, and rehearsing. She was big in the fifties. Water shows, like me. A couple bit parts in Esther Williams films. Impressive, I guess, if you're a know-nothing schmuck from Siberia or somewhere down where the sun don't shine."

She smirked and picked up a wad of doggie doo, inspected it, then bagged it. "The coaching gig faded out a couple decades ago when the young wannabees started looking for someone with more contemporary connections. Now, she makes costumes or something like that, I really have no idea. The old bat's always been ridiculously hush-hush about what she's up to. As if it could be of interest to anyone but her."

Evidently done with their duty, the pups skittered up, begging for treats. Carrot-top doled out orange and green mini-bones. "Oh, such good sweetie pies. Good, good babies." She clucked at them like a mother hen.

Then she dug around in the big pocket of her muumuu and presented Wu with a leopard-themed business card. "Just in case your mother would like to talk about the Wisteria House Community."

"Very kind of you." He glanced at the card—*Mavis Zucker, Stylist to the Stars.*

Wu's cell buzzed and he ignored it.

She tipped up her sunglasses to study him again, more closely. "And you are . . . ?"

Her eyes reminded Wu of watery blue marbles. "Oh, I'm Charles, uh, Charles Chan." He couldn't believe he'd said that. "Thanks for your time, Ms. Zucker."

His cell phone buzzed. He pulled it from his pocket and glanced at it—Casey Abbott was on the line. More of nothing to tell her. He'd call her back later. For now, Wu stuttered out a quick promise of getting his mother in touch with Mavis regarding the condo, and headed back to his car.

With a faint spark of optimism, the detective was anxious to follow up on Jones's aunt Cloris-Edna. She worked in showbiz. So did everybody here, but the thought of the crushed gold beads and strands of golden cloth embedded in the chunk of arm they'd found niggled at him. She was a costumer and lived in Camarillo, just down the freeway from Ventura.

He texted the aunt's information to the office and crossed his fingers that they'd find something.

Back in his car, Wu rolled up the windows and turned on the air. The seats were hot as a deep fryer even though twilight cooled the landscape. Brilliant orange bougainvillea still flamed on trellises against Wisteria House's cream-colored stucco walls. His mother, had she been alive, might have actually liked it here.

He pulled out of the lot turning back toward Sherman Way.

For a nanosecond, Wu began to fantasize about what could have been if his sister had survived, but that only made him sad. He checked his cell; Casey Abbott had called several times.

The detective dreaded telling her that he still had nothing more on Isabelle's disappearance. He knew what it was like to be desperate for anything that could offer a shred of hope, however small. He hit *Call Back* and Casey immediately picked up. "Casey, I'm sorry but—"

"Listen to me," she whispered. "I'm at the Ventura Place Mall, trolling for sex traffickers, and I'm onto somebody."

Wu's blood pressure shot up about fifty points. "You're *what?*"

"Sex traffickers. I couldn't just sit around anymore waiting for something to happen. I forwarded you pictures. Got my eye on somebody. He's Hispanic, lots of tats, around twenty-five. Chatting up lost-looking kids, trying to seem really nice and familiar."

"Jee-zus-Christ, Casey. Get the hell out of there. These people are serious shitholes."

"Look at the pictures, Mac." Her words were ice. "You should have gotten them by now."

Too pissed off to speak, Wu didn't trust what he'd say if he opened his mouth. He brought up the four photos she'd texted.

His blood pressure jacked another few notches. The sound

of pumping blood hummed in his ears. "That's one of *my* people. Detective Beno Ramirez. Undercover. Dammit Casey, let us do our work. You're just making it all the more difficult."

Wu's car crawled down Topanga Canyon Boulevard toward the 101. It was nearing 7:30 in the evening but rush hour never stopped.

Casey snuffled. "You didn't tell me you had people."

Wu blew out a frustrated breath. "Yes, we have people all over this. Trust us to do our damned job."

The last of the four photos caught his attention. Someone in the background twanged a chord, felt familiar. An older dude, ballcap askew over messy metrosexual bleached-blond hair.

Wu mopped sweat from his forehead. "Casey?"

"Wha—what?" She stammered amid tears.

"Listen to me." Wu was all business now.

Her crying grew louder over the phone. "Mac, I didn't mean to—"

"Casey, *listen to me.*"

She blew her nose. "I'm listening."

"Grab a table near the exit, by the sushi place, and stay there. Talk to no one. I'm giving Beno a heads-up but don't show any interest in him. Eat, have dinner, look busy. Stay clear of the blond asshole in picture four. I'll be there in thirty."

"What's goin' on?"

He disconnected before she could say anything more. Wu called Beno and directed him to set up a tail on former Agent Sonny Bartlett.

When Wu finally hit the 101, he popped a cherry-colored bubble onto the dash and lit it up, traveling as fast as a stone moves through a sludge-clogged drain.

Forty-five minutes later, he careened into a handicap parking space at the Mall, hung a tag, then felt guilty that he'd be putting some poor guy in a wheelchair with a heart condition at risk. Wu backed out and re-parked on the edge of the nearby Macy's loading dock.

He sprinted toward the food court entrance. There, waiting for him near the sushi bar, were Casey Abbott and Bea Middleton, deep in conversation. *Huh?*

Chapter 23

Wu slid into a molded plastic chair across from the women. What was the sticky stuff that caught at his pants? He didn't want to know. Heartburn bubbled in his diaphragm. He'd been living on coffee and antacids for too many hours. He scanned the food hall. Beno was gone, and he hoped, out tailing Bartlett's ass.

He turned to Bea and struggled to level his voice. "What are you doing here?"

She folded her arms across her chest. "I knew that would be the first thing you'd say."

"You're supposed to be in Santa Monica with your kids." Why was he always pissed at her? Maybe he'd never had a partner who'd matched his tenacity—and who was, all too often, one damn step ahead.

"It so happens, detective, when Casey couldn't get you on the phone, she called me. My ex scored last minute, second-row Lakers tickets behind Beyoncé and Jay-Z, so he came by and got the boys. They took Uber. I took his Porsche. Sucker really flies when the traffic opens up."

Casey's damp eyes dripped black mascara. "Thank you both for coming. I was starting to lose it." She swiped at her cheek, revealing fingernails painted an orange even a rotting pumpkin would find cringe-worthy.

Wu scowled, focused in on Casey and gave her his complete attention. "Please, for God's sake, never do anything like this again. You may have blown an undercover we've had in place for weeks. You understand how serious this is?"

She nodded, face as bleak as a winter storm.

"This kind of Lone Ranger shit could get somebody killed."

Casey looked defeated and miserable. Her short auburn hair poked up from her skull like plastic bristles on a brush. He wanted to pull her into his arms and comfort her, but knew only too well he had little reassurance to give. Wu closed his eyes and stretched his neck, rubbed at pressure points. "Too many civilians involved in this. It's getting out of control. Bad things can happen."

He heard fear darken the pitch of his voice. Were they already too late—as it had been for his sister? Probably.

Bea let out a long sigh. "You find out anything from following Jones?"

Clearing his throat, Wu took a sip of water from a cup Casey pushed his way. Then, he filled them in on his visit to the Wisteria House condos and the information he'd learned about Jones's aunt Cloris-Edna.

A group of baristas and young customers from the nearby coffee bar howled with laughter at the antics of one of the cashiers. Spilled coffee beans bounced along the floor like spent shell casings. Wu winced.

"You have someone looking into this Cloris woman?" Bea asked, ignoring the disturbance.

He gritted his teeth "Yes, ma'am, we thought that would be a good idea."

Bea rolled her eyes.

Wu continued. "Also, got an interesting call from HQ as I was driving in. The director of a local shelter notified the station that two of her runaway girls had been hit on by a middle-aged dude driving a Range Rover. Plates were registered to, get this, Untamed Adventure Tours Ltd."

"Shit, that's got to be Bartlett again." Bea shut her eyes for a moment and pinched the bridge of her nose. "He seems to love the Range Rover. Gives the illusion that he's a rich and rugged. A decent pimpmobile, right?"

Wu could almost see Bea's synapses clicking as mental gears meshed into place. Then her face lit up.

"That cop from Palmdale? The one we think snatched up Isabelle—and was found murdered?"

"Yeah. Hobbs something, like that movie with Dwayne Johnson. What about the dude?"

"Maybe Bartlett did him, and now he's stuck having to be the pimp-meister until they can grab another creep to take over the job. His moves, like trolling the mall, letting a housemother ID his car—all seem pretty amateurish, even desperate."

"Good point." Wu choked out a begrudging acknowledgement. *Why hadn't he thought of that?*

Casey sat up straighter, clearly struggling to regain focus. "Maybe that means there's going to be a sex tour event happening soon. He needs more victims, like fast. That guy in photo number four? Bea said that's Agent Bartlett—he was chatting up a couple of pretty blonde twins. They seemed to dig him." She wrapped her arms around herself. "Oh, my God, he's trying to abduct them." Casey began to hyperventilate and her lips took on a blue tinge.

Bea dug into her purse and retrieved a plastic prescription bottle. She opened it and dumped a tiny white pill into her palm. "Take this." She handed it to Casey, who was now panting and shivering.

Casey recoiled as if Bea were offering her a fistful of spiders. "I don't take pills."

"I don't do chemicals either, but girl, you are having a panic attack. I have a friend who gets them all the time. This little med will help so you don't have a meltdown. We need you to be present and lucid. Dr. Bea say take the damn pill."

Casey gulped hard, wrinkled her nose, and swallowed. She perched rigidly on the edge of her chair, eyes jittery like a junkie waiting to see if the stuff was good or was going to kill her.

Wu gaped at Bea as if she was the one flipping out. "Am I witnessing a goddamn Ventura Mall drug deal perpetrated by my supposed partner?"

She scowled and pursed her lips. "Gimme a break, choirboy. Gotta use anything in the arsenal in times like these. I've given a bigger dose to my cat."

He tried not to smirk and checked his cell phone. "Come on, Beno let me know what's happening." Nothing.

Bea plowed onward. "So, let's get back to business. It's my turn to report."

Wu glanced toward the nearby tables—all empty. "Your kids find something?" He checked his watch again. "Mall closes in ten." *Why hadn't Beno called in yet?*

"Okay then, hush-up and let me talk." Bea made a zip-your-mouth sign. "Looks like the high school copy room is the SAMOHI version of the office water cooler. Hayes heard Jones whining to Dean Pritkow that he'd have to quit his job if they didn't find an immediate replacement for Isabelle. He didn't have time to keep teaching her class. Had another big project he's developing. Something to launch him onto a 'different professional level.'"

"Shark genetics?" Casey pressed her hand against her forehead, perhaps in anticipation of a drug-induced aneurism that would blow her brains out.

"Makes sense, right?" Bea continued. "That's what Dexter and Hayes were massaging him about on the way to the faculty parking lot, schmoozing about how they wished they could have an opportunity to be interns on important research. Such weasels."

Wu felt vice-like pressure begin to close tight on the back of his skull. "Oh, God. More civilians involved, and underage, too."

"I grounded the dastardly duo for a week, starting tomorrow, for interfering when I told them to back off."

"Glad to know they'll be safely off the grid." *If only.* "Now let's get out of here." Wu stood as a mall security guard headed their way pushing a broom. Multitasking. Wu'd be pushing a broom soon, too, the way this case was going.

Chapter 24

After Bea took off for Santa Monica, Wu and Casey stood on the sidewalk outside the mall entrance. A security car the size of a shoebox cruised slowly to a stop in front of them. When Wu flashed his creds, the mall cop nodded and continued on his route through the sparsely populated parking lot.

"Would you mind, uh, following me home?" Casey asked Wu. Her eyes were watery and pleading. "I'm so freaked out right now." She swiped at a tear and the drippy black mascara streaked further down her face.

He wanted to wipe it away but resisted. He was a sucker for a damsel in distress, especially one whose situation pulled deeply at his heartstrings. "Of course. Let me walk you to your car, then I'll follow you and make sure you get into your house safe and sound."

"Thank you, Mac. Sorry about the undercover thing. Isabelle's usually the impulsive one, not me. Tonight, I just went for it, and it was a disaster. I was never much of an actress."

He smiled and shrugged. "Well, it definitely wasn't a good

choice, but you were pretty convincing. Even Beno didn't pick up on you at first, and he's good."

"I know desperation isn't a place to make smart decisions from."

"I hear ya. Been there a time or two. Don't beat yourself up over it. Feeling like you're doing nothing while a loved one is in danger is a totally fucked-up situation."

They walked along an empty parking row toward Casey's Camry. She slipped her arm through his. He looked down at her and wanted to kiss her ridiculously smudged face.

When they reached the car, she pulled out the fob and pressed unlock. Wu opened the driver's side door and helped her in. "My ride's over there." He pointed a couple rows south to a generic silver sedan. "Swing by and I'll tail you."

"Thanks again, Mac."

Even with runny makeup, hair like a squirrel's nest, and orange nail polish the color of bacteria, Casey Abbott was hard to resist. Letting a personal attraction cloud his focus right now was nuts. Not to mention unprofessional. For the sake of Casey and her sister, he'd walk her to the door, make sure the house was secure, then say goodnight. It was a welfare check. All by the book.

He slid into his vehicle and started the engine. Moments later Casey drove by and gave him a wave. He pulled out after her. The streets weren't busy this late on a weeknight and it took them less than fifteen minutes to get to her place.

Casey pulled into the carport next to her small stucco cottage. Wu parked in front on the street and walked up the sidewalk, meeting her at the tiny porch lined with terra cotta pots overflowing with blooming succulents.

"Cute *casa*," he said.

"Thanks. Bought it with what my mom left me plus all the hard-earned savings I'd stashed over the years. Come on in, I'll give you the tour."

"I'll do a quick check and make sure all's secure."

"That would be amazing." She inserted the key in the lock and pushed the door open.

The cat yowled and rushed up as Casey flipped the light switch.

"I'm sorry to be so late, mister Sebastian. Let me get your goodies." Black as licorice, the feline had two headlight-sized yellow eyes.

Casey stepped into a pale blue kitchen, the tint of a misty morning off the coast. The countertops resembled cast sand interspersed with beach glass. All very artistic and modern-looking without feeling cold. Sebastian meowed, then opened a cabinet next to the sink with a paw and sat there until Casey reached for the kibble container. She dumped morsels into his bowl. He smacked his kitty lips and dug in.

She turned to Wu. "I'm going to wash my face before you check out the rest of the place. My skin feels like it's coated with dried Elmer's glue. Care for a beer in the meantime? I've got a Bud Light and a couple Dos Equis."

Don't do it. Be professional.

"Sure, why not. Dos Equis sounds good."

Casey went to the fridge and retrieved a bottle, handed it to Wu then disappeared down a back hall. Running water sounded in a bathroom.

He twisted off the cap then took a long, cold swig. Tasted like heaven. But he was here to do a welfare and safety check for a local citizen. He wandered through the small, tasteful living and dining room, examined the windows which appeared to have been recently replaced with locks in good shape. Pride of ownership was evident.

He sat down at the dining room table and finished his brew. Studied an assortment of Abbott family pictures from happier times on the wall across from him. Sebastian jumped onto his lap and curled up, all the world was his rightful throne. Wu scratched him behind the ears. The cat commenced purring like an idling leaf blower.

Casey joined them with a beer in hand, an extra for Wu, and a bowl of tortilla chips with guac dip on the side. Dressed in a fresh white T-shirt and running shorts, her legs were fantastic. Her face shown soft and clean without the grungy makeup. He hadn't let himself fully see this, see her, before. Probably for self-preservation's sake, but the woman was amazing—beautiful, smart, nice. *Shit.*

"So, how does everything look here in the front rooms? Any security issues I should take care of?"

Oh, yeah, welfare check. "All is cool. I see you replaced the windows. The locks are solid. Good job."

"Was quite a hit to the budget but there were these rusty, metal-rimmed relics from the forties that rattled even when a truck drove by. I was afraid that one day they'd just fall out and shatter."

Wu nodded. Drained the last drops in bottle one and reached for number two. Maybe they could keep talking a few more minutes about home improvement like on HGTV, then say *adiós.*

Casey took his hand and led him over to the couch. Dumped from his cozy spot on Wu's lap, Sebastian whined in protest. He strutted into the kitchen where he leaped onto the counter and then atop the refrigerator where he settled into a round kitty bed.

"For some reason he insists on sacking out up there," Casey said. "King of the castle from the high tower."

She and Wu sat side by side. She picked a chip from the bowl and popped it into her lovely mouth. *Crunch.* "Do you think she's still alive?"

So much for home improvement topics. *Your sister's probably dead,* was not something he could say. Wu put down his drink, sighed and chose his words carefully. "As you describe Isabelle, she's resourceful, and determined. I'm going forward with this investigation believing she's alive and ready to use her smarts to help us find her."

Casey leaned against his shoulder. He put his arm around her. She smelled of lavender soap.

"You never talk about what happened to *your* sister," she said.

He tensed and was quiet for what felt like a long time. The question was inevitable.

"I'm sorry," Casey pulled away. "I didn't mean to make you uncomfortable. We'll talk about something else besides our kidnapped siblings. Like, uh, what do you think about the Charger's chances this year?"

Wu smiled and rubbed his forehead. "You're probably one of the few people in the world I should be able to talk to about this, but I've been heavily into avoidance. Probably not good."

"Whatever works for you." Casey began picking out peanuts from a small bag of trail mix.

"When my sister, Brianne, disappeared, she was eleven— walking home from her dance studio about eight blocks from our house." Wu took a long swig of beer. "Was a safe neighborhood. I was fifteen and was supposed to meet her but my soccer practice ran late. She didn't wait for me. Resented that my mom insisted on having her big brother around 'interfering with my life,' as she felt it. I never saw her again after bickering at the breakfast table that morning."

Casey took his hand and held it. Said nothing; which said all that was needed.

He continued, comforted. He let out a long, sad breath. "I wish to God I knew what happened to her. Probably never will though."

"Oh my God, that's horrible. I'm so sorry, Mac. Not knowing must be the worst."

Casey's gaze drifted out the living room window into the darkness beyond.

"But let's concentrate on positive thoughts," he said. They sat quietly. Then, Wu held up her hand and examined the nail polish, rolled his eyes, and shook his head. "Worst color ever."

"Oh, come on—Cardi B wore it at the Grammys."

"Like I said, worst color ever."

Casey laughed. Wu realized he'd never seen her actually smile. It was a sight he wanted to see again.

She turned to him. "I'm going to be uncharacteristically impulsive again even though it got me into big trouble earlier at the mall." Casey's voice was low. "Any chance you'd be willing to spend the night with me?"

He felt his heartrate speed up. *Talk about big trouble.* "I think you'll be fine, Casey. You've done a good job here with security."

"No, Mac, I'm not asking for protection from my local cop. You're a special man. I like you. A lot."

She was dizzyingly close. His lips brushed hers. Electricity arced between them.

Wu's breath caught in his throat and he pulled her body to his. "Once in a while, impulsiveness suits you, Ms. Abbott."

The next kisses were deep, endless, wild.

He spent the night.

Chapter 25

Isabelle Abbott woke gasping for breath. Racked with terror, she tried to scream but couldn't fill her lungs with air. The sound she made was a weak wheeze. Desperately, she prayed to regain a sense of calm and forced herself to take slow, shallow breaths. Confined in a dank, dim room and wrapped in the hideous straight-jacket, Izzy knew she wasn't going to last long before disintegrating into a drooling zombie.

Only a few days ago, she'd encountered the high schooler, Celeste, in the same horrific restraint. Izzy'd sworn she'd never let that happen. She was tough, assertive, a budding oceanographer studying at one of the finest schools in her discipline. But then, events took a deep dive into where there was no light or air.

The near-death experiences in the aquarium had gnawed indelible wounds into her psyche. She began to shiver uncontrollably and focused on calming dense waves of panic.

Izzy now knew that being uncooperative would get her killed. If she were to save herself, she'd have to play the role of perfect supplicant until the time was right. Then, she'd strike with everything she had. Could she take Cloris-Edna out with a sewing needle? Strangle Oscar with a shred of plastic kelp?

And what in the world was Halliburton Jones doing here? Tears of frustration oozed from her eyes. *Be strong.* She had to control what little she could. Her survival depended upon it.

The sound of a scuffle arose from outside her room. Girls shrieked, Oscar cursed, then his taser powered up. Izzy could barely draw in enough oxygen to gasp in repulsion. She bit down on the inside of her mouth and tasted blood. Oscar's evil routine had begun. First came a buzzing sound, like when a moth hit a bug zapper. *Bzzzzt.* Then, the body of an electrocuted human being hit the floor. Confusion erupted, garbled words echoed high and fearful, then a door slammed down the hall.

All was quiet. *Hello new mermaids! The next victims had arrived.*

A short time later, someone tapped on her door. Izzy shuddered. Nobody tapped, they barged right in, weapons of abuse blazing. It opened a crack. A shadowy figure blew his nose.

"Miss Abbott? Isabelle? Are you awake? We need to talk."

It was Halliburton Jones—she'd recognize that faux choirboy voice anywhere. Sweat rose cold on her already icy skin. *What was the treacherous asshole up to?* She'd crawled to him, begging, and he'd turned away. But here he was.

The man stepped into the room, eyes open wide, adjusting to the gloom.

Would her former colleague show some mercy after all? As a glint of hope rose in her chest, the bindings immobilizing Izzy's body seemed to contract, as if she was being crushed by a boa constrictor. Her heart hammered and she struggled to speak. "Please, get me out of this straight-jacket." She *had* to convince him to help her. He was her only chance.

His eyes blinked as fast as wasp wings. "Oh dear, I had no idea. But yes, yes, let me untie you."

He stepped over to her cot, fumbled with the hooks and

Velcro, then peeled her out of the abomination. It fell to the floor.

She sucked in air and panted. "Thank you. Oh God, thank you." Izzy's body, particularly her arms, were numb and non-functional. She rubbed them best she could before they turned necrotic and dropped off.

"You need backup, Doc?" Oscar inquired from outside the door. Blue light from the aquarium window made his bald head shine like planet Earth from space.

"I don't think so, Oscar. Miss Abbott and I are old friends. We'll be discussing research, scientific inquiry. She's quite accomplished. I'm trying to talk dear auntie out of sacrificing her this week."

Oscar sneered and skulked off down the hallway.

"You're part of this, Halliburton? What is a respected scientist doing in this hellhole?"

Respected, my ass. She wanted to drop him to the floor and pound his brains out on the wet cement but knew that kind of tactic would be futile. She'd be caught, and was sure she could not survive anymore sadistic punishment. Manipulation and flattery had to be her new best friends.

The professor grudgingly settled on the cot across from Izzy. His back was ramrod straight, and after adjusting his glasses, he clutched his hands together in his lap. "The funding I have been able to get from this, uh, enterprise is allowing me to pursue truly groundbreaking research."

As if in a confessional, his words rang overly somber. *That's where the hell he should be, on his knees pleading forgiveness for this obscenity of a place.* Izzy was rocked with a strong pang of nausea. She gagged out the words, "You know how much I've always admired your work, but this sounds extraordinary."

His nostrils flared with excitement, his hands unclenched and he said, "Few so-called prestigious organizations have the vision to explore truly ground-breaking ideas."

"'*Many great truths begin as blasphemies.*' George Bernard

Shaw, I think." Izzy prayed he'd begin to see her as an ally.

"Yes, yes, perhaps you understand." His eyes sparkled behind the lenses of his glasses. "That's why I'm always turned down for significant support. I've had to make compromises, but the results of my intelligence studies will impact humanity. His eyes glittered. "Logic dictates that sometimes, the few must sacrifice for the many. Yes, indeedy, sad but true." He turned his head toward the window into the aquarium tank. The freaky, bioluminescent great white glided by, then disappeared.

Adoration for the specimen shone on the professor's face.

Izzy gulped. *I'm dealing with an insane narcissist who thinks he's saving the universe.* "Shark DNA, correct? You know I'm quite familiar with it. Perhaps I would be able to contribute."

Izzy had to make a connection. Now. Jones was one of those people always desperate for praise. That was her weapon.

His face shrouded in shadows, the professor's nasally voice dropped to a whisper. "I must obtain a laboratory assistant, and I thought I could talk the powers-that-be into letting me use you."

Adrenalin pumped through Izzy's veins. Yes, she had to get the lab job. *Use me, you sonofabitch!* Grasping at the tenuous opportunity, it was a functional air hose when she was drowning.

"Science is my life, Halliburton. We share that." She paused for impact. "Let me help you in this important research." She smiled at him "I'm so much better at science than water ballet."

No response. She kept talking. "I was just awarded a National Science Foundation fellowship, but I hadn't told you yet." It was mostly true—she was a finalist but they hadn't yet announced the winners. Maybe she'd already won and would never know. She swallowed tears and pushed on. "Maybe, working together, we could bring your research the legitimacy and recognition you deserve."

Izzy could see that the NSF comment sparked his interest. He turned toward her. Was the scale tipping in her direction? How else could she add weight?

"Halliburton, you know I'm smart and capable, a whiz at technology. You need me, and I need you. I'd be the perfect assistant as you secure your, your legacy."

He rose from the cot. Hand on the door latch, he turned to her, arrogance in his ball-bearing eyes and a condescending smile on his lips. "I'll talk to Auntie."

Then he left.

The old bat was his aunt? Would Jones return with her consent to let Izzy be his lab assistant? Or would Oscar show up with her mermaid costume?

Chapter 26

It was 11:30 p.m. when Bea finally arrived back at her Santa Monica bungalow. The lights were blazing and she found Dexter asleep on the couch next to a pile of textbooks and an open laptop. So much for the energy conservation he was always talking about.

At least the dinner debris had been appropriately stashed. An old episode of SNL streamed on TV. She shut it off, shuffled the books onto the coffee table, and placed a plaid afghan over her son's long, unconscious body. One of his beady eyes squinted open, then rolled back into his head. Bea smiled and bent to kiss his cheek. God, she was going to miss those big ugly feet hanging over the end of the couch when he took off for college.

Bea climbed the stairs to her bedroom with a plate of leftovers and closed the door behind her. She didn't want to let Dexter see her get all weepy and maudlin about her child leaving. She wiped her eyes on her sleeve.

As she headed for a cushy chair, a call came in from Wu. Had his undercover guy nailed Bartlett? "Mac, what's up?"

"We lost Bartlett in the hills above Camarillo. He had two girls with him. He took the Land Rover off-road and left our Chevy in a ditch with a broken axle. My Cap is gonna love the repair bill. If he doesn't fire my ass first, I'm gonna see if I can get a department drone authorized to fly over the area."

Bea growled in frustration and sat down on her bed. Bartlett had dodged the bullet again, and the clock was ticking.

Wu continued. "Given the direction he was going, I think our target area might be somewhere around Point Hueneme, part of Naval Base Ventura County. Used to be where the Construction Battalion, the SeaBees set up shop."

"I'm well acquainted with it." Bea remembered when that area was home to farm fields, produce stands, and citrus groves, all with spectacular views of the Channel Islands. It used to smell of orange blossoms and onion fields. Now part of the LA sprawl, the wonderful scents were history.

"Where could a big aquarium be hidden over there? Has to be a tie-in to the former Navy construction group." Wearily, Bea unwrapped the plate of cold sweet potato fries and a quarter of an uneaten barbeque sandwich. The sauce still smelled enticing. "Corcoran talked about Jones's father doing secret research on dolphins. Maybe sharks figured in, too. How 'bout I ask Bijan to dig around online and see what he can find?"

"Yeah, good idea," Wu said. "In the meantime, Pete's working with LAPD to get us a search warrant for Jones's condo. Should be ready by morning."

Said detective swaggered into Bea's bedroom from the en suite bathroom practically naked, except for a low-riding pair of basketball shorts and a Saint Christopher medal on a gold chain around his neck. "Surprise, beautiful."

Bea suppressed a startled gasp. He slid onto the arm of the chair next to her, nuzzled his face into her neck, and wrapped his arms around her shoulders. She smiled and moved her dinner from her lap onto a side table.

She struggled kept her voice even. "I'll be in contact with

him first thing tomorrow and make sure he's got everything we need." Bea pressed into Pete's warm body, and he pulled her closer.

"I guarantee I got everything you need, sweet mama," he whispered *sotto voce*.

She elbowed Pete in the ribs.

"Okay, later, Bea. We'll get this asshole," Wu promised. "We're breathing down his neck."

"I hope you're right. Night, Mac." Bea clicked off the call then turned to her lover. "My, oh, my. What are you doing here, officer?"

"Just stopping by to discuss the warrant, and thought I'd hang around and do a body search." Pete smirked and began his exploration.

A smile flickered on Bea's lips. Despite being exhausted, crawling into bed with Pete Anthony was feeling like just what the doctor ordered. But business first. Saving Isabelle and the others was everything. "What's the skinny on serving the search warrant for Jones's condo?

"I got it." He pulled her over to the bed and snuggled deep into the pile of pillows. "We'll hit his place at 7:00 a.m., right after he leaves for work. Dexter says he's been absent from class the last couple days, so he might be home with a nasty cold rather than off to Santa Monica. If he's home, there's nothing like a police raid to clear the sinuses."

Bea laughed and nodded. Her son's high school department chair was up to his droopy ear lobes in this sick mess. "I'll text Wu and tell him to meet us there." She pulled out her phone and tapped in the message. Got a thumbs-up icon in reply.

She heard Dexter tromp up the stairs and turn toward his room.

Pete licked his lips. "Now come my Nubian princess, the Roman warrior king awaits, sword drawn and ready for battle."

"Just can't get enough hand-to-hand, gotta go for the steel?"

A sleepy voice sounded from the end of the hall. "Oh, my

God. You two're ovah the top—so *dis-gust-ing.*"

Bea cringed, always horrified that her baby boy knew about his mother's occasional less-than-platonic relationships. She grimaced, got up and tiptoed toward the shower.

Pete snickered at her heels.

—

The morning dawned damp and cloudy. Bea, swilling caffeine to keep her eyes open, pulled onto the ramp and followed Pete's car up the Ventura Freeway toward Topanga Canyon Boulevard in Woodland Hills. For once, the worst traffic was moving in the opposite direction.

When they turned into guest parking at the Wisteria House Condominium Community, Wu had already arrived. He stood inside the security gate, chatting with a female octogenarian whose hair was wrapped in a glittery blue turban. She wrangled a gaggle of small dogs on equally sparkly leashes. When Bea and Pete approached, he pulled away from the woman. She followed, but Wu warned her off. Begrudgingly, the oldster shuffled down the sidewalk, pausing to glance over her shoulder toward Jones's condo and the potential action.

An LAPD deputy, thick-bodied, Hispanic, and in his mid-thirties, waited for them near Jones's front door. He was introduced as Officer Kevin Aguilera. Next to the officer slouched Walt Eisenstein, slim with a bushy white beard—the property manager. A jumble of keys, key cards, and tools hung from a belt around his bony hips.

Bea was introduced by Pete as a police consultant helping to identify evidence.

Wu noted that Jones's car was not in its space. "The old lady says he's been gone for more than twenty-four hours. Left with a swarthy-looking bald dude who drove a big-ass van."

"Doesn't sound like Bartlett," Wu said.

Pete nodded, then motioned for Aguilera to start the process. The deputy pounded on the door. Then he shouted, "Police.

Open up."

Aguilera performed the knock-and-announce routine a few more times, then directed Eisenstein to open the door. After a lengthy struggle to find the right key, the property manager was able to let them in. Aguilera called out once more, then entered first, gun drawn, followed by Pete and Wu.

Bea fidgeted outside on the steps chewing a fingernail and hoping no resistance surfaced while law enforcement cleared the premises. The sparkle-turbaned dog-lady watched from behind a spindly hibiscus. Bea scowled her disapproval. The old woman sniffed and adjusted her sunglasses for a better view.

Finally, Pete yelled, "We're clear, Beebs, come on in."

Bea entered and shut the door behind her. She mounted five steps up to the main floor of a sunny, open-design townhouse. Blonde oak flooring spanned a thousand square feet of living room, dining area, and an updated kitchen with stainless steel countertops fit for a science lab. A dozen six-foot folding tables lined the perimeter of the great room, all dusty with open spots where equipment must have been placed until very recently. Three mismatched desk chairs had been pushed into a corner. Light-blocking window curtains had been pulled back.

The cops reholstered their firearms and Aguilera finished up a radio transmittal. Pete, the senior officer on the scene, issued assignments. "Wu, take the upstairs, Aguilera, the basement. Bea and I'll start processing the main floor. Treat it like a crime scene, no smash and toss. Booties and gloves at all times."

While Pete rummaged through drawers, cupboards, and the fridge, Bea went straight to the kitchen garbage can, which brimmed with discarded file folders. "Remember, people," she said in a loud voice, "we're looking for anything that ties Jones to DNA research, the military, weapons, sex crimes, mermaids, receipts for purchase of scientific equipment, accounting docs. That's the laundry list."

Wu hollered from the second floor. "Shit, I've already found a weird collection of mermaid stuff, lots of Ariel action figures in his bathroom."

Bea cringed and said to Pete, "I remember that Casey Abbott saw a Little Mermaid statuette in the window of that Ventura koi shop—the place that was actually just an empty storefront. Wu and I also saw an Ariel in Jones's office at SAMOHI."

Pete paused and chewed his lip. "This Jones dude some kind of mermaid freak? Acting out fucked-up snuff fantasies with live women?"

Bea shuddered. "The little weasel almost seems too bookish and bloodless to be deeply sexually motivated. Feels like he'd be more into raising money to buy research stuff. But who can tell what insanity is going down?"

"*Who knows what evil lurks in the hearts of men?*" Pete recited.

"*The Shadow knows.*" She smiled and recalled the 1930s pulp novels. "Wish I could be *The Shadow* and skitter into this man's sick brain."

"You can, my dear, by using your own considerable devices." He pulled several crumpled receipts from inside an empty Cheerios box and handed them to Bea.

She flattened the crumpled papers and studied them carefully. "Gas and snacks from the Shell station over near the Cal State Channel Islands campus. Just a few miles from Port Hueneme. Are we tightening the noose?"

"Dunno. Think there might be some kind of old aquarium over at the college? It used to be a mental institution. Maybe they had a swimming pool or something." Pete continued digging in the array of trash he'd spread across the floor.

Bea rubbed her neck. "I don't want to think about the 'or something.' God only knows what water tortures were perpetrated in asylums back in the day. I'll drop by there as soon as we're done."

Pete nodded agreement.

After an hour it was apparent that Jones had cleared almost all potentially incriminating contents from his house. Wu bagged the Little Mermaids. Pete would have County PD scan for trace and run any fingerprints though AFIS.

After finishing up and sending Aguilera on his way, Bea, Wu, and Pete congregated in the parking lot.

Wu looked grim. "Maybe we can snag some ID from the van driver that Mavis Zucker spotted leaving with the doc yesterday. Got some video footage from the manager, Eisenstein. Old bird doesn't think it quite covers everything we're looking for, but we'll see what we have. I'm taking it over to HQ now."

"I need to get back to the office." Pete glanced at his watch. "Got a warrant to serve in Monterrey Park before noon."

Bea looked up from her phone. "I'm heading over to the Channel Islands campus and see if I can talk to the science department chair. Just Googled her—she should know about the area resources related to ocean studies. Will be in touch soon, gentlemen. *Tick-tock.*"

Chapter 27

In the shady courtyard outside the Student Union, Bea sipped iced tea at a patio table beneath a bright red umbrella. Birds chirped, students chattered, and sun dappled the gardens of bougainvillea and flowering succulents. The beautiful Mission-style, palm-tree-lined, Cal State Channel Islands campus, built largely in the 1930s, looked like a picture postcard. Visitors would never guess that at one time it was a mental hospital serving the largest patient population west of the Mississippi.

When the Cal State system bought the place in 1998, Bea hoped the ghosts of the tortured souls once housed here would be exorcized by enthusiastic students studying toward healthy futures.

Her phone vibrated, and she checked the message. The department chair was waiting for her at Sierra Hall. She grabbed her belongings and headed across the quad. The new, three-story science building embraced the campus's Mission-style architectural roots. Airy and whitewashed with a central concourse open to high wood-beamed ceilings, Dr. Sharyn

Fawcett's office was on the top floor. It had a breathtaking view across the Oxnard Plain to the mountain foothills and Anacapa Island, twelve miles off the coast.

"Looks like you could practically swim over there," Bea said while shaking hands with an athletic-looking brunette in her early forties. She smelled vaguely of saltwater.

"I have, several times." Dr. Fawcett smiled. "Please, have a seat." She motioned toward a wingback chair upholstered in a Native American rug motif. Beautiful Chumash baskets sat on shelves amid ocean-born objects and academic journals.

"Thanks so much for making time to see me. I know you're very busy." Bea noted stacks of test papers and reports covering the professor's wide desk. Thankfully, she didn't see any Little Mermaid figures.

"Happy to help, Ms. Middleton. I know you can't share a lot, but I take it police are involved and that time is of the essence."

Bea nodded. "I mentioned that I'm a journalist consulting with Ventura Metro and LAPD on this case. Anything we might discuss is off the record. Just so you know."

Fawcett nodded and leaned back in her seat, fiddled with a conch shell containing paperclips. "You asked if I knew Dr. Halliburton Jones. I actually met him at a Santa Monica High School college night a few months ago. Seemed very enthusiastic about his students. He didn't mention anything about a new research project, but we scientists can get all hush-hush when we're competing for grants and awards."

Bea smiled. "Understood. My business is pretty damn competitive, too. Doesn't always bode well for cooperation, sadly."

Fawcett put down the shell and leaned toward Bea. "So, you said you're looking for a private aquarium or something along those lines?"

Bea nodded. "A tank that could hold a large shark, like a great white. Any leads on something like that?"

Fawcett's eyebrows raised. As she pondered Bea's question,

her gaze drifted out to sea. Strains of the band America's old hit, "Ventura Highway," played from a radio on the windowsill. She steepled her fingers. "Would have to be a substantial place to keep such a large species healthy. You're looking for the big kids—like 50,000 gallons on up. There's Cabrillo and Aquarium of the Pacific, but they're in San Pedro and Long Beach, and open to the public."

"Yeah. Would be hard to be cooking up any secret research sauce with thousands of tourists trooping through every day."

The professor was quiet again. Her phone rang but she ignored it, continuing to think. "I read somewhere there used to be an ocean research institute that was once part of the naval base."

Bea's chest tightened with anticipation. *Was this the break they needed?*

Fawcett continued. "Supposedly, it's long gone. The tanks were filled in decades ago. Was built for a top-secret project that cost tons and never provided anything useful. Turned into a big old embarrassing boondoggle, but what else is new with government contracts? The military walked away from it and pretended the whole mess never existed."

"Who told you about this?" Bea tapped notes into her cell.

"My brother. He was stationed at Hueneme for three years. Loved the ocean almost more than I do, if that's possible."

She laughed and cut a quick look at a photo on the wall. A handsome young man and Dr. Fawcett, both in wetsuits, posed with giant tortoises at what appeared to be the Galapagos Islands.

"Your brother?"

She nodded. "K.J. was killed in Yemen."

The news hit Bea like a blow. She flashed to Dexter peacefully sleeping on the couch—life was a damn fragile thread. "I'm so, so sorry."

"Happened a long time ago, but I still think of him every day. Anyhow, I've told you what I know about the supposed ocean facility. Not much, sorry." She paused and tapped her pen on the desktop. "There's a guy at the base named Mike Perry, Naval Sea Systems Commander. He was my brother's mentor. Been there for years. Gotta be very near retirement. Maybe he can tell you more."

Fawcett accessed the contact list on her terminal and texted Bea the link. "I'll shoot him a message right now saying to expect your call. And good luck with this. I know you can't fill me in, but I feel your urgency."

Bea thanked the professor and hurried out toward the elevator, dialing Perry as she went.

—

Izzy carefully cleaned the test tubes and loaded them into a drying rack. In the few hours she'd been at work, her brain was already less jammed up with the sludge of adrenaline and terror brought on by the sick, torturous swim practice. Lab work was familiar stuff that offered her a semblance of control over her environment. The comfy scrubs she and Jones now wore also helped settle her down—she'd never recover from being bound in that straight-jacket. Despite a deep, soul-wrenching shudder, Izzy was beginning to think more clearly, not like a mermaid victim, but like the scientist she was.

The light in the lab was dim thanks to the gooseneck desk lamps over each piece of machinery. Jones flipped the switch on a centrifuge which emitted a low whirr, then turned to his new assistant. "First, we'll extract the DNA gathered from our specimen using phenol chloroform and my state-of-the-art robotic system, the MaxEPC-16." His eyes lit up like a kid with a free pass to Toyland. "The process takes barely two hours."

"I'm very familiar with the extraction process but I've only done it manually. Took three or four hours, at best. Your Max sounds like a real time-saver." She would act like the lowly acolyte until she could find a way to escape and bring this house down.

"Indeed, it is. Oh, yes, with these new pieces of equipment the quantitation, amplification, and electrophoresis—all together should take no more than a half day." He clapped his hands together.

"Fantastic!" She actually was impressed. "I had no idea you were so forward thinking."

"Oh, yes, yes indeedy." Jones's skinny chest puffed up and he preened at the praise. He ran his hand up and down the side of a shiny new genetic analyzer as if caressing a lover. "My research on DNA, cross-species intelligence, and stem cells will be revolutionary." He picked up a sharp, shiny surgical tool from the countertop and dropped it into a beaker of sewer-yellow disinfecting solution.

Izzy fought a disgusted flinch. Feigned a shoulder scratch instead. She would love to grab that instrument and slit his throat but the time wasn't right. Yet.

The pulsing of electronic music bled though the wall of the lab, just off the mermaid practice tank where she'd almost drowned a few days earlier.

Jones grimaced and pressed his forehead. "The party has begun. You should be grateful I've chosen you to assist me."

"I'm *profoundly* grateful." Her heart hammered. How long could she keep this assistantship deal going? "Thank you *so* sincerely. Like I told you earlier, science is my life and I'm grateful to be mentored by a true pioneer."

Slather on the bullcrap.

The professor smiled, and Izzy sensed he'd begun to loosen up after wondering whether he'd made the right choice to take her on. She wanted to ask about "the party," but was afraid her curiosity would stoke his doubt again—*Abbott's too nosey to be a safe choice.*

But then he spontaneously offered up the information.

"If you're going to remain working with me, you might as well see what's going on. It's really quite remarkable, even more amazing than that Canadian circus everybody raves about.

Oh, yes, indeed, Cloris-Edna is quite the theatrical savant. No elephants and dancing dogs, but we have some very special fish and thrilling, cutting-edge effects."

Effects like blatant sexual assault and murder? Izzy's skin tingled with dread. She glanced toward a dark corner of the lab to hide the revulsion on her face. The stainless-steel countertops and the necropsy slab in the middle of the room reflected tarnished silver in the shadows.

She followed Jones to a door that opened onto a high crossover surrounding four aquarium tanks. Each giant vat stood three stories high. They'd been arranged in a circular layout around a central atrium viewing area on the ground floor below.

Jones closed the door quietly behind them. They tiptoed around the platform in almost total darkness.

Thwarted fight or flight instincts squeezed Izzy's esophagus. She peered down into the theater where the audience of five men with dark beards and white pajamas reclined in sumptuous lounge chairs, each in its own little compartment, like pictures she'd seen depicting luxury sections on international flights. Several figures in dark robes circulated among "the guests," as Jones referred to them, bringing various forms of food, libation, drugs of choice, and what looked like sex toys. The terrifying quasi-film director that Cloris-Edna had called Standish, was among the servants.

The music swelled, spotlights intensified, turning the color of fresh blood and strobing with fierce pulsations. Then, the entire theater went black. The music changed to sultry, moaning, minor chords. Images began to flicker in the air, then fully materialized. What was she seeing? A new technology?

"Are those holograms?" Izzy whispered.

Jones shook his head. "Cutting-edge augmented reality, AR. Not holograms. This isn't Disney World."

Izzy's mouth went dry. Completely real-looking naked mermaids and small teasing sea nymphs with pointed teeth began an obscene dance of flirtatious sexuality, which soon changed to something much darker and brutal. Big screens came alive with high-def videos of women in stunning mermaid costumes being violently raped. She looked away, but not before catching a fleeting glimpse of the woman, Black Pearl, who'd been in her rehearsal group.

No! Izzy stifled a scream and stumbled away from the railing over the tanks and theater. Had a young woman been murdered before her eyes? She clutched her stomach. *That could have been me. Still could be.* She tried not to hyperventilate and sink into full panic-attack mode. *Stay in control of yourself.*

Oblivious to her reaction, Jones described the upcoming highlights of the performance as if he were giving a lecture to a classroom of bored high school students. "Soon the center rotunda will fill with warm water, up to the very edge of the chaises—five feet, three inches above the floor. I'm in charge of all waterworks including maintenance of the aquaria. No small job, mind you," he snorted. "Mermaids, professionals to whom we pay a great deal of money, swim through and cavort in every which way with the guests."

"These women haven't been kidnapped?"

"Oh, no. The involuntary group, of which you are still a tentative member, perform later."

Involuntary—no shit. Izzy shuddered. The murder of young women by voracious predators must be the highlight of the men's trip.

Jones followed her gaze down into the atrium but continued, non-plussed. "Tomorrow morning the men go deep-sea fishing out of Ventura Harbor, then back here for the climax of their entertainment experience before they head off to Indonesia."

The professor's voice dropped to a whisper, as if muttering to himself. "After it's all over I clean up the mess. Auntie still thinks I'm some kind of hired help, but that will soon change, oh, yes."

Izzy willed herself away from a vision of what he meant by

"*the mess.*" Instead, she focused on technology. "Where are the light boards and all the techie stuff for these effects? Must be a very sophisticated rig."

"Oh, yes—state-of-the-art. Looks like the control deck of a spaceship. Would make NASA jealous." He smiled and gestured toward a thin slash of light where a gray metal door hung slightly ajar at the far end of the room. "Through there."

"I'd love to take a peek!"

"Well, I don't think—"

"Sounds *so* fascinating." She clasped her hands in appeal.

Jones scratched his head. "Well, okay. I guess if we do it quickly. The magician in there, Ozzie, is a lead animator for a major studio. The man has what some might call, profane proclivities. But he also has a brilliantly creative mind. Quite an *artiste*. We're lucky to have him."

"I'll bet." *So damn lucky to have a psychopathic 'Oz the Great and Terrible' spinning fucked-up illusions behind your curtain.*

Izzy and Jones tiptoed quietly the length of the industrial-style metal catwalk. He knocked softly on the door, then pushed it open.

The entire production booth smelled of weed and saltwater. White powder dusted the control unit. Izzy figured it was cocaine.

Probably mid-thirties, the tech wizard had the dried-apple appearance of someone who'd lost a lot of weight and then had too much extra skin hanging from his frame. He wore a sleeveless T-shirt with a Little Mermaid cartoon on the front. Raised his long-nailed, coke-spoon pinkie finger in greeting. "Hey, Doc." A waxy Salvador Dali moustache spread narrow wings beneath his drippy, red nose. "Wha'up, man?"

"Just wanted a quick look-see," the professor said. "Don't want to bother you, know you're occupied."

The wizard's rapacious grin stopped Izzy in her tracks. A narrow grayish tongue flicked from between wet lizard lips. A chilling flux of pure evil raised the primal hairs on her neck.

"No prob, especially when you bring such a fuckin' hot piece of—"

Jones cut him off. "This is my laboratory assistant, Miss Abbott."

Izzy edged back. She'd scream if the hideous ghoul tried to touch her.

Oz shrugged and turned to the console, flipped a few switches then said over his shoulder, "Doc, remind your bitch aunt that I got a new projection system coming up through the canal this afternoon. I need asshole Oscar and that wimp Stand-bitch to unload it. Heavy lifting ain't in my contract."

"Yes, indeedy. Will take care of it right away."

The wizard's cellphone rang. He plucked it from the sound board and answered, voice low. "Yeah, sweet cheeks. Whatchugot?" He hunched his back and turned away from Izzy and Jones, indicating a need for privacy.

The two ducked out of the control room. Jones softly shut the door behind them. "Busy man."

Izzy gritted her teeth. *Yeah, it's tough being a misogynistic, drug addicted, snuff porn animator these days.* She wrapped her arms around herself to quell waves of anxiety. "What canal is he talking about?"

"We have our very own underground waterway. It's accessed downstairs below the control room. Runs a mile-and-a-half out to the beach." Halliburton sighed as if he was saying too much, but couldn't stop. Izzy knew he loved to be the expert, the man in-the-know.

"All quite hidden, yes, indeed. Built in the early seventies by the Navy's engineering battalion. Part of a top-secret project. We sometimes use it for deliveries of certain entities."

Izzy filed that information away, then again glanced down into the atrium. The augmented reality mermaid orgy was in full swing. And it was just the warm-up.

Water cascaded from spigots below, filling the theater.

Undulating lights in blues and purples lit the floor and bubbles roiled as if from an uncorked bottle of champagne. Shadows of flesh-and-blood, sparkle-tailed mermaids and small live sharks circled what was becoming an exotic island of "guests."

Lucy gulped back a fresh pang of nausea and covered her mouth. Jones would hurl her to the sharks or piranhas if she rained puke down on the jammie-clad sickos. This time, Jones noticed her discomfort and, tittering, quickly guided her back into the lab.

"Not the dramaturgical type, are you?"

"DNA is definitely more my thing," Izzy said, struggling not to choke.

But the show did give her an idea, an important one. Next time on the crosswalk, maybe the sonofabitch Jones would enjoy swimming with the hammerheads.

Chapter 28

Bea finished off the last swig of tepid latte in the to-go cup from the Student Union, then picked up Wu's call. "I was just about to phone you, Mac. Found info on an ocean research center with an aquarium of some sort that was deep-sixed by the Navy in the seventies or thereabouts. Records are scanty. It was a multi-million-dollar white elephant they wanted to disappear."

"Very interesting. And we've got facial recognition of the van driver at Jones's condo." Wu's voice sounded a tad breathless over the phone.

"Great news. Who is it?"

"Guy named Gorski, Eastern European spook. My researchers are checking it all out and'll update me when they know more. Where are you, Bea?"

"On PCH, on my way to Lucy's. Just left the Naval Command Center at Port Hueneme. Nice chat with the CO."

"I'm on the 101 heading south—meet you at the ranch in thirty minutes."

"Ten-four, Detective." *Was the picture puzzle beginning to come together at last? Or was that too much to hope for?*

Bea stepped on the accelerator. Twenty minutes later, she climbed out of her car and hurried toward the Rancho de la Vega yurt, pups at her heels.

—

Lucy and Sister Catherine Lucia sat on opposite sides of the small kitchen table working on their laptops. Bea could see the familial resemblance when they concentrated. A slight frown on their lips, shoulders slightly hunched, wavy hair askew.

She rapped on the doorframe. "Knock-knock."

"No soliciting." Lucy's eyes remained fixed on her screen. "That includes religious proselytizing, campaign materials, and peanut brittle sales."

"But I like that brittle peanut," Sister said. She stood and walked over to Bea, embracing her.

"Oh, Beatrice Middleton, it's you." Lucy glanced up. "The one who left me out of the loop."

"Ah, quit bitching, girlfriend. It's been a whoppin' day and a half. Wu's on his way. We'll update everybody as soon as he gets here. Plus, you're supposed to be chillin' with our dearest Sister Catherine Lucia."

Sister shook her head. "She no good at chiller."

"Like my *tía*." Lucy smiled as the old woman sat back down. "We've been researching Cloris-Edna Jones. What we found is pretty interesting, Beebs."

"She lived with Halliburton at the condo we just searched," Bea said. "We didn't find any evidence that ol' Cloris, or any woman, had been there in a long time. No clothes, no memorabilia, no female stuff."

A car door slammed over near the barn. The dogs yipped, and the Maddie and Bugle welcoming committee ushered Wu into the yurt, pressing open the screen door for him. He rewarded each with a vigorous ear scratch.

"You look exhausted, Mac," Lucy said. "Take a load off." She gestured toward a wicker rocker with fat cushions. "There's a couple beers, iced tea, and water in that mini fridge next to you."

"Thanks, Lucy." He pulled out a can of Coors, popped the top. "Feels like things're speeding up, finally." He took a long swig and settled into the chair. Shut his eyes and savored the moment.

Bea was camped out on Lucy's bed. "I've tried to get Pete on FaceTime, but he's not answering. Let's start and I'll fill him in later." She closed the laptop.

"Yes, ma'am." Wu let out a deep breath. "We got a good freeze frame of the guy who helped Jones move his stuff out of the condo. Name's Oscar Gorski, forty-six years old from Santa Ana. Came over from the Ukraine with his parents when he was twelve and immediately got involved in gang life. His sheet's a mile long starting in middle school. He somehow worked as a mall security guard, then for half a decade as a correctional officer at the federal lock-up in Lompoc."

"How the hell did he pass a background check to get that kind of a position?" Lucy asked.

"Great question. It looks like he took his straight-arrow cousin's ID and posed as Oswald Gorski, age forty-five with an A.S. degree in Criminal Justice from Orange County Community College. The physical resemblance between Oscar and Oswald is striking. Problem is, the cousin's dead."

Bea groaned. "Suspicious causes?"

"You guessed it." Wu finished off the Coors.

"Is Oscar still working at Lompoc?" Lucy pressed her hand against her growing baby bump.

Wu shook his head. "Dude was fired four years ago for suspected drug trafficking and black market sales of everything from earbuds to tennis shoes, but they couldn't make it stick."

"Got an address on this guy?" Bea asked.

"Nothing current. He's been a ghost for quite a while. No bank account, no credit cards—must do everything in cash. He has a current driver's license but the residence listed is actually a nail salon in Long Beach."

"I wonder how he hooked up with Halliburton and Cloris-Edna." Bea turned her attention to the intense clicking sound of Sister's slim fingers flying over the keyboard.

"I have idea," Sister said. "Everybody in LA movie star, *sí?*

Lucy rolled her eyes.

Sister ignored her. "I go to S-A-G site. You know S-A-G? Screen Actors Guild?"

"Yes, we know." Bea shot a quizzical glance Lucy's way.

"Oscar Eduardo Gorski, member begin 1973. Maybe do movie with *señora* Cloris when he a child."

Lucy, Bea, and Wu suddenly sat up straighter.

Chapter 29

Lucy, Bea, and Wu gathered around Sister Catherine Lucia's computer to view a headshot of a boy around ten years old—Oscar Gorski's cousin, Oswald. He had minor film credits for two pictures—the blockbuster, *Jaws,* in which he played "Boy on Beach," and then he appeared as "Bobby" in a subsequent unreleased Warner Bros. picture entitled *Frenzy of the She Sharks.* By the time he was eleven, the kid's career appeared to be over. Maybe he decided to take up baseball or band instead.

"Brilliant work, Sister." Lucy patted the old woman's shoulder. "A real Miss Marple."

Everyone agreed.

Bea pulled up the same site on her laptop. "Look at the credits, unbelievable. Cloris-Edna Jones starred in *She Sharks.* Let's see if the reel still exists in WB's film archives." She continued typing.

"You think they make more shark movie?" Sister asked. "Kill girls?"

Bea remained intent. "A longshot, but maybe. Could be

parallels in that movie that give us a clue as to what they're doing now."

Lucy sat back across the table from Sister. "Beebs, if you can't find more online, Dr. Lydia Woodley was head of the UCLA film archives when I was a student. Taught a couple classes I took, and we became friends. She's long retired but still lives in the area—Studio City, I think. She is, or was, a total movie maven. Maybe she could advise us."

"Call her." Wu stood, bounced up and down on his feet, appearing revived and ready to go. "Tell her we can come right over."

It took Lucy several phone inquiries and about fifteen endless minutes to secure Woodley's contact information. She punched in the number.

"It's been ten years since I've spoken to her. I hope she remembers me." Lucy chewed on a thumbnail. The phone rang. "Maybe she has dementia—must be in her early nineties. Won't even remember the name of the café in Casablanca, let alone an unreleased, schlocky B-movie from the seventies."

"Hello?" The voice was low and scratchy.

"Hello, Dr. Woodley?"

"Yes."

Lucy slowed her speech and enunciated loudly. "You probably don't remember me, but this is Lucia Vega calling, from your film history classes."

"Lucy! Oh, my goodness, it's been years. How are you, dear?"

Lucy gave Bea a thumbs-up.

Woodley continued. "So lovely to hear from one of my favorite students. I've seen your work on TV. Really impressed with the documentary you shot and produced with Michael Burleson last year. Saw it on Showtime. Stunning piece. You deserved that Emmy nomination."

Lucy felt herself flush with pride. "Your approval means a lot to me." *The old gal seems to have all her facilities, not to mention a very discerning eye!*

"Intensely compelling. What are you working on now?"

"Something very different. And that's why I called. I'm trying to find information on an old, unreleased film called *Frenzy of the She Sharks*. Stars a Cloris-Edna—"

"Cloris-Edna Jones." She tsked. "The synchronized swimmer, Esther Williams wannabe. We're about the same age, you know. I met her several times. Most unpleasant. Friedkin said she couldn't act her way out of a Speedo, but cut a nice figure in the pool. I'd have to agree."

"Interesting that you remember her after all this time."

"I remember everyone, hon. But why is Cloris-Edna of interest?"

"She might have ties to a murder investigation I'm involved in researching." Lucy glanced up at her colleagues in the room, all appeared anxious to hear the conversation.

"A murder, you say?" Woodley was quiet for a moment. Lucy heard the sound of a keyboard clack in the background. Another oldie who refused to let the digital revolution pass her by.

"May I put you on speaker, Dr. Woodley? Detective Wu from Ventura Metro, and several of my colleagues are with me.

"Of course. Hello, everyone." They exchanged greetings. "I got very good at conference calls and Zoom meetings during the pandemic. Now, about that film—it was shut down, never finished. Happened with so many during that time. I'll never forget talking with Jack and Harry, you know, two of the Warner boys, about the studio pulling the plug on several shark movies. After Jaws in '75, the bigwigs thought anything with teeth and a dorsal fin would spawn a quick buck."

Her keyboard was back in action. "Huh. Looks like we don't have any of the dailies in the archives. Not sure what happened to the footage, probably destroyed. No one wanted to take responsibility."

"What was the problem? Bad script? Lack of funding?" Lucy guessed.

"Yes, all that, but mostly, a young actor playing Cloris-

Edna's son was killed by one of the sharks. Turned out they hadn't gotten permits or approval for any of their animals or stunts. Obtained the sharks through some shady broker. The boy fell into a holding tank and was literally eaten alive."

There was a collective gasp. Lucy gripped her stomach. Even the baby seemed upset.

After signing off with Woodley and setting a future lunch date at Jerry's Deli with her former professor, Lucy disconnected the call.

"A dead boy?" Sister's eyes caught her niece's. "Must be very *traumática* for señora Cloris."

"Indeed, very upsetting and maybe ended her Hollywood career." Lucy slumped back into her chair, deep in thought. Then she turned to Sister and said, "we need to know more about Camarillo State Hospital."

Sister nodded toward her screen. "It say here, *Rest Home to the Stars.*"

—

Halliburton Jones never looked forward to conversations with his aunt. They always seemed to end badly for him. This was turning out to be more of the same. He dabbed a sheen of perspiration from beneath his nose with a cotton hanky.

"And what do you think you're going to do with her, Halliburton? Keep her in the lab like a pet dog, forever? Girl's a tough one, she's going to keep using you until she escapes and blows our entire enterprise, including your precious research."

"She's a brilliant student. Science is her life; she can be brought around. When Miss Abbott fully appreciates the kind of work I'm doing, she could end up being on our side and not care about what supports our funding. Lesser of evils—you know the old saying."

"Dream on, nephew."

The old woman paced back and forth across her studio in black spandex pants, high-heeled patent-leather ankle boots, and a silver caftan that billowed like an open parachute. She stopped, placed her skinny arms on her hips and planted her feet.

She was Cruella de Ville's evil clone. Jones suppressed a shudder.

"After this week," Cloris-Edna continued, "Oscar's assistance will have to suffice. I can release Standish to help you once in a while as well, but the girl has to go."

Jones wheezed as if he'd taken a blow to the stomach. His knees threatened to collapse. "You *cannot* be serious."

"I'm deadly serious, silly minnow. We are on the verge of great success. There's even talk of opening franchises in the Philippines and Thailand. Miami, too. In less than a year, we may be able to retire from this tawdry operation and move to Paris as we've always dreamed."

Jones ground his teeth, his fists opened and closed. *She'll be dead by the time that happens. I'll make sure of it. And I never wanted to go to Paris.*

"Now clean the aquarium, dear. Quite a mess from last night, and the new group arrives in two days. The word is really getting out there among our elite clientele. We've received five-star reviews on the Deep Gulp app. Now get the detritus to the crematorium in Sylmar, and then you may go back to the lab and work on your little projects."

She clacked over to him on her spiky heels, bussed him on both cheeks, then waved her bony hand in dismissal.

Chapter 30

Lucy felt as if her brain was about to explode. After Bea and Wu took off, she and Sister had labored over their laptops for several hours, pursing the possible connection between Camarillo State Hospital and Cloris-Edna Jones.

"So, my dear aunt, what have we got?" Lucy reached into the mini-fridge and grabbed a thermos of the red raspberry infusion that helped ease uterine tension. She rubbed her tummy and tried not to be concerned by the usual light contractions. Just routine stuff. But even routine stuff scared her.

Sister rose from her chair and stretched. "We know Señora Cloris stay at hospital in late seventy. She listed in newspaper as patient who is movie star." Sister tapped a button and the articles began to print out. "Was maybe she there *por dos años*. That a long time, no?"

Lucy nodded and leaned against the door jamb. The sun hung low on the horizon, turning the meadow golden and back-lighting flitting insects. The hint of ocean coolness began its creep through the canyons at this waning hour, softening the bright harshness of the day.

"Let's get out of our *oficina,* Sister, and go for a little walk." Lucy stepped outside. "Will do us both good. Too much sitting and concentrating." *And too much brutality and mayhem.*

Sister followed her niece out the door and took her arm. The dogs had vanished, Howard the cat slept on Lucy's pillow, and Elsa was off to have dinner with a friend in Agoura Hills. Strolling with her aunt in the quiet dusk scented with the sweetness of nearby creek willows, Lucy's frayed nerves calmed.

The women followed a dusty fire road toward the arroyo. The lower trunks of majestic live oaks along the trail were scarred with blackened bark from the wildfire that had raged through the chaparral months ago. Lucy felt comfort in the big trees— they'd been on this land for a hundred years and would likely continue to weather the storms for a hundred more. Grasses, sage, yucca—all had begun to regenerate and thrive. As a human survivor of that inferno, she struggled to do the same.

But even the idyllic stroll couldn't pull her attention away from the horrific situation facing Isabelle Abbott and the other young women. Kidnapping, sexual violence, and murder— they all seemed to be perpetrated by the cabal of Agent Sonny Bartlett, Cloris-Edna Jones, her nephew Halliburton, Oscar Gorksi, and whatever minions they had helping them. There'd been mention of a Central American connection, Honduras, but nothing had surfaced. Bartlett had clearly raked in millions trafficking in black market exotic animals. Had that provided enough funding for their sick enterprise? Or were there other money sources still hidden away? And how had he hooked up with the Joneses?

Deep in thought, Lucy tripped over a pothole in the road. Sister barely kept her from falling, and almost took a tumble herself.

"You okay, Lucia?" The old woman's face clouded with concern.

"Sorry! I'm fine, thinking about this whole awful mermaid

case. Are *you* all right? I almost knocked both of us over." She squeezed Sister's hand.

"Yes, *mija*. I a tough old bird, balance good." She chuckled. "We head back now—a nap for both of us."

Lucy detested naps, but knew her aunt was right. The twinges in her uterus were becoming uncomfortable. Overexertion was likely the culprit. A rest and her aunt's tincture of crampbark would ease the contractions.

Just as the women turned toward the yurt, Lucy's dogs galloped to greet them. As Maddie rushed up, Lucy reached to scratch her dog's velvety yellow ears. Clamped in the pup's smiling jaws was something gruesomely familiar. Lucy cried out. *Another body part? Isabelle Abbott? God, no.*

Sister crossed herself.

Lucy grabbed her iPhone.

—

It was less than a day before the Los Angeles Regional Crime Lab had the DNA results on the newly discovered physical evidence. Bea was relieved when Pete Anthony put the analysis request on highest priority.

Pete, Bea, and Wu sat with CSI Demi Brown in a far corner of the lab's cafeteria. It was mid-morning and folks taking coffee breaks began to trickle into the new, modern facility.

"Thanks for turning this thing around so quickly," Wu said.

Bea watched the usually health-conscious detective swill a Diet Coke and bite into a frosting-coated cheese Danish. She looked at him and shook her head. He ignored her.

Wu continued, crumbs flecking his day-old beard. "Casey Abbott was sure relieved when I talked to her a couple minutes ago. None of the new body parts belonged to her sister."

But they belonged to some poor soul. Bea vividly recalled the dump site—was the same as last time. Again, the oak-shrouded gulch immediately off Mulholland near Lucy's ranch was thoroughly investigated and the most recent specimens were carefully collected by CSI Demi Brown and his crew. Motion-activated cameras were positioned in several trees overlooking the area. Hopefully, any additional disposal would be recorded if the "Trashman," as Bea called the perpetrator, tried to discard morbid refuse again.

Demi examined the report he'd pulled from a file folder and sipped his latte. "I think we got the remains of not one, but two women this time. Weird thing is, the DNA's almost the same, but not quite. You've likely got a set of identical twin girls."

Bea felt goosebumps raise on her arms which had nothing to do with the morgue-cold air conditioning of the cafeteria. "Agent Bartlett was hustling two young women at the Ventura Mall—pretty blonde twins, maybe sixteen."

"Oh, hell." Wu pushed the cheese Danish crumbs away and looked ready to puke. "Fits the description of the girls who disappeared from the runaway shelter in Ventura."

"I thought identical twins shared the same DNA," Pete said.

Demi shook his head. "Nope, we used to believe that. In this case, there was a 95 percent match. And twins don't have identical fingerprints. We recovered three digits from the remains and were able to nab IDs on these kids because their prints were in the system. One had pled guilty to a DUI, and the other had been arrested for shoplifting."

Wu let out a weary sigh, ran his hands through his short black hair. "Syd-nee and Char-lee Marshall from Moab, Utah?"

"Bingo." Demi passed copies of the report to the two police officers. "Sorry, Bea, can't distribute this to the media."

She'd already had all the bad news she needed.

"Cause of death also the same as last time? Shark attack?" Pete asked.

"Again, not exactly. The water that soaked into the skin samples wasn't from the ocean. We found that it fit the chemical profile of a freshwater river, but not one from around here."

"Like from where?" Thoroughly depressed, Bea glanced at the photos of the two girls. "The Central Valley? Sacramento?"

Demi shook his head. "Like the Amazon."

"The fuckin' Amazon?" Pete's usual poker face turned incredulous. "Not death by shark, then?"

"Ah, man." Demi frowned. "Likely death by piranha—lots of very hungry ones. Vicious little bites. Verified by our forensic biologist this morning."

Stomach knotting, Bea felt as sick as Wu looked. She gripped her coffee cup with both hands. "We have *got* to find the place where all this insanity is going down." She turned to Wu. "Y'all sent a drone out to check the spot where Bartlett's Land Rover disappeared with the two girls. Anything show up?"

"Tracks evaporated right off the bat. Fire roads, hiking and mountain biking trails, game paths, all crisscross the area. And the drought has made the ground so hard that prints, even heavy vehicle traces, don't show up. Lots of high-end residences up there. From the air, none appear to house anything like a big aquarium."

"Unless the facility's underground," Bea said. "The CO at the base thought that could be possible, but again, they're thin on records. I'll check in with Bijan, see if he's had time to come up with anything."

"I gotta get back to the office." Wu rose from the table. "I'll go over those drone images again."

"Oh, and one more thing." Demi stood and pushed his hands deep in the pockets of his white lab coat. "The girl's tox reports showed presence of succinylcholine."

"What's that?" Bea winced as if anticipating a blow.

Demi cleared his throat. "The kids were paralyzed but alive and likely lucid when they were attacked by the piranhas."

Bea's throat tightened. Once again, this all felt too close to home—like when Dexter had been abducted and terrorized in Savannah. And when her daughter had sneaked off to a dance audition in what turned out to be a porn studio. *Isn't this kind of stuff supposed to be fiction?* She blinked away tears and followed Wu and Pete to the parking lot.

Chapter 31

At Ventura Metro PD Headquarters, Wu slumped in his chair, staring blankly at the pile of papers, files, and fast-food wrappers littering his desk. His usual strict order was breaking down. It was late morning, and most of the staff was in the field. He'd begun to doze when he was startled by footsteps behind him. Disoriented, he reached for his gun.

"Whoa, partner!" Beno Ramirez, the undercover detective who had been working the Ventura Mall, held up his hands in defense. "Somebody needs to lose the caffeine and get some goddamn sleep."

"Ah, shit. Sorry, man." Wu dropped his hand from the Glock and offered a guilty shrug of his shoulders. "Yeah, I'm outta here. This case is driving me nuts. Days are zooming by and it's still just smoke and mirrors. In the meantime, girls are getting tortured and snuffed by some lunatic fish freaks."

Beno sat down next to Wu. "Hey, bro, you told me to go through the mermaid files while you were out." He reached over and tapped on a pile of Manilla folders. "I checked those drone shots, too. *Nada.*"

Wu nodded. "Thanks, man. We need fresh eyes."

"This thing's the most fucked-up crap I've ever seen."

"No shit." Wu rubbed his neck. "Catch anything we missed?"

"Maybe. Since I'm off mall duty, I dropped by the runaway house and talked to the director. Thought I'd give that another shot."

"Yeah, I got your text. Good move. What'd she say?"

"Told me she first noticed this asshole Bartlett outside the pancake house off Telephone Road where the twins worked. So, I decided to get me a pile of hotcakes this morning, and there he was."

"What? You saw him?"

"Yep. He scored nice personal attention from the manager—felt like a regular, or an occasional who tips good."

Wu frowned. "Our people showed the manager a recent photo. He denied ever seeing Bartlett before."

"The lying bastard. We'll bust him for something. Send over the health department. Anyhow, I struck up a conversation with Sonny boy."

"And?" Wu opened his desk drawer and pulled out a bottle of Advil. Popped a couple and washed them down with what was left in a stained cup of day-old coffee.

Beno grimaced. "And, I said I'd seen him at the mall food court. Mentioned that I hung out there on occasion. He acted a little squirrely when I said it. Then no more talk. We just ate our cakes—they were damn good."

"Thanks for the restaurant review. Then what?" Wu ran his hands over his face as if trying to scrape away the exhaustion.

"I paid my bill and left."

"What? You didn't tail him?"

"I planted a bug under his back bumper. He was driving a 2013 Highlander this time. Licenses plates traced to a dead cop from Palmdale. Name's Hobbs—supposedly sold it to Bartlett two weeks ago."

"Shit."

Beno held up his cellphone, turned the screen toward Wu. "Right now, dude's at the Barefoot Bar at Point Hueneme."

"That's real good, Beno. Maybe this is the break we need." A sharp pain stabbed Wu between the eyes. "But I've said that about fifty times before."

"Maybe fifty-one's the charm. Persistence pays, man. Now go home and rest that ugly mug of yours. You look like shit."

Wu stood and grabbed his black nylon backpack. "Meet you here later to run the scenario."

"Roger that, bud. We're gonna nail this sonofabitch."

—

Bea slid into the black leatherette chair behind her desk and gazed out toward the Hollywood Sign in the distance. The atmosphere was clear and the city gleamed fresh as a newly painted theater set. This was the Southern California of New Year's Day Rose Parades. Like most things in Tinseltown, it was a brilliant illusion. Bea couldn't shake the image of Bartlett with his carefully highlighted and artfully messy surfer boy hairdo, seducing two vulnerable kids from Moab straight to their hideous deaths.

She turned to the pile of messages overflowing her in-box and began to sort through. That's when her boss, Winfrey Chambers, decided to stop in for a chat. He stood in the doorway waiting for an invitation.

"Come on in, sir." Bea gestured to a chair across from her desk. She always felt a tad intimidated in his presence, like she was never doing quite enough.

"Haven't seen you for a few days, Miss Beatrice, and you haven't checked in. Want to give me an update?"

"Sorry, Win, but this has all been coming at me really fast."

He adjusted his sweater vest and touched his bow tie. "Is this story tying into the new take on human trafficking that I'd asked for?"

"Yes, absolutely." She filled him in.

He sat and listened intently, remaining quiet after she'd finished. Then, Winfrey stood and scratched at his close-cropped gray hair. "If this story's as big as you say, if it's international in scope, I think we should turn it over to the global news desk."

Bea gasped—couldn't believe what she was hearing. "No! You can't do that." Her heart hammered. "We're so close, we've been working day and night to wrap it up before more young women are murdered by these monsters. And it's all taking place in our backyard—it's local news. You can't—" She took a deep breath and tried to collect herself before saying something stupid.

He gave her a long, hard look. "Okay, Bea, I'll hold off for now, but I need something in the next few days with a true local angle, or it's time to hand it off."

"Thank you, sir." She was hyperventilating as he turned and walked out into the newsroom cube farm. When her cellphone rang, she grabbed it from her pocket, hands trembling. It was Bijan. Bea didn't answer immediately. She needed a moment to calm down. When the ringing stopped, she pressed *Call Back*.

Bijan immediately picked up. "Lunch, sweetie? Got some news."

"What? Spill. My boss is all over me for results, and we're nowhere." She didn't like the shrillness in her voice.

"Settle down, my Bea-bop-a-liscious one. I'm feeling ya, but no goodies over the phone. Meet me at Cha Cha Chicken, 1:30 sharp and bring that cute Chinese detective with you."

—

Near the corner of Ocean and Pico in Santa Monica, Bea and Bijan lined up among the swimsuit and flip-flop-clad beachgoers to order their coconut jerk chicken and sweet potato combos. Seagulls stood watch above the restaurant's awning, ready to swoop down and pilfer food from distracted diners.

Bea and her ginger-bearded friend wandered among the

picnic tables looking for an empty spot. She resisted the urge to grab Bijan and immediately shake the information he was hoarding onto the sidewalk. Instead, she tried to appear patient, a quality that was not among her top ten.

"Bijan, doll, you're lookin' pasty as bread dough. Y'all gotta get out of that dark studio more often, and not just to eat." She slid onto a hot pink picnic bench, and Bijan planted himself across from her. Caribbean music played from a tinny loudspeaker.

"And you're looking as brown and yummy as a pumpernickel bagel, girlfriend. Mmm-mmm."

"Bijan, is being compared to a bagel supposed to be a compliment?"

"From me? *Absolutemente.* And where's Detective Woo-woo?"

"He's tied up in Ventura."

"Oh, I like the sound of that."

Bea huffed, held her plastic knife like a dagger and stabbed the chicken breast. "Bijan, focus on aquariums, mermaids. What gives?"

He leisurely popped wedges of fried sweet potato into his mouth.

"Bijan. Talk. People are dying."

He choked on the reality and coughed. "Jesus, Bea. Sorry. I sometimes lose perspective working in my cave. The whole world seems like a video game."

"This is no game, man. This is murder. Now, tell me what y'all got." Bea suddenly felt too stressed to eat, and she was a dyed-in-the-wool stress eater. She pushed her plate away.

"Okay, I scoured the clear net, the dark net, and finally came across something interesting on an obscure government website. Looks like a top-secret aquatic research facility, located in the hills above the Navy base, was closed in 1978. Subsequently, it was sold to a company called Agua Adventures LLC. Names on the sales docs—Simpson S. Bartlett and Cloris-Edna Jones."

Bea felt cold hackles rise.

Bijan wasn't done. "The Camarillo State Hospital connection Lucy and her nun aunt discovered seems to be the common thread. Bartlett's grandmother was in the facility, in the same wing as Cloris-Edna Jones back in the late sixties."

"Oh my God—probably where they all met."

Bijan nodded and swallowed a big bite of coconut chicken. "And the Jones family was loaded. Cloris-Edna was the sole recipient of the family fortune. Jones, Halliburton & Hyde Chemicals out of Montreal was sold to Monsanto for a major profit. The old broad seems to have been a sharp money manager. She had a widowed older sister who died of breast cancer. That's when Cloris moved to LA with Halliburton in tow. There was a small article in the social section of a local paper that hit on that."

Bea chewed on her thumbnail. "Starlet Cloris must have had enough *dinero* for nannies and private schools to keep young Halliburton entertained while she worked at her movie career."

Bijan eyed Bea's barely-touched lunch. He was more predatory than the seagulls. "Gonna finish that honeybun, or can I pick?"

"Pick away. I feel like I'm gonna puke. But what about the facility—the aquarium? Any info on where it might be located? We've got to get there before someone else dies."

Bijan fumbled with his iPhone while inhaling Bea's leftovers.

"Just texted you the location and copied Lucy, Pete, and Woo-woo. It's on Dos Vientos Way, up in the unincorporated Ventura County hills. It's also possible there was a tunnel from somewhere off Point Mugu to the so-called Institute. I found a reference to it, but nothing more. No blueprints. That's all I got, sweetheart."

"Big boy, that's incredible information. You're saving lives, real ones. Thank you, baby." Bea jumped up, laid a smacking kiss on the big man's forehead, and rushed off to her car.

Pulling onto Ocean Avenue heading west toward Pacific Coast Highway, she dialed Wu.

Chapter 32

Bea banged on the door to the detective's Mediterranean-style condo, six blocks from the Ventura Pier. "Damnit, Wu. I know you're in there. Didn't you get my texts? My calls?" She pounded again. A neighbor's curtain fluttered aside. Bea waved to a gray-haired woman.

The old woman called through the screen in a smoker's gravelly voice, "Stop that damn pounding, missy, or I'll call security." The curtain was yanked shut. A bird cawed from inside the apartment sounding remarkably like the Wicked Witch of the West when she was melting.

The detective's door slowly opened. Macintosh Wu, dressed in a pair of striped boxers he'd obviously slept in, yawned and straightened his off-center eyeglasses. "You've just met my guard dog. How did you know where I live?"

Bea crossed her arms on her chest, jutted a hip. "Beno. He couldn't reach you either."

"I needed a few hours. I'm not somebody who can run on zero sleep."

"Me either. Wish I was." Bea cleared her throat, eyes darting to Wu's undies. *Nice bod.*

"So, what's the breaking news?" He opened the door wider so Bea could step into the narrow entryway.

"Bijan found an address for the research institute, had a big-ass aquarium at one point. It's in your texts."

"Whoa, awesome." The detective's bleary eyes brightened.

Bea continued. "And get this, the facility was sold to Sanford Bartlett and Cloris-Edna Jones in the late seventies."

"No shit?" Wu reached for his phone then seemed to suddenly realize he was chatting with Bea in his underwear. "Make yourself comfortable inside. Let me get some clothes on and then you can get me up to speed on the details."

Bea stifled a wisecrack about boxers vs. briefs, and wandered into Wu's sparsely furnished living room. She parked herself in an overstuffed leather chair beneath an impressionistic painting of a golden Buddha while Wu hopped in the shower. She pulled a photo album from a bookcase next to the chair and slowly paged though Wu's life. An attractive couple—arms around a smiling boy and younger girl with long dark braids at a beach somewhere. Then, at birthday parties, Christmas, a Chinese New Year's parade. The girl was likely Wu's missing sister. He'd shut Bea down any time she tried to broach the subject.

The shower turned off. A dresser drawer slammed. Bea quickly returned the album to the empty spot on the shelf.

Minutes later, Wu appeared wet-haired in pressed khakis and a light blue button-down shirt. He slipped into a shoulder holster and inspected his Glock like he'd probably done hundreds of times before.

Bea filled Wu in on the rest of what she'd learned from lunch with Bijan.

"Let's get to the station and examine those drone shots again." He grabbed a sports jacket that had seen a lot of mileage from a hall closet and shrugged into it. "We'll blow 'em up on the big screen in the conference room. I'll have Beno start a subpoena request to search the place."

Bea trailed her hand along the edge of the Buddha painting for luck, then followed Wu out into the too bright sunshine.

—

A half-hour later, Bea, Wu, and Beno sat at the end of a long conference table, all eyes to the big screen, watching live GPS from a just-launched drone. This state-of-the-art bird was the best they had. The initial stills over the area had given them little.

The surveillance currently in progress was much more informative. A black panel van had pulled to the rear of the large, Spanish-style mansion on Dos Vientos.

"What do we have here?" Beno asked.

Two figures unloaded what looked like catering goods.

"Probably food for the sick fun and games expected tonight. I hope they choke on it and die. When do you think we'll hear on the subpoena?" Bea sipped Ralph's Market-brand water from a dented bottle.

"End of day at the earliest," Wu said. "Gonna be a crapshoot as to whether the judge'll grant it or not. Gotta admit, our probable cause is skimpy."

Beno raked a fingernail across his front teeth as if trying to dislodge an invisible sprig of lunch remains. "Security there looks tight as shit."

They watched a bald man in dark clothing step from the house onto the front terrace.

"Is that Gorski, the driver?" Wu asked, eyes narrow. "I think it is. Yes!"

Bea clapped. "Very good. Now we know where he hangs. Got you, sucker."

Gorski glanced innocuously around, then stared straight at the drone, at them.

"Shit. We've been made." Beno leaned back in his chair.

Baldie flashed them the bird, then aimed a rifle that had been resting against a palm tree. A collective gasp ripped through the conference room. A moment of static crackled on the screen, before it cut to black.

Beno jumped from his seat as if he'd been shot himself. "Asshole took down our fucking drone! It's brand-fucking-new!"

"Damn." Wu's eyes narrowed in consternation.

Beno sputtered. "It had thermal imaging!" His arms rose to the sky and he shook his fists. "The fire department uses the exact same model for fire-spotting. Took us months to get funding for that baby."

The dude was practically crying.

Wu motioned Beno to a seat. "Pull it together, bud. Maybe we can use this to our advantage."

"What do you mean?" he asked, head in hands.

"I'll email the recording to the judge. Might bolster our request for cause. But this gives us the go-ahead to drive over and demand to find out what happened to our CJI Hawkstra II."

"And maybe arrest that scumbag?" Bea rubbed her hands together in anticipation.

Wu nodded.

Beno jumped out of his seat again. "Let's boogie."

—

Another day ticked by like a slow-mo timebomb threatening to detonate. It took Bea and the Ventura cop crew forty-five minutes to reach the Dos Vientos mansion they'd identified as the possible former government ocean research facility.

Wu pulled up to the decorative wrought-iron front gate and pushed a call button. A small brass plate announcing Piscem Auratus had been fixed to the surrounding stucco wall above the call box, next to a camera. There were several lenses aimed their way.

Bea surveyed the grounds through the fence. The place was beautifully xeriscaped with cacti, yucca, bunchgrass, and manzanitas plants. Flowering oleander hedged the shaded walkways. A lush fountain with a bare-breasted mermaid in the center spewed water from the conch shell she held above her head like a prize.

"Yes?" A gruff female voice sounded from the speaker.

Bea wondered if it was Cloris-Edna Jones.

Wu cleared his throat. "VMPD here to investigate the shoot-down of our drone. The perpetrator stood on your terrace and took it out with a high-powered rifle."

There was a pause. "Impossible. You have the wrong house."

"We have a digital recording, ma'am. We'd like to speak with you—here or at the station. Your choice. It's against FAA regulations to destroy a drone in service."

"Especially an expensive one belonging to law enforcement," Beno growled.

Wu continued. "It's also against county regulations to discharge a firearm in a residential neighborhood."

Another long pause.

The gate began to groan open.

Wu steered along a circular drive lined with palm trees. An aquamarine swimming pool sparkled from across a boulder-strewn lawn, artfully softened with flowering groundcover. Jasmine and the salty tang of the ocean scented a gentle breeze. Hummingbirds were busy at feeders. The residence resembled a posh Palm Desert resort.

Bea shuddered at the thought of what might be going on in the bowels beneath the sumptuous façade. As Wu drove, she videoed the grounds with her phone. "Are you gonna confront them, Wu?"

"I just want to rattle the cage, not send them running." His dusty, bullet-gray vehicle was a blight on this bright manicured landscape. "We'll talk to the old woman, then wait and watch. Once we have the warrant, boom-chukka-boom."

"We can't afford to wait." Bea pulled the mermaid fountain into close-up though her lens, just as Lucy would probably do. Rusty stains on the statue's face looked like bloody tears.

"We have no choice but to wait," Wu said. "If we're gonna take them down, we go by the book, line by line. Nobody gets sprung on a technicality on my watch."

He parked the car next to a stone terrace that led up several steps to an imposing front door. The thick teakwood had been expertly carved with sea creatures frolicking amid the waves. No body parts appeared to be bobbing in the surf.

The door opened just as Beno was about to press the bell.

A crone of perhaps ninety years stepped out onto the portico. She teetered on four-inch-heeled black ankle boots. Black leggings led up to a short purple dress that draped her twiggish body like a loose tablecloth. Gold chandelier earrings pulled her long silvery earlobes practically to her bony shoulders.

"Hello, ma'am. I'm Detective Macintosh Wu, Ventura Metro Police Department." He held up his badge, as did Beno. "These are my colleagues, Officer Martinez and Ms. Middleton."

"Good afternoon." She paused to study them, mouth twisted in distaste. "I'm Miss Cloris-Edna Jones." Her enunciation was stiff and formal. She didn't offer her hand. "I'm sure you're mistaken about this, this what? So-called drone? Why would it be flying around here anyway? I'll have you know, we in the hills don't take kindly to having our privacy violated."

"The man who shot it down—shaved head, late thirties—we think his name is Oscar Gorski."

Miss Jones's eyes popped wide, then squinted into mean, knife-like slits. "I'm sorry but my man-servant is gone for the day. I know nothing of his guns. And his name is not Oscar Gor-whatever. Now, please, I must ask you to leave."

Something caught Beno's eye and he momentarily disappeared. He called out from near the pool. "Well, lookey here."

Bea watched as he reappeared on the terrace with a major chunk of the mangled drone in hand.

"What is *that?*" Jones asked, unable to mask her shock.

"What's left of our drone." Beno sneered and dropped the

wreckage at her feet.

She jumped back as if he'd dumped one of her dead mermaids on the doormat, steadying herself on the doorjamb.

"I don't know anything about whatever it is you have there. But you may take it and leave. I'll ask my man about it in the morning. I'm sure he was just enforcing our security. I'm an old woman and I live alone, so he's very conscientious."

"His name and contact information, please. We need to see the gun registration, too." Wu pulled out a notepad and planted his feet.

"I'm sorry, officer." She stepped back into the foyer.

"Detective."

"Yes, whatever. Contact my lawyers. They can provide you with any information you need. Now, if you'll excuse me, I'm beginning to feel quite faint."

"I'll bet you are," Beno mumbled.

Wu drilled him with a cautionary glance then turned his focus back to the old woman. He was all business. "The name of your attorney, please, ma'am?"

Jones tottered back into the house and re-emerged seconds later with a business card. She handed it to Wu. Her long, sharp claws were lacquered the greyish hue of dead flesh.

Bea gulped, recalling the horrific, discarded body parts.

Wu pocketed the card.

Bea couldn't turn away from the frightening talons. Strains of pulsating sound bled through from somewhere deep inside the residence.

"You're into techno music?" Bea asked.

"Goodbye, detectives." Jones frowned and slammed the door shut.

Beno picked up the drone's remains and toted the mangled metal and plastic to the car, Bea and Wu followed. He placed the wreckage reverently in the trunk.

"That was interesting," Wu said. "At least we met the old bitch, but we still don't have much."

"*Au contraire.*" Bea pointed at two spent shell casings on the ground next to a ceramic planter. "Must have dropped as Gorski shot from the terrace."

Wu smiled. "Very good, Ms. Consultant. You're more than worth the high salary we pay you."

"They're in plain sight so you can legally bag 'em, right?"

"Roger that, Ms. Middleton." He bent down and took several photos *in situ* with his cellphone. Texted them to VMPD HQ. "Okay, Beno, bags 'em. And let's pray the paperwork to search the place for Gorski's weapon comes through before they clear the hell outta here."

"What if it's denied?" Bea asked.

Wu checked his watch. "Then, I guess we're gonna have to go freelance. You good with that?"

Bea nodded, a faint smile flickered on her lips. "I've done some of my best work freelancing."

—

Sonny Bartlett pulled his Rover into a parking space at the edge of the small lot that serviced his office building in Malibu. His was one of only two vehicles, the other being a small luxury SUV with Nevada plates.

It was half past midnight and this part of Cross Creek Village was quiet, illuminated only by display lights from shop windows down the block. The Arroyo Building was dark except for wall sconces in the small lobby. Bartlett slid his keycard though the scanner. The glass door clicked and unlocked.

Although the night was cool, he wiped perspiration from his forehead and headed for the stairway to the second floor. Why had Arnaldo Barahona, also known as *El Tiburón,* wanted this secret meeting? An emissary from the Honduran cartel, he coordinated and contracted with sex adventure providers around the world. Barahona was probably here to personally thank the mermaid crew for their exceptional performance.

He took two stairsteps at a time, then strode quickly down

the hall to his office. The door was wide open. Not a positive sign. Barahona was early and evidently thought he had the right to break in. Bartlett paused, took a breath, and walked through his small anteroom into the inner chamber.

Barahona sat behind Bartlett's desk, smoking a cigar, and perusing a stack of paperwork. Short and built like a weight lifter, his features were thick and unattractive. A long keloid scar bisected his right cheek. He wore a gray velour track suit and gold neck chains right out of 1980s Compton.

The nerve of the bastard. Bartlett gritted his teeth. The intrusion was outrageous but he couldn't confront the asshole. The guy and his minions controlled the business. For now. But that was going to change. Bartlett had plans to take the mermaid operation solo. He forced a smile. "I see you've made yourself comfortable."

Barahona tipped his cigar ashes into a ficus planter on the desk. "I have, thank you." He had only the slightest Spanish accent.

Eyes black holes in the dimness of the office, Barahona was lit only by the computer screen and a small desk lamp. A slight rustling noise came from across the room. Another man sat in the dark, a duffle bag at his feet. Two against one. Bartlett couldn't get a fix on the dude's appearance.

Barahona steepled his fingers. His rings were big as golf balls. "We're unhappy, Agent Bartlett."

"What?" He wasn't hearing this right. "I don't understand." The niggle of concern as he'd entered the building intensified.

"A dead cop, the abduction of a high school teacher with law enforcement and reporters among her confidants, your poor attempt at recruitment. It's not working. None of it."

A wash of frigid fear turned Bartlett's blood cold. "You don't understand. I can explain—"

Barahona slapped the desk. Paperclips jumped like popcorn from a plastic container.

Bartlett became excruciatingly aware of the open ledger.

Fuck. His mouth went dry.

"And most importantly, I see you've been keeping two sets of books." Barahona took a long suck on his cigar. The ember flared.

Bartlett winced.

"Who else has access to these records?" Beneath a thick unibrow, the man stared at Bartlett. His small teeth clenched on his cigar like shark chops on a mermaid's ass.

Bartlett struggled not to hyperventilate. "Uh, no one."

"No one?"

"Well, my assistant, Oscar Gorski, has a key to the office for emergencies." Bartlett was beginning to see stars. Was Gorski a fuckin' mole?

Barahona nodded. "He works for me, not for you. Capiche?"

Bartlett nodded like a dashboard bobblehead on a rough road. The man in the corner unzipped his duffle and withdrew objects that Bartlett couldn't identify in the gloom.

"With all your success over the last two years, we wondered why you weren't pulling in more. Aside from poor management, I now see why."

Bartlett gripped the edge of the desk. He'd kept the ledger separate, recorded everything by hand to avoid any online exposure. Had cell phone pics of every page on a thumb drive he kept in his filing cabinet. It'd been a mistake. Was nothing immune from the scrutiny of the Honduran and his tribe? Could Gorski have broken in and sent the info to Barahona?

"Listen to me. I have a plan, a good one," Bartlett said.

"You have thirty seconds." Barahona again tapped ash into the ficus.

Bartlett struggled for words. He had no defense.

The man across the room stood, a tool in hand. A buzzing sound cut through the thick quiet of the office. Bartlett turned toward the only way out of the office. A third dark figure materialized. The dude slouched against the door jamb. What looked like the silhouette of a pistol with a silencer hung from his hand.

Shit. Bartlett's throat tightened, and he forced out hollow words. "So, uh, when you I and spoke last year about a second mermaid venue, you weren't too receptive. So, I decided to hold back some funds—"

"Seventeen million?"

Sweat ran down Bartlett's neck. "Significant funds . . . to develop a new site. I figured once I had the property identified and the enterprise ready to go, you'd be pleased. No, thrilled. I even have a place cued up near Miami." *If only.* "That seed money I, uh, borrowed, and much more, will be back in your pocket within eighteen months. A win for all."

The Honduran's eyes narrowed. "Ah, so your little independent endeavor would ultimately benefit my enterprise?"

"Yes, yes, exactly." Bartlett stood and crossed his arms on his chest in attempt to regain a shred of leverage. He was a man on crumbling gravel at the edge of a cliff.

"I don't think so, Agent Bartlett."

Barahona scowled. With the flick of a finger, he indicated for Bartlett to sit. Grudgingly, the agent complied.

The little spark of hope in Bartlett's chest flared and fizzled. Even he realized how bullshit it sounded. He was fucking ripping off the Hondurans. It was that simple. And that stupid.

"I'm disappointed, señor. I expected a more creative answer." There was a long pause as Barahona studied the open ledger. The buzzing pulsed again like a dentist's drill.

The man with the instrument stepped into the pale light. He was meth-addict skinny, with a drooping black mustache, and a stringy beard threaded with gray. Tats covered everything. Even his ears had ink. He turned on a headlamp which was momentarily blinding.

Barahona's thick lips curled into a soulless smile. "Stand up. Pants to your knees, Agent Bartlett. And bend over the desk. Spread your legs, gonads out."

"What the fuck?" Bartlett was incredulous. "I'm telling you

208 | SUE HINKIN

everything I've done, planned, is in all of our best interest. You're making a big mistake here. If you stop and think about it for even a second, you'll see I'm right."

The boss man was unmoved. "You can hold on to the ledger if it gets too, uh, difficult."

The buzzing noise sounded. Bartlett's intestines roiled, but he refused to soil himself. He tightened every sphincter, groaned, and dropped his pants.

Barahona cleared the desk, then pushed Bartlett down so the agent laid with his torso sprawled across it. Ass high in the air, he was sweating like a fountain. Were they going to take his nuts?

Bartlett started blabbering. "You've got this all wrong. I've been one of your best operatives." His desperate words spilled like blood from an artery of a dying man. Bartlett knew they were worthless, lying pissant excuses. "Together, the sky's the limit. Don't do this. I'm begging you." How did he ever think he'd get away with double-crossing the organization? He clenched his anus again.

"Anything come outta there, I gon' make it extra hard on you, bro," the man with the instrument growled. The Honduran pressed the ledger into Bartlett's hands. "You may begin, Guillermo." Barahona leaned back in the desk chair for an advantageous view of the procedure. "This is a small warning, Agent. If there is ever a next time, there will be no warning at all."

The tool buzzed and bit into Bartlett's tender flesh. He cried out in agony.

Chapter 33

Cloris-Edna paced her studio, kicking and stomping the gold cloth that had fallen to the floor near her sewing machine. She grabbed a ceramic head topped with a curly seafoam green wig laced with shells and hurled it at the wall, recoiling as it shattered. A sour smile on her lips, she threw another and another until there was a pile of multi-colored tresses among the ruins of broken skulls and painted faces. Her kohl-dark eyes narrowed with mean satisfaction.

Standish, who'd been dutifully organizing the makeup tables, dropped an open container of glitter, mouth slack in fear. His narrow shoulders shook and his hands went to cover his genitals as the old lady picked up another missile.

Halliburton slinked in with Oscar right behind him.

"You fuck-ups!" She screamed and threw a head toward Oscar, barely missing him. He held up his hands to protect himself.

Shards sprayed across the floor as Bartlett limped in, balancing on a cane. The detritus crunched beneath his shoes.

The old woman frowned. "What's with the cane?" she demanded. "Not a stylish look on you. What happened?"

Bartlett grimaced and his eyes flitted toward Oscar. The man's face was implacable. The agent had no evidence that the piece of shit Gorski was the mole, only a feeling in his aching motherfucking gonads. "The Hondurans are unhappy. Motherfuckers. They think they own us. We're on a short leash until I can figure out a way to make them pay." Turning his attention to the mound of wigs and broken heads, the skin beneath his fake tan itched. "What the fuck is this about?"

Cloris-Edna stopped pacing. She licked spittle from her thin lips. "Hero here shot down a goddamn police drone."

Oscar winced, looked away.

"A drone?" Bartlett looked ready to throw up. "You're shitting me."

Oscar shrugged. "The asswipes were spying. How the hell was I supposed to know it belonged to the cops?"

Cloris-Edna took a deep breath and threw one more wig mannequin against the wall. No more left to hurl. The heat of her rant began to cool. "And they have his *name,* his goddamn *name.*"

Bartlett aimed a killer stare at Oscar. "Of all the dumbass things you've pulled, this is the worst, except for the books."

Gorski frowned. "What are you talking about?"

Bartlett sneered and raised his cane at the man. "You know exactly what the fuck I'm talking about."

"Stop your imbecilic squabbling," Cloris-Edna demanded. "Listen to me! We are completely compromised. We have to close up and get out of here. Immediately."

"But my research!" Halliburton bit down on his knuckles.

"To hell with your research, child. Our entire dream is being be wiped out, extinguished." Cloris-Edna pressed the back of her hand to her forehead as if in a swoon from a vintage romance movie. It was one of her signature poses.

"The climactic experience for our guests has already begun."

Oscar's voice was low and menacing. "We have to finish it."

"Then go and see to it, you idiot. Get more champagne, Standish. The show will go on. The minute it's over, have the limos waiting to wisk them to the airport." She glowered as they gaped at her. "Don't just stand there, you two dunces, move!"

They fled the studio, Oscar the bowling ball and Standish the pin.

Cloris-Edna resumed pacing, despite her worsening balance on the stilettos. "This will be our last group of visitors. We'll have to cancel six months of lucrative bookings from the world's elite. We have nowhere else to open shop, not yet, anyway."

The old woman's knees began to sag. She held out her hand and Bartlett rushed to her side. "You're way overreacting, dearest," he said.

"Don't patronize me, you bad, bad boy!"

"Sorry." Bartlett rolled his eyes. "But you need to settle down. Those cops know nothing except that Oscar Gorski might be working for you as a security guard. No big deal, all perfectly legit." He helped the old woman ease onto her desk chair.

Her focus whipped Halliburton's way, and he flinched, ready to take the punch.

"What do you think, Nephew?"

He gulped. "I, uh, agree with Sonny. I think you're overdramatizing. I mean, what really do they have?"

She frowned. "You had better find out. Is there anything else I should know,, Halliburton?"

He shook his head, a bit too emphatically.

Cloris-Edna silently assessed him. He was weak, a silly pseudo-scientist like her brother, Keaton. She'd indulged them both. It had to end. As sweat began to bead above the minnow's chubby upper lip, she glared down her long nose. Time to pull the plug on his foolishness. She straightened her shoulders. "You must get rid of your lab assistant. Immediately."

"But—"

"You have no choice. She'll perform tonight. Go, Halliburton.

Now."

"But—"

"Now!"

He shuffled from the room, hunched like a beaten dog.

Cloris-Edna continued to Bartlett. "After today's final show, we'll halt our production and figure out what we're going to do next. We'll tell everyone we're developing new and exciting aspects of the experience. Raise our prices."

"Nice idea but the Honduran involvement is a cluster fuck for us. They discovered the second set of books and hurt me, bad." Bartlett glowered. "How do you think they knew about the money laundering?"

Cloris-Edna wiped her mouth with a shred of gold charmeuse. "I trust my people."

Bartlett's face hardened. "I don't trust Gorski."

She examined her fingernails. Two were badly broken. "Then we'll get rid of him."

Bartlett nodded. "In the meantime, I'll use my contacts to see what I can learn about this Detective Wu. I know Bea Middleton. She's a tenacious bitch. We may need to apply pressure."

"What are her vulnerabilities?" Cloris-Edna asked, seeming back in control of herself.

Bartlett raked a hand through his surfer do and leaned heavily on his cane. "The people closest to the woman are her children and her best friend, a photographer named Lucy Vega—very pregnant and living in a yurt in a remote Malibu canyon."

Cloris-Edna stretched her neck and stood up straight, emulating the starlet she used to be. She pulled a tube of red lipstick from her pocket and reapplied a slash of color.

"Remote is good. Let's think this through carefully. We can't afford mistakes. We'll rattle Miss Vega's cage, driving attention her way and creating a diversion, should buy us some extra time to get out of here."

Bartlett nodded and left the crone alone in her trashed studio.

Chapter 34

Izzy worked single-mindedly in the lab, trying to block out the suggestive music and the unholy crimes being perpetrated as she filled beakers. In her peripheral vision, she saw Jones slink in from the hallway, dressed in blue scrubs.

She looked up. "Dr. Jones, you'll be happy to know that the PCR reaction is complete. The amplified DNA was nicely separated, and the variations are easily distinguishable. The polymer you suggested functioned well with the capillary electrophoresis."

"Good, very good, indeed. But . . ." He plucked at his shirt as if the baggy fit was too tight.

Izzy paused. Why did he look so upset? She was sharing information that should make him pleased.

"The data's running as we speak," she continued. "The complete DNA profile of *Piscem Auratus* will be finalized and graphed shortly. Replication looks promising."

Jones leaned heavily against the stainless-steel counter. His hand gripped the electron microscope as if clutching a life preserver.

"It's over." His words were choked.

"What are you talking about?" Panic fluttered beneath Izzy's skin.

"They've pulled the plug on my research. On my life's work." He swiped a tear with the back of his hand.

"What? Why? Did I do something wrong? I assure you I've been meticulous." Her life depended on being indispensable to him.

"This has nothing to do with your competence, Isabelle. Forces beyond my control are at work. Your services are no longer needed. The project is being shut down."

"But we're just getting started." Her chest was a birdcage with a wild raptor fighting to escape and pluck out the professor's rat-like eyes.

"I'm sorry, Isabelle. Oscar will be here soon to take you to the studio. Costume fittings, makeup, rehearsal—you will be performing tonight."

Izzy's vision darkened; her breath came hard. "I'm going to die? Tonight? Ripped apart by your monstrosities?"

Halliburton shrugged. "Again, I'm sorrier than you know, but there is nothing I can do. Perhaps you could file your notes before Oscar arrives."

Izzy's anger at his indifference incinerated the panic. Fire pulsed through her fingers.

If she was going to survive, she had to kill him. Now.

Lurching toward the door to the crossover above the aquarium, she was pretty sure he'd follow. He did. He was a sucker for any opportunity to gaze lovingly at his fish, particularly *Piscem Auratus*—the golden, luminescent great white shark. The doc was like a new parent constantly astounded by his offspring's never-failing brilliance.

High above the atrium, Izzy pressed against the cold metal railing that circled the tanks on the catwalk and provided safety and support for feeding and care-taking procedures from the crossover. "But what about your great white and the others?"

"They'll be left behind." Jones gulped hard. "If the authorities manage to secure this place, hopefully, they'll rescue my dear ones before they perish."

He was clearly more concerned about his specimens' welfare than with the mayhem they inflicted on living humans. But could she kill a person herself? A man? Halliburton Jones?

Izzy leaned over the rail. The magnificent shark of gold prowled hungrily. She would not be its next meal.

It was now or never.

Izzy stepped back to gain momentum, then launched herself, striking the professor with everything she had. He cried out and clutched at her, catching a handful of her sleeve as he tumbled over the railing.

He scrambled to hoist himself back onto the catwalk, dragging Izzy down in the process. "You ungrateful bitch!"

Before she lost purchase and plunged to death along with him, Izzy shrugged out of her shirt. As it fell into the aquarium, Jones managed to grab her long ponytail. Shrieking as her hair ripped from its roots, she clawed at his grip. With her hair clutched in his hands, Jones propelled himself with a strong kick, then released her and snatched the lower of the two parallel railings with both hands. Little explosions popped in her vision. Izzy's scalp felt like it had been blowtorched.

He began to crawl over the railing and back onto the crosswalk.

"No!" Izzy dropped down and beat at his fingers, bit his hands. Imagined she had a mouthful of shark teeth instead of blunt incisors. Blood slicked the rail but he held fast. The great white broke the surface, its ghastly jaws wide. Her discarded pink scrub top disappeared. An *hors d'oeuvre.*

Izzy continued her assault on the professor's grasp. She was doing damage. He was beginning to falter. His thumb looked broken. Good.

The door to the control room flew open, banging loudly

against the metal wall. The crossover grid vibrated as Oz the Terrible rushed to join the death match. Barreling toward Izzy, he raised a heavy flashlight, ready to swing.

Izzy sprang away from Jones to sidestep Oz's attack. With her fist, she smashed him hard in the ribs as he flew by. The air whooshed from his lungs. He lost the weapon. It crashed and spun toward the edge of the crossover within Bartlett's grasp.

The wizard was beyond out of shape, but the professor wasn't. She and Jones both lunged for the weapon.

In one fast movement, he snatched it up and hoisted one leg securely over the lower railing.

Izzy leaped toward him and fought again to dislodge his hold. The translucent great white thrashed below in anticipation of a feast.

Like a jumping spider, Oz was suddenly on Izzy's back. Pressing his fingers around her neck, strangling her, he ripped at her clothing. She stumbled backwards, nailing him in the gut with her elbow. He groaned and his grip loosened. She smelled vomit.

As Izzy grappled with Oz, Jones gained better traction on the railing and was nearly back onto the crossover. He raised the flashlight and swung it at her head. She ducked. Oz didn't.

Jones landed a full blow across the bridge of Oz's nose. The animator crumpled to the floor, wailing in agony. Crimson bloomed on his face and speckled his superhero T-shirt.

The doctor again tried to clamber over the top railing. Flashlight still in hand, he was inches away from making it back onto the catwalk.

Angry shouting sounded from the lab.

A renewed shot of adrenaline coursed through Izzy's shaking body. Red sparks of fury pocked her vision. She slugged Halliburton Jones full in the face, then kicked him hard in the chest. She slammed her shin painfully into the rail in the process, but she'd made contact.

The flashlight dropped from his hand onto the lip of the

crossover.

This time it was hers.

His legs slipped from the railing and he dangled above the aquarium. Loud music continued to blast and lights strobed from below. Jones's fingers trembled, bloodless with the effort it took to maintain his hold on the lower railing. The shark's fearsome jaws snapped at his feet. The doctor's eyes met Izzy's. Desperate, disbelieving.

She shattered his hand with the bloody flashlight.

His shriek rent the atrium. He clawed at the air. A second later, a splash sounded from below. Churning water, screams, gasps for breath that would never come again.

"Feel what those girls felt, you asshole!"

She limped toward the control room. Oz, eyes swollen almost shut, was curled up on the floor of the crossover, whimpering.

Izzy slammed the control room door behind her and hit the lock. Over the production console, big screens showed clients clapping appreciation at the unexpected show. In high-def color, Professor Halliburton Jones was eaten alive by the love of his life, *Piscem Auratus*.

Chapter 35

Behind her, loud pounding on the door to the control room began. Izzy's heart raced. She rushed out the back door and down the steps to a subterranean level where a four-by-six-foot metal hatch blocked access to the canal and her only shot at escape.

The hinges on the hatch were caked with rust. She pulled hard, to no avail. She pulled again and again until she dripped with sweat and her arms quivered. No movement.

The seconds ticked by. The door above wouldn't hold Bartlett and his blood-sucking cronies much longer.

Izzy was determined to put every ounce of the energy and grit she had left into what might be her last opportunity to open the hatch. This was it. The thought of dying in this miserable stairwell was too much to bear. The final pull was for her life.

Isabelle Abbott took a deep breath, growled, huffed, and yanked so hard her shoulders felt like they'd popped from their sockets.

The hatch flew open.

Momentum knocked Izzy onto her back. Her head banged hard against the concrete floor. Pops sparked in her peripheral vision like bullet blasts but she steadied herself, rose, and stumbled into the gloom ahead.

The briny smell of saltwater filled her lungs. A dim light illuminated a wood plank dock. Above, in the control room, she heard the sound of frenetic voices and the lock being jimmied.

Izzy secured the hatch behind her, then turned and took stock of the empty mooring. There was just enough space for a small yacht or fishing boat. Clearly, she wouldn't get any kind of *Pirates of the Caribbean* ride out of here. Only pure evil trolled these waters.

This time of year, the ocean temperature hovered in the low sixties. She knew it was probably even colder in the darkness of the cavern. Swimming out was her only hope, but how long could she last before hypothermia set in? An hour? Expenditure of body heat from the physical exertion of her flight would cut that time in half, or more. What was the distance from this inky cul-de-sac to open ocean? Had Jones said a mile-and-a-half? Would she make it?

Above, she heard the control room door crack open. Angry voices filled the outside stairwell, and footfalls thudded down the cement steps. She had to act immediately.

Slipping into the oily water, the cold snatched her breath. The sound of Bartlett's people banging against the recalcitrant metal hatch chilled her even more. The hinges shuddered, barely holding.

Izzy gritted her teeth and plunged downward into the cave's cold black gullet.

—

Oscar, with two squat-bodied henchmen and bloody-faced Oz, pried the hatch open with a crowbar and a heavy-duty screwdriver.

"Faster, we gotta move faster," he grunted. Sweat beaded

his face.

They pushed, pulled, and beat on the metal until the door finally began to move. Moments later, the entry groaned open, twisting on its corroded hinges.

Just behind the men, Cloris-Edna growled and covered her painted red lips with her bony hand. Standish trembled at her side. Oscar leapt onto the empty dock.

The water was quiet, just a gentle lapping as the tide slowly rose. Condensation dripped from above.

"Shit. She can't be far." Oscar raised his AR, sprayed the small cove with gunfire and waited for anything dead to float to the surface. One silver-bellied barracuda bobbed up.

He turned to Cloris-Edna. She nodded, her face contorted.

"Let out the hammerheads," he roared to his comrades.

—

An hour later, Oscar, angry and agitated at the Abbott chick's escape, drove Bartlett's fancy Land Rover conservatively at the speed limit on his way to the Lucy Vega ranch assignment. He would not be stopped by the pigs for a random infraction. He knew traffic stops had ruined many a well-planned exit.

He rolled the unfortunate events of the last few days over in his mind. How had something so good gotten so fucked? Ol' Bartlett's rage and frustration were even beyond his own—— right off the Richter scale of pissed off. The Abbott girl's breakout had been outrageous. Devious bitch. She should've been the first to die. But now, with the hungry hammerheads loose and on the prowl, there was little chance her body would ever be recovered. This fiasco was all Hobbs's fault for recruiting her, but thanks to Bartlett, the cop was now rotting in an isolated desert arroyo.

Gorski couldn't believe the agent thought he was the mole. It had to be money-grubbing Halliburton. The doc's death was a relief actually. Always whining about his research funding—he was beyond tedious. The girl had done them a favor by tossing him in the tank.

Oscar glanced at his watch. Their getaway boat would enter the canal within the hour to pick up Cloris-Edna, Bartlett, Standish, and their hangers-on. Pacific access to the waterway had been there for decades without discovery. It was the perfect back door—too treacherous an outcropping to approach, it had little to offer the curious beyond a seemingly inaccessible rock face covered with seagull shit.

And then there was the money, lots of it. Bartlett seemed to trust Cloris-Edna to secure their online accounts and scrub any incriminating evidence. Maybe it was Cloris-Edna who was the leak, hoping for a nice payoff from Barahona. Wasn't she too old to be able to enjoy all that extra payola? The hag was definitely the brains of the operation. She'd sent the sex tour clients on their way with happy loins and a bottle each of delicious two-century-old vintage champagne a Baltic wreck diver pulled off the ocean floor in 2010. She knew how to make a business successful. But she was devious as hell. Whatever, he'd have to watch his back.

Oscar shifted his thoughts to the task at hand, He wasn't about to let another smartass broad slip through his fingers today. Although Cloris-Edna was hellbent on clearing out of Piscem Auratus immediately, they still needed a bit more time. Lucy Vega's disappearance would be a distraction that would give them what they needed to get away free and clear. A chopper would be waiting off the island to transport their Piscem group to a small airport in Palmdale for the final adios.

Oscar would join them in Palmdale after dumping Lucy Vega in the desert near Hobbs. He had to admit, offing a pregnant woman was a little spooky, but he'd done worse. After that, they were on to South America, the first leg of their escape. Next, it was Indonesia where there was no possibility of extradition, even if the cops eventually tracked them down.

It'd been a great run, but now it was time to pull up stakes in search of new opportunities. An isolated island in the Indian Ocean the old bitch raved about could be a primo location for their special brand of tourism. Maybe she deserved Barahona's bonus.

He glanced at his speedometer—ten miles over the limit. He eased off the gas. Oscar smiled as he turned inland onto Kanan Dume Road toward the Vega chick, alone at her remote rancho.

o-o-o

Slumped in the pungent and grossly stained backseat of Wu's county-issued ride, Bea dreamed of a cup of coffee and rubbed her aching head. She was no good at stakeouts—too ADHD to sit still. The warrant hadn't come through—not enough supporting evidence. All they could do was maintain surveillance and hope for some mitigating action that would give them enough to file another request. They had to get the hell inside Piscem Auratus *ASAP*. If something didn't give soon, it would be time to work outside the box.

Wu pushed his seat way back to give himself leg room as he caught up on his report writing—talking to himself and grumbling as he wrote. Beno played some violent-sounding videogame on his phone when suddenly there was silence. He lurched up straight. "Shit."

"What?" Wu sounded irritated.

They were all irritated, patience frayed.

"The bug I put on Bartlett's car? It was moving down the coast, but it just stopped."

"Where?" Bea asked. "At a grocery store? Probably buying bulk wet wipes for his sicko's excretions."

Beno gulped. "Uh-oh. He's at . . ." He turned toward Wu, his face paled. "Oh, fuckinay."

"Wanna be more specific?" Wu grimaced and closed his laptop.

"Turned inland on Kanan Dume." Beno twisted in his seat and looked over his shoulder at Bea. "He's at the Vega ranch."

Her stomach plunged like an untethered elevator. "Oh, my God." Bartlett was going after her closest friend who was isolated, pregnant, and vulnerable. She grabbed her cell and punched in Lucy's number.

Beno snatched the cop radio and called for reinforcements.

Wu careened out of his parking space down the street from Piscem and rocketed toward PCH.

Chapter 36

In the early evening cool of the yurt, Sister Catherine Lucia watched Lucy doze in the chaise next to a table where the nun had spread an array of medicinal plants she'd found growing wild on the ranch. Atop a drying rack lay dusty green valley oak for diarrhea relief, oleander for heart problems, asthma, and ringworm, and Cleveland sage for pain control.

Lucy tossed restlessly. Sister didn't like the pallid tinge of her niece's skin or the tepid dampness of her forehead. An hour previously, she'd administered a dose of black haw and partridgeberry to ease the cramping that had come much more frequently over the last day. The nun had been on the phone with Lucy's physician who basically said—wait and watch. In her long tenure as a nurse and *curandera,* Sister'd done just that with enough pregnant women to know when things weren't right. Elsa should be home in an hour—she'd drive them to the hospital in Santa Monica. Ready or not, this baby wanted out. God willing, he would be alive and well, and so would Lucy.

The sleeping patient's cellphone quietly chimed. Sister took a look—Bea was calling, likely to check in for an update and to offer words of encouragement. Sister turned off the phone. Lucy could call her friend back after she woke from her needed nap.

Sitting back in her chair, the old woman continued reading the third Brother Cadfael mystery. A fifteenth century monk who had seen the ills of the world before withdrawing to a monastery where he had a medical practice involving plants, potions, and sleuthing. Sister swooned as he concocted a poultice of herbs, clay, and charcoal. A character after her own heart.

She barely heard the vehicle roll slowly across the gravel drive outside the yurt. The dogs barking brought her back fast to Rancho de la Vega. Locks clicked and a car door opened. She heard Maddie snarl. That dog never snarled. Then a loud yelp and whimper as if she'd been kicked.

The old woman rose, put down the book, and went to the doorway.

A stocky, densely-muscled man with a shaved head strode toward her from a shiny black SUV. He smiled. It was a lizard's smile—taut and predatory. She knew it well from her years as a *curandera* among drug dealers and corrupt officials in the Guerrero foothills. Sister shuddered and stepped back into the yurt. Closed and locked the door. She'd lived her life among dangerous men. This was one.

Sister reached for Lucy's cell phone but before she could hit 9-1-1, the man burst through the flimsy barrier, gun drawn.

He batted the phone from her hand. It bounced along the floor and skidded into a corner.

Lucy woke and cried out, tried to rise from the chair. The effort was too much. She sank back down and licked her dry lips. She wiped away sleep. Her eyes narrowed and focused on the intruder. "Who are you? What do you want?"

"Get up, Miss Vega. We're going for a ride."

Sister Catherine Lucia helped Lucy stand and wrapped her small arm around her niece's waist. "Can you no see she pregnant and very sick? She no go for ride. Lucia's health *mucho* dangerous, baby, too."

Oscar hesitated for an instant, recalling the reality of Lucy's condition. He swore under his breath. In that moment, Sister leaned against her drying rack and pocketed a hefty pinch of flaked oleander leaves.

"I don't give a fuck. The bitch is coming with me." He waved his gun in the air.

Sister clung tighter to Lucy. "She no go without me."

Oscar sneered. "Your choice, old lady. Die with her. Now move."

—

"He's still there," Beno said. "Bug hasn't moved."

Wu clutched the steering wheel so hard his hands were becoming one with it.

They raced by Leo Carrillo State Beach, lights flashing. Surfers stripping out of wetsuits barely paused to note the speeding car. A mother grabbed her youngster who was about to cross the highway from the campground.

"Just heard from Pete." Beno glanced at Bea. "He's on his way with a couple of County Sheriff's black-and-whites. Just turning onto Kanan."

Knowing Pete was almost there, Bea felt her anxiety dip for a second, then amp back up, realizing they could have a volatile hostage situation. Those didn't always end well. As they flew by Zuma Beach, she shut her eyes and prayed.

Finally, they turned onto Kanan and came upon a cruiser parked at the foot of the road up to Rancho de la Vega. Wu slowed and pulled in next to the county squad. The officer approached Wu, who flashed his credentials.

The broad-chested guy waved them on through.

Pete Anthony emerged from the yurt as Wu skidded to a stop at the barn. Two local cop units were parked next to Pete's vehicle. The officers were patrolling a perimeter and stringing yellow crime scene tape.

Bea jumped out of the car and ran to Pete, threw herself into his arms. "Is she okay?"

He said nothing but held her tightly. She stepped back, trembling.

He took her by the shoulders. "She's gone. Sister, too. And it doesn't look like they went quietly."

Beno and Wu immediately joined Pete and Bea. Beno gaped at his phone tracker. "Says Bartlett's car is still here." He looked around, searching for something to pin the agent to this location.

Pete extended his open palm toward Wu. A mud-encrusted item that resembled a garage door opener was in his hand. The GPS bug.

Bea pressed on her chest as if she were trying to keep it from exploding.

Pete frowned. "Found it over by the yurt."

Wu paled. "Shit." His jaw clenched and unclenched. "My guess is he's heading toward Palmdale. That's where they found the body of Cole Hobbs, the cop pimp. Nice airport up there for a quick getaway out of the metro."

He checked his phone. "The warrant just came though. We're into Piscem Auratus." He took a deep breath, blew it out, then locked eyes with Pete. "Beno and I are heading back to oversee the search of the aquarium compound."

"Okay, good," Pete said. "Lucy's abduction is LA County so we'll take it from here. You and I'll coordinate."

"I'm with you, Pete." Bea turned and jogged toward his car.

He started to protest, but knew better. "Okay, let's roll. We've got an APB out on his car."

Wu gave his LACSD colleague a thumbs-up. "Today's the day we're taking these fuckers down."

"Roger that, detective."

Chapter 37

This time Beno took the wheel. Wu rode shotgun manning communications. First to his captain, "I need backup at Piscem Auratus. The warrant's good for a full search. Roll SWAT and dispatch an ambo on call. Have no idea in hell what we're gonna find."

The approach strategy was discussed and locked in with a thumbs-up from brass and the support teams.

Next, Wu called Casey. Ordinarily he wouldn't bring in a civilian, especially one with so much at stake, but this was not an ordinary situation. If there was anything at Piscem Auratus that could be identified as belonging to Isabelle, or any clue as to her presence or absence, Casey would be more likely to spot it than his investigators. They needed information without delay.

She picked up on the first ring and was out the door as they spoke.

It was over an hour before everyone was in place and ready to launch.

Wu was on point, SIG Sauer P220 drawn, with Beno at his

heels and SWAT just behind them circling the house to secure the perimeter. The detective stepped onto the porch. "Ventura Metro Police. Open up!"

He shouted it twice. No response.

"Breach the sucker." He motioned to a beefy duo toting a metal battering ram between them. They swung it hard.

The heavy, artistically-sculpted hardwood door barely moved. All that happened was that a bas relief carp got its head bashed in.

They swung repeatedly, until the jamb began to splinter, and finally gave way.

The door fell inward and the SWAT team swarmed into the house followed by Beno and Wu. Like a finely choreographed dance squad, they cleared each room.

"Looks like recent guests." Beno pointed to rumpled sheets and a side table stacked with Asian porn magazines and Ventura-Santa Barbara tourist brochures.

Wu nodded. "Let's get crime scene in here, STAT."

Beno made the call over the radio. Moments later, Demi, Meghan Li, and several of their colleagues appeared from standby, suited up and ready to go. Casey had followed them in. A stab of fear for what she might see rattled Wu's chest, but better to have her here helping than off alone, thinking about going rogue again.

Already, he could sense her antennae sweeping the pricey, hacienda-style surroundings.

"Casey, like we discussed, stay back until we call all-clear. Understand?" His words felt hard, but they had to be.

She nodded agreement and stood aside to give the CSI and their photographer room to work. Meghan handed her a pair of blue protective gloves and booties to slip on.

When the house was secured, another formidable barrier in the form of heavy metal double doors blocked access to the inner facility. After bludgeoning them to no avail, the experts set an explosive that finally did the job. Acrid, stinging gunpowder filled the hallway.

Wu, Beno, and half a dozen SWAT team members disappeared through the charred opening. Their footsteps pounded down wide steps. At the bottom landing there was yet another set of doors.

The battering ram guys stepped up again but not before Wu tried the push-handle. The doors swung open.

"Hot damn." He quickly assessed the environment.

Three corridors spun off from a brightly-lit foyer hung with vintage movie posters of Esther Williams and a slim brunette who was probably Cloris-Edna Jones back in her glory days. An array of autographed head shots of old-time actors and actresses in swim suits were meticulously lined up like synchronized swimmers rising from the aqua blue walls.

Casey wondered, "Was every mermaid destroyed an act of revenge against her failed career?"

Beno shrugged. "Who the hell knows about any of this psycho shit."

Wu split the shooters into groups and each crew headed down a dark hallway, firearms ready. Canned techno music leaked from overhead speakers, and the air smelled strongly of fish and brine. Detective Wu, Beno, and two sharpshooters moved stealthily into an area marked *Piscem Auratus Aquaria*.

"Bastards love their Latin." Beno hissed.

Fluorescent lights blazed overhead as they entered what looked to be a lab with empty counter spaces that likely had contained equipment. Halliburton Jones was a shark DNA researcher—this had to be his lair. Chairs were overturned and papers strewn across the floor. A stack of Petri dishes looked ready to tumble.

Wu directed SWAT through a portal and onto a scaffold-like platform that circled high above four multi-story aquariums—like a watery pie cut in quarter slices. Moments later, the team called 'Clear.'

Casey again trailed them in and moved to peruse the empty

lab. Before Wu could reprimand her for following without his say-so, she turned and held up a round wad of blue cloth.

"Izzy's ponytail scrunchie. I'm sure it's hers. She was here." Face pale, Casey turned back toward the countertops, eyes scanning for more evidence. "Maybe she was working with Jones on some kind of research project."

Detective Wu could hear the trepidation in her voice.

"Wu!" Benno called from the aquarium area. "You gotta see this."

The detective jogged to the doorway, Casey at his side.

Beno's eyes were wide. "There's blood everywhere on this fuckin' catwalk."

"Oh, my God. Izzy's?" Casey clutched at the collar of her T-shirt and steadied herself against the cold, white-tiled wall.

Wu gulped hard and questioned himself again for bringing her in, but she'd identified her sister's hair thingy confirming Isabelle's presence. "Beno, get Demetrius down here."

Wu saw Casey creep over to what appeared to be a tangle of bloody, long hair stuck to a railing around the tanks. She reached toward it then quickly pulled her hand away before he could call out a warning not to touch anything. "My sister has long hair."

Jaw clenched, Wu peered into the atrium below where a crime scene tech moved slowly around the room's perimeter, video camera on her shoulder. Then, his focus shifted to the closest ocean blue tank immediately on his left. "What the hell is that?"

A translucent golden shark the size of a school bus, prowled at the shadowy bottom among rocks and sea weed. Casey moved next to the detective and they observed the predator glide through the water, restless, agitated, and likely hungry.

"Looks like a great white," she said. "Probably genetically engineered to look like, uh, like golden glass. Amazing. Izzy was off to buy a koi with this appearance when she disappeared."

Wu scrutinized the creature. It was surreally beautiful.

"Maybe this monster's a leftover from when the military ran the place. Could relate to Dr. Jones's research."

Beno joined them on the deck. The radio on his shoulder squawked quietly.

They moved on to the next tank clockwise around the circle. It held a stunning tableau of glittery kelp, giant shells, corals, and schools of small, colorful exotic fish. Overhead, oxygen tanks were attached to air hoses.

"Obviously a set for some kind of undersea mermaid show. I remember a description in one of those deep web photos Bijan dredged up." Wu wondered, Had Isabelle been one of the stars?

Wu, Beno, and Casey moved toward the third aquarium. It contained a school of at least a hundred-silvery black fish with roundish bodies the size of large pizzas. A prominent underbite of shark-like teeth made for a horde of menacing grins.

"Shit, those are goddamn piranhas." Beno grimaced.

Farther to their right was a half-empty tank. A single, hammerhead shark circled, then disappeared into the blackness of an open hatch at the bottom of the aquarium. How many others had been let out?

Before Wu could look more closely, a SWAT duo emerged from a door at the far end of the crossover. A short, wiry gunner named Killebrew said, "Looks like a control room in here for some kind of high-tech visual effects and a kick-ass sound system. And downstairs there's a metal door that was ripped off its hinges. Opens onto a dock and that underground channel you told us about. No sign of anybody. I think they rabbited."

Beno stepped aside and finished a conversation on the radio. He turned to Wu. "All's clear in the rest of the building. Some freaky stuff, though. Demi wants to call in the feds to help process things."

Wu nodded. "Okay. We'll need all the help we can get with this shit."

Beno made the call then followed Casey and Wu carefully around bloody footprints and into the TV-station-type control room. A black hoodie had fallen onto the floor next to an ashtray overflowing with half-smoked blunts. The smell was pungent. A partially opened duffle contained technical manuals, bottles of medication, and something silky and red. Trophy underwear swiped from a mermaid? Who knew. Demi's crew would handle it.

Eight large, high-def monitors surrounded the operating console. All were dark except for one in the center that held an undulating image of busty mermaids with orgasmic faces of popular Hollywood stars.

"How the hell do they do that?" Beno was momentarily dumbfounded .

"Augmented reality, AR." Wu's eyes narrowed. "Live-action and digital information is integrated. Flip on the goggles and you're sucked into a totally realistic environment. Seen it used for firefighter training. Figures that it'd be hot shit for porn."

Casey disappeared down the stairs toward the canal. Wu frowned and dashed behind her. "Hold up, Casey."

He and Beno stepped though the ruptured hatch. A crowbar lay on the dock in the semi-darkness. Wu perused the mooring. To the left gaped a large dark tunnel, perhaps thirty-five feet both high and wide. Plenty of space to accommodate a getaway craft.

To the right, a smaller cavern opened in the direction of the aquariums.

Casey knelt down and picked at something lodged between the wood slats.

"What do you have there?" Wu asked.

Casey slowly rose. "These were my grandmother's." She held a small, creamy pearl earring in her fingers. "Izzy never took them off. She left us a message, Mac. She's trying to swim out."

A mighty splash broke the water below the dock. Casey teetered and stumbled. Wu grabbed her and pulled her away from the edge.

A fin sliced the dark surface of the water, then a broad bony head like a truck fender with small headlights on each end emerged and disappeared into the channel.

Chapter 38

They left the traffic behind when Oscar turned onto the rugged Angeles Forest Highway north of the suburban communities of La Cañada Flintridge. The sun had disappeared below the western horizon and the misty blue of twilight had faded to black. A waning half-moon silvered the landscape like mercury on pennies.

Lucy had travelled this winding, dangerous route over the San Gabriel Mountains and into the Antelope Valley a handful of times. The country was rocky and barren and the drop-off from the south edge of the crumbling road shoulder was terrifyingly precipitous. The opposite side brought walls of decomposing granite, flat dry washes, and an occasional trail used for off-roading.

Tall green trees, like those in the Eastern U.S., did not grow in the parched Angel's Forest. The leggy scrub oak and cacti that survived here welcomed scorpions, fire ants, and rattlesnakes—but not humans.

Cell reception was also zip. They were on their own.

Lucy's contractions were no longer random but came at regular intervals. With her hands miserably zip-tied to the base of the passenger-side headrest in front of her, she breathed into the spasms.

Sister, pressed to her niece's side, had protested vehemently and launched a passionate homily on her arthritic wrists as Oscar tried to cuff the feisty old woman.

He winced as if her torrent of words were fingernails scraping a Catholic school blackboard. "Too bad you don't have arthritis of the damn mouth," he said. Finally, just to shut her up, Oscar relented, figuring the scrawny, gray-haired bitch could do little harm.

Lucy also sensed that he had a shred of discomfort about manhandling a nun. She'd seen the Saint Christopher's medal dangling from his tree-trunk neck.

"She in labor, *señor*. You must take to hospital. Baby too small, need help."

"Babies are the least of your worries, Sister." Oscar said as he munched on potato chips.

Lucy's pain intensified. This was something new, not the irritating cramps of the past. These contractions were the real deal and were escalating unbearably.

She panted through each new wave. Sister rubbed her niece's shoulders and neck and whispered support.

Lucy moaned. A gush of liquid soaked her loose, pale yellow dress and the back seat.

"Her water break!" Sister scrambled for something to sop up the flood. She pulled a sandy beach towel from behind the car seat. A couple of stained fast-food napkins came with it. The smell of amniotic fluid was earthy and pungent.

"Oh, shit," Oscar whined. "Can't believe this is happening to me."

"No, you asshole, it's happening to *me!*" Lucy cried out. Another pang squeezed her diaphragm like electric pliers. She gasped and tried to focus on Lamaze-style breathing. Sweat slicked her face.

"How long to *médico?*" Sister rolled down the window a few inches where it stuck. Oscar had the child lock activated.

He took a quick sip from a Starbuck's cup and growled. "There's no fuckin' *médico,* Sister."

Abruptly, he pulled over to the side of the dark road, killed the lights, and got out of the car.

Lucy gasped and clutched Sister's hand. *This is it. He's going to murder us and dump us here. I'll never get to see my child.* Tears welled in her eyes.

The labor took her breath away again. Even thoughts of death faded into the background.

With the sound of pee hitting rocks at the side of the road, Bartlett let out a groan of relief. Sister leaned forward, snatched his coffee from the front console and dropped something into the cup. She swished the liquid around, then put the top back on the drink.

"What was that?" Lucy gasped, panting.

"*Adelfa*—you call it oleander, *mija.*" The old woman crossed herself and murmured something about forgiveness. "Dunno if he drink it, but maybe. Will make the heart very sick. I got no other weapon."

"You're a bleeping genius." Lucy grabbed her aunt's hand again. She wasn't ready for another brutal contraction, but nature is ruthless.

"About two minutes apart now, maybe less. Bring legs up if you can, *mija.* I check *cerviz,* see if *el niño* peek out." She pressed the cabin light switch.

"Turn that damn thing off." Oscar growled as he zipped his pants and returned to the car. He slid in and slammed the door.

Sister obeyed. Lucy knew her aunt had seen enough. The infant wouldn't tolerate confinement much longer.

Their kidnapper took a sip of coffee and grimaced but still drank more. "Fuckin' cold."

"*Señor,* you let Lucia hands go. She giving birth, can no

run away. *Por favor*, please, *señor*. The Lord no wan' to hurt pregnant woman and helpless *bambino*."

He banged on the steering wheel, then jumped from the car again. He pulled out a long serrated knife. Sister threw her arms protectively around her niece and winced.

He cut Lucy's zip ties. "No more talk, hear me? Be fuckin' quiet, *silencio*, or I cut more than zip ties." He pricked sister's cheek with the tip of the blade.

She crossed herself.

He glowered and returned to the front seat, flicked on the headlights, and pulled onto the empty desert highway.

Lucy slumped back and rubbed her bruised wrists, struggling to return feeling to her fingers.

"*Sí, sí*, señor, no talk, no talk—but how long to *médico?*" Sister Catherine Lucia persisted, her voice increasingly strident. She placed her hands atop Lucy's belly and gently prodded. "Need help, need help, *señor*."

Oscar snarled. "I said, shut the fuck up!" He took another swig of coffee and turned on an oldies radio station. The reception was staticky. A county singer crooned about small town girls and broken hearts. "God damn Bartlett for getting me into this," he grumbled.

Seat belt," sister whispered to Lucy. She pulled at the buckle.

"No, I can't—"

"You must." Sister strapped them both in.

About three sets of contractions later, the car began to swerve. Oscar struggled to stay in the lane.

He rubbed at his eyes. Muttered "What the hell?" as he finished the coffee.

Two more contractions and he turned left onto a dirt road. Lucy caught a glimpse of the lights of Palmdale shimmering far in the distance. Vomit rose in her throat as the SUV bumped over potholes.

"Where you take us?" Sister demanded.

"Someplace where you won't have to worry 'bout nothing

much longer." He scrubbed at his face, now filmed with perspiration. "Shit. What's happening?"

Lucy squeezed Sister's arm.

The SUV veered off the track, hit a berm of loose gravel. Oscar violently overcorrected.

Lucy's shoulder banged hard against the door. Pain radiated into her chest. Then, a round of spasms hit like lightning. One after another. She felt a rush of warm liquid again soak her thighs. This time the coppery smell of blood assaulted her nostrils.

Oscar sped up. The driver's side of the SUV ground against a cliffside flanking the road. Pebbles fell through the partly-open window.

Sister gripped Lucy close and began to pray loudly, making sure God heard her.

"Shuhhh the fuhhh up!" His words slurred and his body twitched.

Sister shouted out the Lord's Prayer. *"Padre nuestro que estás en los cielos . . ."*

"I can't breathe." Oscar gurgled, let go of the wheel and clawed his chest.

Then the SUV lurched forward, sideswiped an outcropping of boulders, spun sideways, flipped over, and rolled like dice on a game table.

Chapter 39

It seemed like she'd been swimming forever. The darkness was complete and Izzy couldn't stop shivering in the dank cold. She rested her hand against the edge of the cave wall—it was the only way to keep her bearings. Sharp barnacles scratched at her skin. Then, something rough and sandpapery grazed her legs.

A hot stab of panic pierced the chill. She brought her knees to her chest and froze. Her dulling senses sharpened.

What had touched her? A sea turtle? A reef shark? What species would venture into a dark cave? Or was she becoming hypothermic and hallucinating? *No, this is dead real.*

Another touch, firmer now. A splash. Had they released the hammerheads? Izzy's intestines loosened.

Maybe the creature would just investigate and move on. She remembered the childhood game of statue-maker she'd played with Casey and their neighborhood friends. She never won—she could never hold still. But this time, she had to win because now a wrong move could mean death.

Slowly and carefully, she ran her hand along the water line, above the razor-sharp crustaceans to the slick mossy wall of the cave. She felt an indentation in the rocks, a shallow ledge. Could she gain a handhold to lift herself out of the channel and onto it? And could she do it without seeming like a wounded, tasty, sea otter?

This time she could sense the beast coming at her—a ripple, agitation in the water. The encounter was more aggressive—a jab, a strong nudge—clearly a shark. Her heart raced.

If Bartlett and Oscar had let out the hammerheads, the creatures would be famished. There must have been twenty or thirty in the tank, maybe more. Would they fight over bloody chunks of her body?

There was no time to hesitate. The shark's next run at her could be lethal.

Kicking her leg up over the barnacles, Izzy felt them slice at her skin but she got a foothold. Her hands scrabbled at the slippery rock shelf. She was able to gain purchase and pull herself up, arms shaking from the effort. With her other foot, Izzy dug into the crust of sharp shells with her toes and hoisted herself onto the ledge. It was a narrow indentation—maybe two feet deep and four feet long. Crouched and bleeding, wounds burning like fire, she pressed her back against the icy hard stone, trying to disappear into it. The sharks continued to prowl, frenzied by the blood.

If one of the great fish decided to leap out of the water and grab her, she'd be done for. Izzy began to tremble uncontrollably. The cold, combined with the adrenaline rush, was taking its toll.

In utter blackness, she could sense her chances at survival slipping away. She touched her remaining pearl earring with stiffening fingers.

Find me, Casey. I'm counting on you.

Chapter 40

The SUV tumbled to a stop, upright on its wheels. From the chaos of the crash, all was now still but for the ticking of the engine. The airbags were limp balloons after a bad party and the smell of sulfur and gasoline polluted the air.

Lucy heard the snap of Sister's seatbelt click open. The old woman leaned into the front seat—her hand reached toward Bartlett's neck. She pressed her fingers against his carotid for a long minute. "*Muerto.*" She slumped back and crossed herself once again.

"We gotta get out of here." Lucy yanked the door handle but it wouldn't budge. The window had shattered. She brushed away glass shards and began to crawl out. She gasped in pain and fell back in her seat.

"I go first, help you." Sister struggled over Lucy through the window.

The old woman's face was bloody and her shoulder looked strangely angled and dislocated. Once outside, she clutched the door handle and dropped to her knees. A scream rose from her lips—she had wrenched her shoulder back into place.

Seeing her aunt's agonized face, tears rolled down Lucy's cheeks. Overwhelmed by chaos and pain—she was losing it. And the baby was coming.

"Be strong, Lucia. We must survive." The car door jammed shut, Sister carefully helped Lucy through the window then they struggled over to a flat area well away from the vehicle.

Lucy whispered, "Bartlett probably has an earthquake kit in the back. We all carry them." With the next wave, she gritted her teeth so hard she felt like they were going to snap off.

Sister ran to the car and returned with a plastic storage box. Sure enough—water, granola bars, a small first aid kit, and a solar blanket. She laid out her resources and checked the baby's progress again.

"I see little head. Push soon, *mija.*"

Lucy screamed. "Shit, is it too late for the epidural?"

Sister rolled her eyes. "We no even have tequila." She settled her niece on the soggy beach towel and covered her with the solar blanket.

Lucy gasped between murderous contractions. "Nobody knows we're here. How are we going to get help?" She moaned in pain. "My baby will die!" She fought down the panic.

The nun paused in rifling through the first aid supplies, her face grim in the moonlight. The smell of gasoline was increasingly pungent on the wind.

Lucy grabbed her aunt's hand. "We have to blow up the car, Sister. People will see the blaze. There's hardly any brush for miles, the fire won't spread." Thoughts of the devastating wildfire that leveled her ranch and the fires across the state that brought such cruel mayhem scorched through Lucy's brain. She clutched her belly, turned away, and vomited.

Sister dampened a wad of gauze and wiped Lucy's mouth. Insisted she drink a bit of water. "Okay. Blow up car—how we do it?"

Lucy panted, thinking, trying to organize her thoughts amid

the all-encompassing misery of impending childbirth. A few synapses somewhere in her lizard brain still functioned. "Get Bartlett's gun. Had it in a shoulder holster under his jacket. You'll shoot out the gas tank."

Sister hesitated for a nanosecond then dashed back to the SUV and yanked open the passenger door. Lucy watched her search through the dead agent's clothing. She found the gun.

Next, the nun wrestled the agent's body from the driver's seat and lugged him away from the car.

"Sister . . ." Lucy began to protest.

"No desecrate, must respect," the old woman croaked out. Then she stopped, bent over and gripped her shoulder, stood up and continued to drag Bartlett's dead weight behind a pile of boulders. She crossed herself and scurried back to Lucy, a Barretta clutched in her small hand.

"Do it now." Lucy groaned and tried to sit up. "Shoot!"

"We not safe from explosion. Hide behind rocks. Come, Lucia, one last move. Then, time to push."

Lucy crawled on her hands and knees behind a granite crag that looked like a Stonehenge relic—upright, tall, and pointing toward the heavens. She shivered. *What kind of sign was this?*

Then signs became irrelevant.

She pushed, feeling the baby's head emerge. "Sister, shoot the damn gas tank. Now!"

Sister stumbled from Lucy's side and crouched behind a boulder, using it to steady her hand. She planted her feet, held her breath and took final aim at the wreck.

She emptied the clip into the gas tank. Sparks flew as bullets grazed the metal. Sister ducked down and hunched protectively by her niece.

Silence.

Then a whoosh.

The explosion was deafening. Even sheltered by the rocks they could feel the blowback. The sky lit up like a mortar blast. Gravel rained down.

Then, at the foot of the ancient pillar, little Henry Michael surged into the world.

Sister wrapped the child in her skirt to keep his scrawny preemie body warm. He was as still as the surrounding granite. She administered CPR and he began to breathe. Then he stopped and began again several times. Little puffs, two-finger chest compressions over and over. The fragile lungs fought for air.

Exhausted, Lucy and Sister Catherine Lucia huddled together over the tiny, struggling child and prayed.

Chapter 41

While waiting for the Coast Guard, Wu met with the Channel Islands Harbormaster, a lanky man, thin as a mast with intelligent blue eyes bracketing a long drooping nose. His colleague, a heavily freckled Ventura Harbor Patrol Officer named Dixon, was a husky coil of energy, ready to spring.

A middle-aged male named Hollister, owner of Ventura Pier Sportfishing and Dive Company, addressed the law-enforcement group.

"An hour-and-a-half ago, two men dashed into the shop waving a wad of cash at Ainsley, my reservations clerk. They wanted to rent a fishing boat, but when she demanded a credit card and driver's license they knocked her down and took off with the keys. A smash and grab. I keep the fobs on hooks behind the counter." Hollister clenched and unclenched his fists. "Took my Boston Whaler 350 Outrage. Flies at 40 knots—almost fifty miles per hour—best vessel in my fleet. Shit, I loved that boat almost as much as my dog. You gotta nail those bastards."

"Roger that, man." Officer Dixon bounced on the balls of his feet; a pugilist ready to throw a knockout punch. "Nobody rips off our pier businesses." His eyes went to the Coast Guard patrol craft still a half mile away. He complained, "The perps'll be in Tijuana by the time the Coasties show up."

The harbormaster shook his head, an exasperated frown lined his forehead. "Aside from the local boat rip-off, these are federal crimes happening outside our one-mile jurisdiction, Dix. And our Coast Guard station's the best in the business. Their resources are way beyond ours, so be patient."

"Yeah, yeah. I know." Dixon nodded to Wu and the harbormaster. "Anything we can do to help bag these creeps, we're here."

Wu felt a pang of empathy for his frustration. "Thanks, sir."

The harbormaster lowered his voice as Dixon stepped away to check his cell phone. "Guy's a bit of a hothead, but he's a damn good seaman. He and his crew'll be on backup for you guys."

The radio on his belt came to life. A boat collision on the peninsula, capsized catamaran. Drinking involved and people in the water. "Dix, let's boogie. We're off to the rescue," he said. "Best of luck, Detective."

So much for backup.

Wu shook the harbormaster's hand and thanked him for his help. Dixon saluted and jogged toward his patrol boat. Hollister returned to the dive shop, still muttering about his Boston Whaler.

Casey and Beno chatted with Ainsley, the young woman from Hollister's shop—a local college student with blonde dreadlocks and a toned swimmer's body. The security camera nabbed a fuzzy shot of one of the men who attacked her and swiped the keys. Beno texted it in to HQ hoping for positive facial recognition results.

Wu joined the group as Beno brought up the freeze frame of Oscar Gorski he'd received days earlier from the LA County Sheriff's.

"According to Ainsley's description," he turned to Wu,

"sounds like the perp could be Bartlett's enforcer." Beno held the phone toward the woman for a good look.

Removing her sunglasses, the clerk studied the picture, and shook her head. "Huh-uh. Not him."

Damn. Beno brought up a photo of Halliburton Jones.

"Nope. The dude was tall, bleached blonde hair, fifty trying to look thirty."

Beno glanced at Wu, showed her the photo of Agent Sonny Bartlett.

She pursed her lips and nodded. "That's the dude. For sure."

Bingo.

She continued. "The other guy was a squirrelly little worm. Stayed off camera. His eyes zoomed around like flies on roadkill. Definitely high. And his face had lost a fight with a brick wall."

Wu smirked and thanked Ainsley for the help.

0-0-0

A few minutes later, Wu, Beno, and Casey boarded a Coast Guard patrol boat from the Channel Islands Station—a twenty-five-foot rapid response craft propelled by twin Honda 225 outboards. They were greeted by a no-nonsense crew of three men and a woman with *Paramedic* embroidered across her shirt pocket. Uniformed in navy blue with orange floatation vests and USCG baseball caps, the officers exuded competence and professionalism.

Once onboard, introductions were made. Beno, Casey, and Wu were outfitted with life jackets and then the powerful engines revved. Captain Dutch Visser, fortyish and blond with a SIG Sauer at his hip, hit the gas and turned the craft southeast toward Point Mugu Navy Station and Port Hueneme. It was there that the islet likely the door into Bartlett's lair, lurked offshore.

Alone at the bow, Wu's chest tightened with anticipation. Overhead, a Jayhawk helicopter tracked their movement toward the location identified on the map Bea had received from Dr. Fawcett. Beno chatted with the paramedic, a young African

American woman named JoJo Palmer. He filled her in on what they might encounter ahead.

Wu watched a brown pelican fold its awkward body into a sleek missile and plunge toward the water in pursuit of an unsuspecting meal. As the bird splashed down and re-emerged, flopping fish in its beak, the waning sun touched the horizon. Gold spread across the dark line like shimmer on a blade. White-sheeted sailboats began to gather and converge on the harbor after a perfect day on the water. Perfect, if you weren't Isabelle Abbott, that is. Wu knew her survival was a longshot. He hated that fact.

The water was choppy and Wu found the cool, salty spray on his face bracing. Casey remained in the cabin looking over the map with the navigator. She glanced out the window toward the bow and caught his eye, gave him a thumbs-up.

Wu nodded, distressed at what would likely be the grim outcome of this rescue attempt. Even if Izzy'd managed to survive Bartlett and his murder-the-mermaid scheme, the sharks and hypothermia were equally as lethal.

Chapter 42

Captain Visser joined Wu on the bow. "I told the ranger on Anacapa Island we're on operations. The area's overseen by the National Park Service so we'll keep them in the loop. You never know—these pirates could end up heading their way."

Wu nodded. Visser continued. "I reviewed the map you provided and turns out we do know about this islet—really just a big rock, part of the brown pelican rookery. It's barely a quarter mile offshore and has some kind of cave entrance. The ranger says it's been closed off with serious iron grating for years, decades."

"Surprising it has remained so isolated."

"We really don't monitor that area often. It's off-limits to park visitors and the general public. Because of the treacherous currents, it's near impossible to land a boat or even get close. Seems like the spot has slipped through the jurisdictional cracks. The Navy controlled it at one point."

Wu chewed at his lip, tasted salt. "How do you think these assholes have been getting their boats in and out if it's so hazardous, and locked down?"

"My guess is somebody's a helluva boat pilot, and they've got to have altered the entrance. Maybe now it opens electronically, by remote." Visser rubbed at his leathery forehead and adjusted his sunglasses. "If the gate's secure, we have the breaching tools you asked for and we've piloted this rig though hell and back a number of times. We can do this."

"Thanks, Captain. I'm just praying Ms. Abbott's sister is still alive."

A dozen bottlenose dolphins danced in the wake of a yacht heading back toward the harbor. Visser grabbed his binoculars and peered out across the Santa Barbara Channel.

Wu glanced back at Casey. Her gaze seemed fixed on the carefree dolphins.

Twenty minutes later, the Coast Guard boat circled the rock. Waves clashed violently and pounded the sheer, inaccessible cliffs that dripped with grayish heaps of guano. There was one small area that held a narrow, vertical slot, like a long crack in the face of the cliff. Elephant seals lazed on flat rocks at the base.

Overhead, the chopper texted birds-eye-view photos of the area. There was indeed a slot, larger than it seemed from their perspective on the water. The boat's helmsman cut the motor and puttered slowly toward the break. Wu overheard discussion of approach strategies. None sounded good.

Visser returned to the cabin and took the wheel. Casey joined Wu on the bow. She gripped the gunwale and Wu put his arm around her shoulders. He could feel her body shaking. "Let me get another jacket for you."

"I'm not cold. I'm scared shitless and trying not to be a basket case."

He pulled her closer and she nuzzled into his shoulder. He felt the weight of her dread. "You're doing great, Casey. We wouldn't have gotten this far without you" But Wu knew there were no words to comfort her.

The boat was battered hard but Visser was clearly a master

mariner. They passed the seals on the starboard side. The big animals honked out tepid alarm, but none moved to abandon their comfortable positions.

The slot loomed shadowy in the dusk. Visser positioned the boat perpendicular to the rock face. Sharp boulders protected the gap like the shark teeth that had torn the mermaids apart. A wave slapped the boat from the stern, then the craft rose and surfed through the gap toward what they hoped was the inner channel into Piscum Auratus. Casey screamed and stumbled toward a padded bench. She held on tight.

After a breathtaking rollercoaster ride that gripped the bowels of those aboard, the craft emerged into a small, relatively protected inner cove. Wu let out a ragged breath; his knees were like jelly. Salt spray dripped from his face and dampened his clothing.

He examined the sheltered rock walls. Less than a hundred feet away was a barred gate like Wu'd seen on another island—Alcatraz.

Casey, now pale with fear, appeared about to faint. Wu reached for her but the paramedic, Palmer, got there first. She coaxed a bottle of water into her hand, offered optimistic words, and asked for Casey's help in bringing first aid supplies on deck.

Wu gave her a grateful nod as she led Casey back into the cabin.

Visser joined him again on the bow. The boat edged closer to the opening—the iron gate was indeed fitted with electronic access. The helmsman maneuvered parallel to the barrier where the other two crew members roped the boat's fenders in tight to the rusty, metal bars. The locking device was now within their reach.

One of the breachers, a crewcut petty officer named Rodriguez, pulled a drill with a long, slim bit from a toolbox. Wu and Visser moved back to let him work. Another officer, taller and younger, assisted by holding a shaky stepladder and manning the gear like a surgeon's assistant. The boat lurched up and down as Rodriquez struggled to fit the bit into the locking mechanism. Once he had it in position, it took less than three minutes to disengage the latch and open the gate.

Overhead spotlights blazing, the Coast Guard boat cautiously entered the narrow, claustrophobic tunnel. Hammerhead dorsal fins spilled from the mouth and cut the water like dull gray razors. Rodriguez joined Wu and the captain on the bow, crouched, guns drawn.

Casey's voice echoed against the dank rock walls. "Isabelle! Sister, we're coming for you!"

With the roiling surf left behind, the water inside the cave rose and ebbed like breath in the throat of a slumbering beast. Colonies of whitish barnacles and darker limpets, sharp-rimmed and invasive, edged the tidal zone. The air was pungent with briny decay.

Another hammerhead raised its mallet-shaped cranium then disappeared beneath the boat. Something pale bobbed ahead.

Wu gulped and held up his hand to slow the craft. The captain idled the engines.

"Grab that net," Wu said to Beno. "Catch that light-colored thing. These assholes are known for being careless with body parts."

"Jesus," Beno said. He holstered his gun and picked up a long-handled net. Stretching out across the bow, he fished the ghostly object from the inky channel.

Driftwood.

They both let out a sigh of relief. Wu signaled to the captain and the boat resumed its careful progress deeper into the cavern.

Casey and the paramedic Palmer, who was now in a full wetsuit, sat together on the portside bench. They held hands and stared into the shadows beyond the glowing searchlights. Except for water lapping against the channel walls and the drone of engines, all was muted and tense.

Ahead on the left, a gray shape rolled from a narrow rock

shelf above the tideline. A little cry, a splash.

Wu's heart raced. A harbor seal? He raised his hand again to stop the boat.

"It's Izzy!" Casey's voice echoed off the walls, tight with panic.

Palmer grabbed Casey before she could launch herself into the water. "Whoa, there, girl. We don't need two victims."

The lights focused ahead. Wu crouched low, service revolver in hand, ready to blast any fiend, finned or otherwise, threatening the floating body.

The paramedic slipped into the water. A dorsal fin rose, then disappeared. Seconds later, Palmer pulled a bluish, deathly limp woman into her arms.

Isabelle Abbott.

Chapter 43

B eno and Rodriguez worked fast to haul Isabelle onto the deck. The paramedic scrambled in behind her just as a large shadowy creature with a battering ram head thumped the boat.

Wu watched the ten-foot shark emerge on the lee side of the boat then vanish back into the channel.

With a cry of deep distress, Casey dropped to her knees beside her sister's motionless body and grabbed her icy hands. Beno pried her away so Palmer could assess the damage and take vitals.

"Her pulse is weak and thready," Palmer said, listening through her stethoscope. "Definitely in shock." She grabbed the oxygen mask and put it over Izzy's pallid face.

Wu winced. Isabelle looked like a bled-out corpse. Her eyelids fluttered but that was her only movement. Pinpoint explosions edged his vision. He imagined his own sister lying there, on the edge of death. While Meghan was long gone, Izzy still had a chance, didn't she?

Trembling, Casey looked as pale as her sibling.

Palmer took the situation in hand again. "Heads-up, Casey," she ordered. "Stay with me, girl. Your sister and I need your help. Get me those warmed blankets from the cabin."

Wu envied the paramedic's way of keeping terrified family members distracted. This woman was the ultimate pro.

After an instant of paralysis, Casey struggled to her feet and rushed to the cabin, returning with an armload of towels and blankets. Palmer checked pulse rate again and they stripped off the Isabelle's wet clothing and wrapped her up.

Casey cuddled tight next to her sister and murmured encouragement into her ear, the one without the pearl earring.

Hamlin was now at the wheel. He threw the boat into reverse, readjusted the lights, and the craft began its retreat from the tunnel. Wu overheard Rodriguez on the radio requesting an ambulance to meet them at the pier.

Visser emerged from the cabin with an IV line ready to go.

"Warm saline," Palmer said. She extricated Izzy's arm from the blankets and hooked her up. She checked her heartbeat and body temperature again, and continued ministrations while Visser took Wu aside.

The captain's voice was low. "Harbor Patrol found the Boston Whaler abandoned near Hollywood Beach in Oxnard. The engine was still hot. We put out a BOLO to area airports for the fugitives. The photos you sent us have been forwarded."

"Thanks, Cap. I'll alert the County Sheriff; they're headed for the Palmdale Regional Airport. Word is these assholes are gonna try to leave the country tonight, fly out to someplace that doesn't extradite."

The captain nodded.

Wu bent down to join Casey and Palmer, kneeling at the altar of the ravaged woman struggling to live.

—

As the road ascended to its highest point before dropping down into the Antelope Valley, Bea spotted a sudden bright flare in the distance.

"Look Pete." She pointed to the north. "Did you see that flash? What the hell?"

His eyes squinted in the darkness. "I see it. Shit."

Bea leaned forward and chewed at her thumbnail. "You don't think that could be . . ."

Pete grabbed the police radio. "Detective Anthony. Just spotted what looks like an explosion, about twenty miles due west of Palmdale off Angeles Forest Highway."

Bea was almost paralyzed with terror as the illumination in the distance grew brighter.

Pete continued on the radio. "Possible vehicle accident. Need medevac. Could have us a pregnant woman with complications onboard. Send backup—potential hostage situation. Driver armed and dangerous. En route, ETA ten minutes."

He continued to talk to the dispatcher. Then, with lights flashing and sirens wailing, he floored it.

"Dunno what we got, Bea, but we're gonna make sure we're ready for anything."

—

Seven minutes and change later, Bea and Pete pulled up to the fiery vehicle wreck. Immediately seeing Lucy and Sister crouched next to a massive boulder, they went to work doing the best they could to stave Lucy's hemorrhaging and support Sister as she struggled to keep the baby breathing.

In less than twenty minutes, Bea stood next to Pete and held up her hand to protect her teary eyes from the chopper's downwash. The sand and dust were blinding and corrosive as the medevac raised Sister Catherine Lucia, Lucy, and the baby up in a wire basket, maneuvering them into the belly of the helicopter. Bartlett's car was still smoldering.

The smell of burning rubber made Bea's stomach queasy. "Sweet Jesus, Lucy gave birth to her son here in the dirt. And there's so much blood." She bent down. Her fingers lightly touched a dark clot. She drew away—this was a crime scene and shouldn't be disrupted. Bea held back sobs. Her chest ached from the effort. She turned and looked desperately into Pete's dark eyes. "I should be with her. There's so much blood."

"No room in the bird for you, sweetheart. The medics need space to work. They brought in a neonatal nurse to stabilize the kid. In no time, they'll be landing at Antelope Valley Hospital— it's a level II trauma center. They have a great reputation." He gently squeezed her shoulder.

Bea felt herself calm just a tad. "I called Burleson. He's on his way."

Pete nodded. "The women and child are in good hands, Bea. There's nothing you can do right now."

"Sarge," one of the uniforms called just as Pete and Bea were about to crawl into the cruiser. "Ya gotta take a look at this."

The man adjusted his Kevlar vest and stretched his neck long like a turtle emerging from a shell. "I think we found where they buried Hobbs. And there's another shallow grave just beyond his. Probably intended for the Vega woman."

Pete looked at Bea. They followed the officer to a sandy clearing about fifty yards from the car wreck. They passed Gorski's crushed corpse, now being loaded into a body bag by two crime scene technicians.

"So, this was where he was taking Lucy and Sister. Was going to kill then and dump them here to rot." Bea snarled, spun around and marched back to the CSI van. As the techs zipped Oscar's remains into the black bag, she kicked his dead carcass with all her furious might.

"Right on, sister," a dark-haired female CSI tech, muttered. "Kidnapping a woman in labor. Deserves what he got."

Bea wound up for anther kick, but Pete stepped between her and the corpse. "Keep it together, Beatrice."

She smiled. "That felt too damn good to pass up."

Bea followed as Pete and his team returned to the shallow graves. The CSI were hard at work recording the scene and collecting evidence samples from Cole Hobbs.

The other trench was agape, awaiting victims who'd refused to lay down and die. Fury, as hard as the rocky gulch, clogged Bea's throat.

"Notify Palmdale we have their MIA detective," Pete instructed the lead officer. "Their people will want to see this."

"Roger that, sir."

"We're on our way to a potential landing strip. Will call in if we need backup."

Bea and Pete took one last look at the rough gravesites, then scrambled back to the cruiser. Its flashers lit the small canyon like bloody fireworks on the Fourth of July. The siren wailed once, and they were on their way into the Antelope Valley.

Chapter 44

After a long swig from a water bottle, Bea rifled through her cellphone contacts.

"What're you looking for?" Pete asked.

"Tell you in a sec." She continued to assault the tiny keyboard. "Here it is. Got a friend who heads the small plane terminal—he'll be onboard to help us if the Piscem assholes show up at the old Palmdale Airport. We hit it off when I covered a story about their commercial airport closure some years back."

"'Hit it off'?" Pete looked like he'd sucked on a lemon.

"Maybe you should let the feds make that call."

"We don't have time for protocol, cowboy. You of all people are an expert at playing it fast and loose."

"Yeah, I guess I gotta maintain my rep."

Pete's cellphone buzzed. He glanced at caller ID. "It's Wu." He went to the Bluetooth speaker.

"Did you find Isabelle?" Bea asked urgently, her hands clasped in prayer.

"We did. She's critical, hypothermic—on her way to the ER

in Oxnard. Touch and go." Wu cleared his throat. "Lucy and her aunt?"

Pete's dark eyes sparked dangerously in the reflection of the car's lights. He filled Wu in on the women, the baby's condition, and Oscar Gorski's death in the wreck.

"Lucy gave birth at the scene?" Wu sounded incredulous.

"Yup, and Sister dislocated her shoulder. Popped it back in by herself," Bea added.

Wu let loose a low whistle. "Sweet Jesus, two tough customers."

Pete quickly concluded his update. After disconnecting from Wu, he accelerated hard, firing up the sirens as they approached the city limits. It was close to midnight, and traffic was minimal.

"There it is," Bea said, pointing. "Turn on Avenue P."

The airport came up fast. Quiet and deserted-looking, it had long been closed to commercial aviation. Even small plane civil flights were rare. With his federal connections, Bea figured Bartlett had somehow faked clearance in order to be serviced out of this site.

Bea dialed Fred Knapp, head of the terminal at what was locally called Plant 42. A former aviation manufacturing site and also black ops Skunk Works, it was still run by the Air Force and NASA out of the City of Palmdale.

An older-sounding male with a curt military tone picked up. Bea tried to communicate the urgency of the call without giving away specifics. He rang through to Knapp's desk, to no avail. Bea wiped perspiration from her forehead as he promised to try and locate Knapp.

After what seemed like hours on hold, Bea's contact came on the phone and she put the conversation on speaker.

"Hello, Bea."

"Hey, Fred. Thanks for jumping on my call."

He cut directly to the chase. "The dispatcher filled me in. The people you're after just boarded a Learjet. I was surprised they didn't use the Fox General Aviation Airport, it's right nearby in Lancaster, but the guy presented himself as a federal agent. Creds looked authentic."

"They're legit—or were. He retired six months ago. Now he's on the lam for sex trafficking and murder."

She heard Knapp suck in a fast breath.

"Who's the pilot?" Bea asked.

"A highly experienced ex-Air Force private contractor, Mindy McIntyre. She has no clue her passengers are dangerous fugitives. Got a young navigator with her, his first trip in a Lear."

"Shit." Pete careened past Plant 42. It was flanked by an ominous-looking F-16 and an array of long-range, supersonic fighter jets on massive display stands. The air route control center for LAX and the western states was a dim lantern in the distance.

"Keep them grounded, anyway you can," Bea said. "I'm with Detective Peter Anthony, LA County Sheriff."

Pete called out, "Knapp, need your help, man. The worst of human pukes are on that fuckin' plane. Palmdale PD and the feds are on the way. We're passing Blackbird Air Park just south of the runways."

"I'll meet you at the terminal in five, but damn, they just lifted off—probably over your head right now."

Pete groaned. He leaned forward to glance up through the dusty windshield. Sure enough, a small jet zoomed overhead, wing lights blinking red and green. "A couple feet lower and I'd grab Bartlett's goddamn balls."

Bea smirked and leaned in close to the phone as if it would bring her face-to-face with Knapp. "Can you get with traffic control? Maybe there's a way to divert them without the passengers knowing."

Before he could respond, Knapp excused himself to talk with someone in the background. Then, "Bea, we'll continue when you get here." She agreed and they both disconnected.

Pete sped to the front of the terminal and slammed his County Sheriff's Ford Interceptor to a stop in the mostly empty lot. The building was a large white box with square columns supporting a dark, glassed-in face. Knapp met them at the door. Medium height with a full head of graying dark hair, the man had a no-nonsense demeanor.

They shook hands, then Bea and Pete followed him past deserted check-in counters and down a long hallway to the airport control room. Three staffers sat at consoles before multiple large computer screens in open cubicles. The smell of burnt coffee hung in the air.

Knapp ushered them into a small office with expansive windows overlooking the runways. The door plaque read *FAA Deputy Regional Administrator*. He sat down behind his desk and gazed out into the darkness, mouth in a tight line.

Bea took a seat across from him.

"McIntyre didn't file a flight plan," Knapp said, frowning. "Unusual, but not illegal, unless they're leaving the country." He did finger gymnastics with a Sharpie pen.

"We think they're on their way to Ecuador or Nicaragua," Pete said. "Probably failed to mention that to the pilot. Those countries have dicey extradition laws—more like suggestions. The creeps'll probably head out somewhere overseas from there. Bartlett has significant ties to Indonesia." He stared out across the high desert. The moon was a waning slice in the clear night sky.

Knapp's desk phone rang, and he grabbed it, listened, and then said to the dispatcher, "give us ten minutes then send them up."

He turned to Bea and Pete. "The cavalry's arrived. Politics never sleeps. But before we all meet, I want a plan. Got to secure your perps and still keep our navigator and pilot safe—she has a husband and two little kids."

"These people are grime." Pete rubbed at a spot on the glass as if trying to make the whole scenario vanish.

Bea leaned forward, arms on Knapp's desk. "It's about a five-and-a-half-hour trip to either country, yes?"

He put down the pen and steepled his fingers, expression thoughtful and intense. "Hang onto that thought, Bea. Let me get the head traffic controller on with us. Gunnar Viglund, he's been through this shit before."

Knapp quickly got the controller on speaker, bringing him up to speed on the situation.

Then, Bea continued. "You could have the pilot in flight for five-and-half hours, get Bartlett and Cloris-Edna all comfy, right? Then land in Tucson. The fugitives will think they're in Managua or Quito. They step out onto the tarmac, and bang, we got them. Crew stays locked in the cockpit."

"The door to the cockpit's just a privacy screen on the Learjet 75," Viglund said. "Flight deck's totally vulnerable. But your diversion idea is a good one. We've had to do it before—not our first rodeo."

"How'd it go? Successful?" Pete asked.

Viglund cleared his throat. "The odds wouldn't be big in Vegas."

Knapp frowned.

Pete left the windows and sat next to Bea. "Can you communicate with the pilot without Bartlett hearing? I've been told anybody can follow air traffic control on a smartphone with the right apps."

"That's unfortunately true," the controller said.

Knapp rubbed at the gray stubble on his chin. "The plane's direction, altitude, the whole ball o' wax can be monitored over a phone. Whether they'll be doing that or not is anybody's guess. But if we let them actually get to South America, you can kiss them goodbye."

"So, we're screwed?" Pete growled.

"Not necessarily." Knapp tapped away on his desktop computer, then responded. "We're back to diversion—we could have the pilot claim a mechanical issue and land outside of Tucson in an hour. Our controller can direct the pilot to a military frequency and review the mission plan."

"Flight Captain McIntyre can require airplane mode on their phones and insist that cellphone use will screw up her navigation system," Viglund said. "If they want to land safely, they'll listen. We can switch back to commercial band as soon as we get her acknowledgement."

Pete shook his head. "Bartlett's a smart dude. He'd be on to that right away."

Knapp squinted at his computer screen. "I'm afraid it might be our only option."

"Copy that, sir," Viglund responded. "Sometimes shit's all you got to work with."

Bea felt like the air had been sucked out of the room.

Then, the posse arrived.

Chapter 45

The Palmdale Sheriff's station captain along with their rapid response team leader, two Air Force brass, and three federal agents crowded around a table in a claustrophobic conference room next to Knapp's office.

Bea realized why Knapp wanted a plan before stepping into this mosh pit of big dogs all scrambling for dominance. He presented the diversion idea to the group. Everyone had an opinion.

Bea checked her watch. Heart hammering, she stood, asserting her right to be heard in a room full of men used to giving orders.

"Listen gentlemen, with all due respect, time is of the essence."

The noise level dropped but chattering continued. Bea looked hard at the group and envisioned a classroom of unruly high school students. Then she got pissed.

"Listen to me, dammit." Her fists clenched into hard knots. "Bartlett could be over southern Arizona in forty-five minutes.

We act immediately, or we miss our window of opportunity. Think about the families who've lost their daughters to these monsters. You have baby girls? Sisters? Want these assholes out there destroying more lives? You need to move. *Now*."

Discussion stopped. Faces turned her way.

Knapp spoke. "Bea's right. Time is not our friend—I think we've already lost our chance for an intercept in Arizona. We can't mobilize fast enough. We gotta bring 'em back here to Palmdale," he said. "I'll direct Captain McIntyre to shut off an engine. She'll radio an emergency and tell the passengers they're landing near Hemet. It's dark and one remote runway looks like any other from thirty-thousand feet."

Knapp paused, then everyone began to talk at once.

He stood and drilled his attention into the overhead clock on the wall. The discussion halted again. "There's no time for a pissing contest over jurisdiction—countdown has already begun."

After some grumbling, the officers from the various factions turned their faces to Knapp and tacitly acknowledged his leadership. He crossed his arms on his chest and nodded. "Okay, then. Let's roll."

Bea and Pete followed him back to the office.

Knapp was immediately on the horn to Viglund. They agreed on a radio frequency to engage the flight crew and then Knapp made contact.

"Mindy, it's Fred Knapp. We have a situation and I need you to listen carefully."

"Roger that." Her response was all business as the operation was laid out. The airwaves were quiet for an instant, and then the operation began.

Pete pressed Bea's shoulder. "Gonna get these motherfuckers, Beebs. And when the jerk-offs are either cuffed or dead, we'll raise a glass to the mermaids."

—

Leaving Knapp and his minions to coordinate the operation, Bea and Pete sat alone in a dark VIP lounge overlooking the runways. All they could do now was wait and let others take action. Her nerves shimmered like a mirage on hot sand. Perspiration dampened her skin and her vision began to pixilate around the edges. Damn migraines. Bea knew very well she didn't have the metabolism to run without nourishment and rest for too long and still be functional. She glanced at her watch. Time dragged by. She took a couple Advil.

"We have at least another half-hour before we see activity." She fidgeted in her chair. "There's a Mickey D's a couple miles down the road. Let's grab some breakfast sandwiches and coffee and bring them back here."

Pete finished up a text and put his phone in his pocket. "You're really going nuts, aren't you?"

"Gotta get out of here, breathe some air. Just for a few minutes. This waiting with nothing to do is killing me." She pressed her aching temples.

"Okay, babe, people's lives are hanging in the balance, but I'll make a fast-food run, just for you."

She punched his shoulder. They exited the lounge down a short stairway and through a double door into the dim, empty terminal. Their footsteps echoed across the terrazzo floors.

At a lone reception desk, a skinny young man in uniform played videogames.

When he became aware of visitors, the guy jerked up straight and shifted his focus to an open textbook under a gooseneck desk lamp.

"Fortnite?" Pete asked.

The guy grimaced self-consciously. "Assassin's Creed."

"Have at it. We'll be back shortly," Pete called to him.

Bea mumbled, "Terrorists could take over the whole building and the kid would still be fighting it out in fantasyland."

She pushed open the glass terminal door. The outside breeze puffed cool and sweet. Bea took a deep, cleansing breath and let it out slowly. Her brain began to clear. Stars salted the night sky and for an instant her mind slipped from the incoming terror with the Learjet to sheer gratefulness for her humble life. She murmured an invocation for the innocents everywhere. The moment was fleeting but provided just enough to get her back on track.

They climbed into the cruiser and drove across the deserted parking lot toward Columbia Way, one of the main streets into the complex. A ten-minute drive to Palmdale Boulevard put them in the heart of the fast-food district.

"There it is." Bea nodded as she fished a wallet from her purse.

Between a closed auto parts store and a twenty-four-hour off-brand gas station with enough bright lights to illuminate a small country, Pete coasted into the drive-thru. In the middle of the night, they were still fifth in line. The driver in the first car appeared to be having a debate with the order taker.

Bea looked at her watch again—twenty minutes until the plane should be at the airfield.

Car number one finally settled the dispute and drove off. The cruiser crawled forward. This was all taking too long. She glanced across at the gas station where a muddy Toyota 4x4 with dark, tinted glass windows just pulled in. She'd thought about getting a 4x4 when she replaced her burned-out BMW, but needed something more economical on the streets of LA.

Pete inched ahead into spot number three.

Just as Bea was about to turn away and count out the money, the Toyota driver's door opened.

A fiftyish man wearing a ballcap hoisted himself out of the truck with the help of a cane, and skulked to the pump. His head swiveled back and forth, scanning the area, sniffing for the scent of danger.

"What the—" Her breathing stopped and the wallet slipped from her hands. *Was this real?* She cried out, "What the hell? Pete, he's getting gas!"

Pete craned his neck in the direction Bea was pointing. "What are you talking about?"

"It's freakin' Bartlett!"

Chapter 46

Pete's mouth dropped open. "I don't believe this." He froze for a nanosecond then pulled out of line and backed into a parking space. He picked up the radio mic.

"Looks like he may have been hurt." Bea snatched her phone and pressed video. Bartlett leaned on his cane.

"Maybe got chomped in the ass by one of his freaky sharks."

"If only." Bea maneuvered to get a better view. The cruiser was behind the order kiosk so Bartlett couldn't see them, but they could see him. She nabbed the license plate number on camera. "You have to shoot out the tires if he tries to leave the station."

"We're not starting a firefight in a public space, darlin.' People could get hurt or taken hostage. We'll follow and monitor."

Bea growled. She knew he was right.

"Lemme get with Knapp." He radioed the frequency Knapp had provided.

The FAA regional administrator immediately picked up and began speaking before Pete could interject. "Detective, the jet's number two engine has shut down and they're fifteen minutes out."

"Listen Knapp, I don't know who the hell is up in that plane but it ain't Bartlett."

"What?"

"The asswipe's down here at the Lucky Skunk gas station getting fuel and fuckin' peanuts. We're following. Let Palmdale Station know and we'll coordinate."

The radio crackled. "You're sure of this?"

"Look at the video Bea just sent you."

"Roger that." There was dead air for a few moments then Knapp let out a low whistle. "Okay, we'll pull the landing op and get Palmdale redirected as soon as you know which way your guy's headed. Wish you had an unmarked."

"No shit," Pete agreed. "Over and out."

Bea watched Bartlett hang up the pump, limp into the station and buy a few snacks, then crawl back inside the truck. The 4x4 turned north onto the boulevard toward Lancaster. Cloris-Edna was in the passenger seat.

Bea's mouth went dry. "Oh, man. I think he's going out to the Fox Airfield. Small planes, general aviation. Knapp wondered why they didn't fly out of there originally."

"Our Agent Bartlett set up a decoy at Plant 42 and he's really leaving from Fox. Brilliant." Pete immediately alerted Knapp via military band on the radio.

The cruiser continued to follow and hung way back from Bartlett. Pete let a couple vehicles slide in front of the black and white, but the sparse traffic this time of night made it tough to keep a cop car invisible.

Two miles south of Fox airfield, Bartlett accelerated.

"We've been made." Pete lit up the flashers and moved into pursuit mode. The 4x4 gained speed. "Damn. What the hell's he got under that hood?"

Bea grabbed the overhead hand hold.

From a side road, one Palmdale Police car joined the chase,

then another.

Pete's radio activated. It was Knapp. "You can back off, Detective," he said. "Palmdale has it now."

"Hell no." Bea shouted.

Pete careened after Bartlett. The souped-up 4x4 made a hard left into what appeared to be a rear maintenance entrance to the airfield. A Gulfstream waited on the taxiway just beyond a chain-link fence. Bea had no doubt that was the plane Bartlett was fleeing toward.

The muddy Toyota 4x4 disappeared around a corner and bowled through the gaping mouth of a small hangar. The big rolldown door slammed shut before the squads could enter.

Pete jumped out of his cruiser, gun drawn, and dashed to a side entrance. Two Palmdale officers sprinted behind him. The door was locked. It took three shots from his service revolver to obliterate the bolt. The door sagged open on one hinge.

Bea grabbed the Glock from her purse and followed the men into a dim, empty hangar. Just behind her, the SWAT crew surged from their van. "They're not in here," Bea shouted. Someone hit the controls for the hangar's main steel roll-up door and it began to rise.

As they moved out onto the tarmac where the jet waited, Cloris-Edna, spry for an old broad, skittered up the steps to the plane like a spider whose rock had just been overturned. Bartlett struggled behind her.

Pete called out, "County Sheriff! Stop! Hands on your head!" He raced to the Gulfstream's steps as they lifted and closed into the body of the plane. For a moment Pete dangled precariously by one hand from the bottom tread, then lost his grip and crashed to the ground. The door shut with a thunk and the engines roared. The plane slowly turned toward the main runway and gained speed.

ARs blasting, Palmdale SWAT strafed the side of the shiny sleek Gulfstream G280. They continued to sprint after the plane, firing heavy rounds.

Vehicles swarmed the runway—local cruisers with their lights strobing, airport security, utility trucks——all blocked the plane's escape route.

The engines finally shut down. After endless minutes, the jet's airstairs partially lowered and the cabin door opened. Bartlett appeared with a male flight crew member clutched to his chest and a .357 pressed to the guy's head.

Bartlett yelled, "We want another plane or I'll shoot the navigator. You have fifteen minutes."

The young man's face was immobile, but Bea noted that his white flight crew shirt was ripped. There had been some kind of struggle.

"It's over, Bartlett. Let the guy go," Pete shouted. The SWAT captain he'd seen earlier in Knapp's office was at his side. Bea moved next to them.

Bartlett yanked his hostage back into the cabin.

"I got an idea," she whispered. "It's a long shot, but maybe it's not Bartlett who makes the calls."

Darting away, she ran crouched low toward the plane.

"Shit, what the hell is that woman doing?" The SWAT captain barked. He moved to follow but Pete held him back.

"Give her a minute. She's partially crazy but her instincts are usually spot on."

The captain, glowering in the dim light, glanced over at his crew and held up a clenched fist to indicate they weren't to move. Yet.

Bea crossed the twenty-yard distance and planted herself beneath the tail where she was out of Bartlett's shooting range. Pulsing police lights reflected in pools of jet fuel leaking from the fuselage. The stench was a dizzying mix of high octane and super glue.

The plane's stairs raised a bit but the door remained open overhead. She heard the old woman's shrill voice lambasting Bartlett and shouted out to her.

"Cloris-Edna Jones! It's Beatrice Middleton——I'm a news

reporter. Your friend Bartlett has really screwed things up with this macho stunt. But if you surrender, I can promise, whether you go back to the state hospital or to jail, you'll still be able to do your productions. I hear they're impressive."

The old lady remained as quiet as the tomb she was going to be planted in if something didn't give, fast. Bea glanced over at Pete and the SWAT leader. Ignoring their angry faces, she took a deep breath, and continued. "Maybe not mermaids this time, but something daring and classic—like satyrs and nymphs. Greek mythology——humans with horse bodies rather than fish, and sexy little faeries. Wouldn't that be fun?"

Nothing.

She paused a moment to frame her next words. "Even iron bars can't hold a talent like yours, Ms. Jones." Bea licked her dry lips. "You're a legend, like Esther Williams."

"I have more talent in my little finger than that insipid bitch had in her entire saggy-boobed body."

Bea's heart raced. Bingo, she'd struck a vulnerable chord.

"Get back in here, you hag," Bartlett snarled.

Cloris's scratchy voice sounded from near the door. "It's over, dear. There's nowhere we can go. You let us be cornered and trapped." She paused. Unintelligible arguing ensued, then she continued. "Beatrice is right, we will take our show to another venue. Don't you know that Beatrice was Dante's lover in the Divine Comedy? I think we should listen to such a clever, passionate woman. And a news reporter to boot."

"Get back here, you brainless shrew," Bartlett's demand hummed with panic.

The airstairs began to lower. Cloris-Edna, black beret tilted jauntily and bloody red lipstick lacerating her lips, appeared on the threshold as if she were Queen at Wembley Stadium. Her hands were raised, not in surrender, but as if she were accepting adulation from a vast audience. The cops had finally been able to get spotlights set up. They popped on as Cloris took her first step.

Bea smiled to herself——perhaps this was the moment Cloris-Edna had been waiting for all her life. The old woman's face would be plastered across every TV screen for at least twenty-four hours.

"I'm happy to talk to the media." She slowly descended the stairs.

Cloris-Edna Jones smiled dreamily, even as SWAT officers pushed her to the ground.

Bartlett appeared again at the door, the navigator still hostage to the .357. "You have ten fucking minutes before I take him out," Bartlett screamed, his voice sounding out of control.

"Drop the gun," the SWAT cap yelled.

No response.

"Give it up, Bartlett. Now! Last warning." SWAT had the plane surrounded. "Put down the gun or we'll shoot."

Bea remained hunched beneath the plane, cold sweat running down her neck. The SWAT circle tightened. Their shadows were long, black staves against the spotlight.

"Eight minutes!" Stumbling back into the cabin, Bartlett tripped and waved his firearm in the air.

The rigid-bodied navigator sprang to life——he lunged to the right and launched himself over the stair railing, landing hard at Bea's feet.

Guns blasted. Bartlett crumbled.

It was over.

Chapter 47

Lucy gazed at her little man with wonder. Now the size of a football at thirty-six weeks, he was finally home. "This is where you're gonna grow up, sweet boy."

Day after day at his side in the antiseptic high desert hospital, recovering from a delivery that had almost claimed both their lives, the earthy feel and sweet, dusty smell of the Malibu ranch was sublime to Lucy. The baby had been inspected and licked by the pups, eyed by Howard the cat with semi-disdain, and all was copasetic. She breathed deeply, closed her eyes, and thanked the great powers in the universe for their survival.

The wind off the ocean puffed and swirled. The smell of sawdust blended with familiar natural fragrances. Elsa, Michael Burleson, and their neighbor across the road, Cheyney Hitchcock, had done an awesome job of keeping everyone on task. The barn was fully raised, the bones of the new house were up, and the framing was almost finished.

The thrill of renewal was piquant, but Lucy also deeply felt the absence of Sister Catherine Lucia who'd returned to

Guerrero the week previously. The old woman had saved Lucy's life. Despite a dislocated shoulder and cracked femur, Sister had managed to apply enough pressure on Lucy's ruptured uterus to keep her from bleeding out. But now, others needed the nun *curandera* back at her rural clinic. Lucy couldn't selfishly ask for more time. Aunt and niece had bonded with a depth Lucy never thought possible. Even thousands of miles and cultures apart, she felt her aunt's comforting presence every moment.

"Our son's got the skinniest little ass I've ever seen." Burleson gazed down at his wispy-haired offspring.

"Next to his daddy's," Lucy said. "Now I've got two of 'em I gotta look at every day. How lucky am I?" She beamed.

"Talk about skinny butts," Bea interjected, you look like you've lost half your body weight, girlfriend. Time to start packing it back on. Take care of her, Burleson."

"Will do, Beebs." He squeezed Lucy's shoulders and scooped the peaceful child into his strong arms.

Lucy still felt weak and was not one to value any kind of thinness over health. But she was feeling stronger every day. And she was home, her loved ones were alive—she had it all.

Elsa and Izzy called everyone to the picnic tables. The dogs arrived first with a pygmy goat named Wilkie. Somehow, they'd figured out how to spring the little dude from his pen. Newly thirteen-year-old Alyssa shepherded him back to his enclosure before he ended up on top of the table with feet in the egg salad.

Wu and Casey held hands, almost desperately joined at the hip. He'd just had an impressive job offer in Denver and was seriously considering the offer. Lucy wondered if Casey would pull up stakes and join him. She sighed and kissed her baby on his warm sweet forehead.

Pete followed Wu and Casey to the table, pitchers of beer in hand he'd just drawn from the half keg. Cheyney, always upbeat with a can-do attitude, limped behind him, struggling with arthritis from decades of body-breaking work as a stuntman.

Vintage Beach Boys music played "God Only Knows" from

Lucy's laptop.

"So, did they finally figure out who all were in the decoy plane out of Plant 42?" Cheyney asked Pete.

"They were two actors from Central-goddamn-Casting."

Cheyney chucked. "No kidding?"

"Each was paid a grand to take a ride to Arizona and back." Pete plunked the two pitchers in the middle of the table.

Cheyney put the red cups beside them. "Hell, they could have been killed, no?"

"Oh, yeah. They're totally shaken—had no idea what they were into, really thought the plane was going to crash and that their lives were over. Pretty insane."

Pete helped Cheyney crawl onto the picnic table bench then slid in next to him. "Thanks to all out work, a costume designer named Standish and a master animator named Oz are on their way to Lompoc. Bartlett's waiting for his supermax assignment and Old lady Jones is in the federal lockup in Dublin up near Livermore. It's minimum security, but we found out the bitch is ninety-five years old. She ain't gonna be running too far on those spindly gams. She's already organizing an inmate's talent show or something."

"Think she feels any remorse at all?" Lucy asked.

Bea shook her head and grabbed a turkey burger from the passing plate. "She's a total psychopath. The girls' abduction, torture, and deaths are just part of a big movie fantasy for her. She feels nothing."

"What about Arnaldo Barahona, *El Tiburon,* and the Honduran connection?" Bea asked.

Pete shrugged. "In the wind. I was told the CIA is on it."

Burleson passed baby Henry to Alyssa who'd been dying to show off her "big sister" skills. The new mom turned to watch Bea's precious daughter dance in careful little circles with Henry happily in her arms. Lucy was momentarily overwhelmed by the undying love and fear parents have for their children.

Bea glanced over at her friend and acknowledged the

unspoken words. She gulped down a wedge of anxiety and went for the potato salad.

Pete stood up and raised his cup high. "I promised Bea as soon as these jerks were either dead or cuffed, we'd drink to the mermaids. So, to those who died——may you find eternal solace in the warm, blue waters of heaven, and may your loved ones find some comfort in the fact that the assholes are off the street forever."

"Hear, hear." They toasted together.

"And to the one who lived," Bea added. "Strong, smart, beautiful Isabelle Abbott——may your life, and all of ours, be a testament to living every day with gratitude, resilience, and joy." Casey and Izzy hugged with tears running down their faces.

"And to the tadpole who lived too." Alyssa proudly held up Henry's baby bottle to make sure even the tiniest at the table was part of the tribute. He shrieked with delight.

Acknowledgments

Deep appreciation to the Rocky Mountain Fiction Writers, home of my amazing critique group at Tattered Cover bookstore in Littleton, Colorado. A shout-out to the brilliant and supportive Colorado crime writing community including my friends at Sisters in Crime-Colorado and the Rocky Mountain Mystery Writers of America.

Props to my husband, Alan Klein, and to my straight-shooting beta readers Lacey Greer Pare', Marlene Simon, and Carolyn Olson. Deep appreciation to Liz Cooke for her editing magic.

Special acknowledgement to the Downtown Denver Aquarium Mystic Mermaids. Kudos for performing underwater in blinding saltwater, wearing 30-pound neoprene tails, dodging sharks, barracudas and 400-pound groupers. You women rock.

Sincere gratitude to Susie Brooks, publisher at Literary Wanderlust. It's a privilege to be part of this great indie team.

About the Author

Sue Hinkin is a former television news photographer, NBC-TV Art Department manager, as well as a college teacher and administrator. A graduate of the American Film Institute and long-time L.A. resident, she now lives in Littleton, Colorado. The Mermaid Broker is her 4th Vega and Middleton thriller. See more at www.suehinkin.com.

CPSIA information can be obtained
at www.ICGtesting.com
Printed in the USA
FSHW011325260221
78978FS